Coming
HOME

a novel

Jennie Hansen

Covenant Communications, Inc.

This book is dedicated to two women who have gone beyond being my editors to become my friends—Valerie Holladay and JoAnn Jolley. Thanks to both of you.

Published by Covenant Communications, Inc.
American Fork, Utah

Printed in the United States of America
First Printing: July 1998

04 03 02 01 00 99 98 97   10 9 8 7 6 5 4 3 2 1

ISBN 1-57734-280-1

Library of Congress Cataloging-in-Publication Data

Hansen, Jennie L., 1943-
   Coming home / Jennie Hansen.
      p.   cm.
   ISBN 1-57734-280-1
   I. Title
PS3558.A51293C65 1998
813' .54--dc21   98-18827
                                           CIP

One

"DR. BRADLEY WILLIAMS TO EMERGENCY. DR. Bradley Williams to Emergency." The disembodied voice repeated itself and Brad slammed his locker door shut with a resounding clang. He winced more from his touch of temper than from the sound.

"Not another one," he groaned as he left the doctor's lounge at a run. He'd already delivered three babies today, the first one shortly after four o'clock this morning. He hadn't seen the inside of his office once all day, and he'd been counting on getting home in time to see his kids before they were all in bed and asleep.

Days like today hadn't bothered him when Cathy had been with the children, but now . . . Now flashes of anger colored his reactions more often than he liked to admit.

Deliberately pushing irritation and disappointment to the back of his mind, Brad mentally reviewed his patients. Audrey Breckenridge should be next, but she wasn't due for another week and her first three babies had all been late. He'd seen no indication that this one would be any different, but in ten years of obstetric practice he'd learned that each baby called its own tune.

Silently he prayed he wouldn't find Missie Madison when he reached the ER. The young woman had already suffered three traumatic miscarriages. She'd never successfully carried a baby for over six months before, and on reaching that milestone she was finally allowing herself to hope. "If she loses this one I'm not sure she'll ever recover emotionally," he muttered under his breath as he swept open the double doors leading to the hospital's ER.

From long practice Brad's eyes ignored the chaos of the trauma center and went directly to a thin figure in hospital greens, her hair spilling from a crooked surgical cap. A seasoned triage nurse, Corbett carried a clipboard and acknowledged his presence with an almost imperceptible nod of her head.

"Four." She pointed with a thick black marker pen to a curtained cubicle, and Brad hurried toward it. As he stepped inside the curtain, his eyes widened in horror as two things registered at once. His patient was little more than a child, a badly injured child with long, straggly blond hair matted with drying clumps of blood. And she was going to deliver her baby right now. Brad knew he would have no time to clean up the battered teenager or prep her in any way. The ER attendant at her side gave him a weak smile as Brad paused only to pull on plastic gloves before taking his place at the foot of the gurney.

Placing one hand on the girl's abdomen, he instructed her to take a deep breath and push out slowly. In seconds a squirming, screaming dark-haired little girl slipped into his waiting hands. After a cursory inspection of the child and a quick clearing of mucus from the tiny mouth and nose, he handed her to a pair of waiting arms. "Get someone down here from the Women's Center to take care of the baby, and prepare to transport the mother to that wing of the hospital as soon as possible." He issued the instructions without turning around.

Deliberately modulating his voice, he assured the young woman that her baby was fine and that she only needed to push a few more times to deliver the afterbirth. As silent tears ran down the girl's bruised cheeks, merging with blood from a nasty gash on her temple, Brad felt his heart wrench. His young patient was scarcely a year or two older than his oldest daughter, Bobbi. A flicker of anger surfaced in the back of his mind as he mentally questioned the sanity of a world where children gave birth to babies. He suspected he'd really lose it if this were his little girl lying here.

Well aware that fathers are often the last to recognize their daughters' interest in boys, Brad mentally paused to reassure himself that his fourteen-year-old, sports-crazy daughter's only concern with boys was whether she could outshoot them on a basketball court. He hoped she would stay that way for at least a couple more years.

As he worked to repair the damage done to delicate tissues, he spoke from the side of his mouth, "Let her see her baby before she's taken to the nursery."

"I don't want to see her," the girl spoke for the first time, her voice flat then rising with a note of near-hysteria. "Take her away. I don't ever want to see her. Give her to some nerdy people who will make her go to school and church and stick braces on her teeth." Her voice disappeared in sobs and Brad reached instinctively for her hand to offer her comfort. As he did he noticed the girl would have probably benefitted from braces herself. Front teeth that twisted inward gave the girl's mouth a pouty look, enhancing her childlike appearance. Brad had already noted that she was young and slight, quite possibly undernourished; she probably hadn't had much in the way of prenatal care, he thought.

"You don't have to see her," he whispered in consoling tones. "But if you change your mind, it's okay. She's small, but seems to be perfectly healthy. She'll get a thorough checkup in the nursery. Right now, I want to focus on you. You have some injuries that have nothing to do with the baby you just delivered. They look as though they need a little attention."

From out in the hallway he heard the familiar sound of a rolling infant crib. He turned to issue instructions to the ER nurse and stopped with his mouth open. No ER nurse stood behind him. Susan A. MacKendrick, M.D., head of the hospital trauma unit and nicknamed "Doc Attitude" by more than half the staff, awkwardly clutched in her arms the tiny naked newborn he'd delivered minutes before. A strange mixture of emotions flitted across her face—fear, hunger, anger, despair, aching need, awe, love.

When Dr. MacKendrick looked up to see Brad staring at her, her eyes were misty, her face tender. Brad almost didn't recognize her. Then the Women's Center nurse entered the room. "I'll take the little one now, Dr. MacKendrick," she said, reaching for the infant.

Dr. MacKendrick appeared almost reluctant to relinquish the baby, but as she straightened from transferring her burden to the smaller woman, her face assumed its usual businesslike mask.

Brad continued to stare at the other doctor, wondering if he had actually seen what he thought he had seen. No, he decided, his imagination was running wild. Dr. MacKendrick—not even her colleagues called her Susan—would ever be caught displaying any kind of emotion. In fact, at times, since Cathy's death, Brad had found himself envying MacKendrick's ability to block out everything except her work. Other times he thanked God that his ability to care hadn't died with his wife.

He realized that Dr. MacKendrick was speaking to him. "As soon as your patient is stabilized, Dr. Williams, notify Corbett and she'll schedule X-rays for her arm." She spoke briskly, her voice revealing none of the emotions he thought he had seen on her face.

Brad started guiltily; he'd only noticed peripherally the swelling around the girl's elbow and the awkward way she cradled one arm with her other hand. He'd been aware of her battered appearance in a general way, but his attention had focused narrowly on the girl as an obstetrical patient first. He'd noted the absence of needle tracks with a sense of relief, but pushed the more obvious injuries to the back of his mind.

"Will stitching the gash on her temple interfere with any post-natal procedures?" Dr. MacKendrick asked, although it was evident that she expected no opposition. She only asked because professional courtesy dictated she do so. Her deft hands were already opening the suturing kit she'd extracted from a small cabinet.

Brad shook his head and returned to monitoring his patient's blood pressure and trying to elicit a few words from the obviously terrified teenager. She had lost a little too much blood, but it hadn't reached a dangerous level. A quick glance at her chart showed almost no information beyond her name, Alice Jones, and he wondered if that were correct.

"Alice," he spoke softly. "Do you have any family I could call? Perhaps your mother?"

"She won't come. She told me to get out; she don't want to ever see me again. I was leaving when I got hit by a stupid car." The girl's voice was flat, expressionless again.

"How about the baby's father?" Brad prodded gently.

"He don't care about me. He told me to have an abortion and when I didn't, he dumped me. He's got someone else now." Hurt underlay the empty tone of her words.

"Count yourself fortunate, young lady," Dr. MacKendrick cut in sharply. "The real tragedy would be if you and your baby were stuck depending on the jerk. Go back to school and make something of yourself. You don't need him!"

Brad was surprised by the other doctor's vehemence. Her words to the girl were the closest to real emotion he'd ever heard from Dr. MacKendrick. Unexpectedly the other physician held out one hand toward him. After a moment he wordlessly placed the scissors in her hand as he tried to hide a twitching lip. Turnabout appeared to be fair play. MacKendrick had played nurse for him; he supposed he could return the favor.

An urgent voice interrupted them. "Dr. MacKendrick! Inbound ambulance, arriving in ten minutes. Gunshot. Fifteen-year-old male. EMT insists that he talk to you."

Susan MacKendrick lifted her eyes and met Brad's squarely. Understanding and something more flared briefly in their gray depths. Responding to her unspoken question, he nodded his head. "I can finish, you go ahead." As smoothly as though they'd practiced the procedure many times, he slipped onto the stool she had vacated and with no loss of motion resumed stitching the gash on Alice's temple.

Four hours later Brad pushed through the double doors and began the long walk down an eerily quiet corridor. Or perhaps it only seemed eerie because the hour was late, and the hall wasn't one he usually frequented late at night. He spent many nights at the hospital, but seldom strayed further from the Women's Center than the cafeteria. He wasn't sure why he was heading back to the trauma center now. He had finished with Alice Jones, who was now settled in the maternity wing. Leaving her with her arm in a bright blue sling, he had next checked on the baby, before talking to the on-duty social worker about his newest patient.

After that Brad had quickly reviewed his other three new mothers' charts. With everything appearing to be under control, he would ordinarily be on his way home, but something niggled at the back of his mind. His thoughts kept returning to that moment in the ER when he and Susan MacKendrick had communicated as easily and soundlessly as one unit. That kind of empathy with another human being was something he hadn't experienced since Cathy, and it had left him with a confusing array of emotions. In one sense, it electrified him. In another, it scared him. That few minutes of rapport had given him a sense of wholeness he'd missed over the past three years, but why had it happened with Susan MacKendrick, of all people?

He knew it wouldn't be that much farther to leave the hospital by the emergency room on his way out. From what he knew of Dr. MacKendrick, she didn't just work in the hospital; she practically lived there. Why he felt compelled to see her again, he didn't know. She had none of Cathy's feminine softness and sunlight. Even before he'd lost his heart to Cathy, he'd never been interested in tall, thin model types like Dr. MacKendrick. His heart caught painfully for just a second as a picture of his tiny red-haired wife's generously curved shape came to mind. Even if another woman did exist like his Cathy, he still wouldn't want her. He'd only ever wanted Cathy.

The quietness ended as he rounded the corner and approached the trauma center. Two deputies supported a belligerent, screaming man who demanded to see his wife. A baby cried and a toddler streaked down the hall with a frazzled mother in hot pursuit. Half a dozen bruised and bloodied teenagers leaned against a wall while emergency personnel moved swiftly between stations, a siren wailed, and two uniformed ambulance attendants rushed a gurney through the automatic doors.

Corbett raised one brow as Brad walked through the door, then she turned back to her clipboard. She too was working late; her usual shift ended at eleven and her replacement should have taken over twenty minutes ago.

"Dr. MacKendrick still around?"

"Just left. Badger's on duty now." Corbett, as usual, wasted no words.

Feeling oddly disappointed, Brad zipped up his jacket as he stepped out into the night. He didn't know what he would have said if Dr. MacKendrick had still been there. He didn't have a clue why he'd felt compelled to come looking for her anyway. Doc Attitude wasn't the type one looked to to rehash a shared, emotionally charged experience.

A harvest moon hung at midpoint in the sky and Brad was sorry he hadn't been on the patio with his daughters to watch its climb over the Wasatch peaks tonight. Before Cathy's death, on warm summer nights the two of them had often watched the moon together as it rose above the jagged mountain peaks before they put the children to bed. Some days his love for Cathy and the knowledge that one day they would be together again were all that kept him going.

Brad regretted that he hadn't spent much time with his girls since they returned to school last month. Bobbi was starting high school this year, Ashley and Michelle were both in middle school, Heidi was now in the third grade, and even little Kelly was in school half a day this year.

A sudden urgency to see his daughters and assure himself they were safe hastened his steps. He understood the prompting and knew it stemmed from this evening's young mother. Once more he faced the fear and doubts that had assailed him at frequent intervals during the past three years since his wife's death. Again it left him feeling inadequate to the task of rearing five daughters without their mother.

Gradually he became aware of a figure moving slowly ahead of him with shoulders hunched and hands buried deeply in coat pockets. Not wishing to intrude on the solitude someone had sought in the privacy of the night, he stopped when the other person stopped. As he debated moving on or seeking another route, something held him motionless. He watched a head come up and a face turn toward the full moon.

Susan MacKendrick! He felt a strange jolt inside. Funny, he'd never noticed before that the tall, ultra-efficient doctor was an attractive woman. The pale moonglow gave her sleekly coiffed blond hair a silvery glow. Not only did her hair sparkle with silver streaks, but so did her cheeks. Was it the slight shudder of her shoulders or some small sound that alerted Brad that the silver streaks on her cheeks were tears?

Without a thought for the unlikeliness of Dr. MacKendrick crying or the possibility she might not want anyone to offer her comfort, he stepped forward.

"Susan," he spoke her name softly as he touched her arm.

She whirled in panic to face him, her eyes wide and staring.

"I'm sorry. I didn't mean to startle you."

"You—you didn't."

He watched her mammoth struggle to control some great emotion. He hadn't meant to frighten her and couldn't help feeling she was overreacting to the surprise of seeing him here. In the back of his mind he experienced a struggle of his own to equate the cool, professional colleague he'd met five or six years ago when she first joined the hospital staff with the vulnerable woman standing before him. With an odd little thrill he realized he'd called her Susan, not Dr. MacKendrick, and the name felt right on his tongue. A swift stab of guilt caught him off guard. He suddenly felt a desire to protect her and he didn't want to feel protective toward any woman other than Cathy, and he certainly didn't want to think of Dr. MacKendrick as Susan.

"You seem upset—distracted." Searching for the right word, Brad found himself inviting her confidence and questioning his own sanity as he did so.

"I'm tired. That's all. We're short-staffed and I worked a double shift today." Her attempt to dismiss his concern only stirred a greater sense of empathy in Brad, or maybe it was downright curiosity. Dr. MacKendrick had a reputation for working double shifts; some of her staff questioned whether she ever went home—or if she even had one.

"It's more than that," Brad spoke softly. "Double shifts don't faze you."

"What is this? Feel a need to play bishop tonight?" Sarcasm laced her voice, and only a slight tremor alerted him to the fact that the sarcasm was her way of hiding her vulnerability.

"I haven't been a bishop for more than three years. I'm a little rusty as a counselor, but we've been colleagues for a long time and it looks to me like you could use a friendly ear. Come on, sit down a minute." He urged her toward a cement planter. A voice in his head told him he should just let it go. He had no desire to see "Doc Attitude" as a woman, let alone a vulnerable one, but something inside him kept him prodding the issue even while he mentally kicked himself.

Her first impulse was to resist. He could see that, but slowly her shoulders slumped and she moved tiredly toward the planter ledge where she seated herself, leaving more than a foot of space between them. Without conscious thought Brad reached across the gap to take her hand. She flinched when his hand touched hers and he considered releasing his hold, then decided against it. He'd grown up in a home, then headed one, where touching was warm and easy, where touching meant concern and support.

A memory stirred of his friend Doug's wife. Megan didn't like to be touched. A childhood filled with abuse had left her unable to accept the casual physical overtures of friendship that others took for granted. Something he couldn't explain told him that Susan MacKendrick shied away, not out of fear, but because her need was too intense.

"I'll release your hand if you really want me to," he told her. "But sometimes it helps to hang on a little bit."

"And you think I need someone to hang on to?" The words were bitter, but she stopped trying to free her hand.

For several minutes neither one spoke. Brad found himself haunted by the tone of her voice. It mimicked almost exactly the bitter, flat tone of little Alice Jones. Was there something about the young girl that had broken through Susan's defenses tonight? Absently he rubbed one thumb across the back of her hand and said nothing.

"I lost a patient tonight," Dr. MacKendrick broke the silence abruptly. "A fifteen-year-old kid with a gunshot wound in his belly." She spoke flatly, devoid of emotion. Brad understood. He'd lost patients too, and had been eaten by "what if's" and "if only's." Quite a few doctors seemed to take losing a patient in stride, accepting an occasional loss as inevitable, but Brad hurt with each one. And it had been worse since Cathy; now he understood only too well the pain left behind.

So it wasn't the girl, then, who had somehow upset the usually unflappable doctor. But something didn't add up. After spending six years in trauma Dr. MacKendrick had certainly lost patients before. Her grief seemed far beyond the sense of loss and failure that inevitably accompanied the loss of a patient. Brad squinted his eyes and thought about what the woman beside him had said—and what she had not said. She had a reputation for doing what had to be done, then getting on with the next case. Something else was at work here.

"Tell me about him," he prompted as carefully as he could.

At first she seemed to ignore him, then the words spilled out as though a dam had burst.

"He was a kid! A little boy called Robbie with dark curls and big, sad brown eyes. He was small for his age. He was conscious when they brought him in and he was crying for his mama. Only," she swallowed and looked away, "he doesn't have a mama. He was adopted when he was just a few days old. The officer who came in with him told me his adoptive parents were killed in a car accident when he was five and he went to live with an aunt. She couldn't handle him and turned him over to foster care. He's been in *eleven* foster homes in the nine years since then. He's been mixed up with a gang since he was ten, arrested twice, and tonight he was shot by a rival gang member, a sixteen-year-old who claims it was self-defense."

Brad shook his head sadly. Gang violence made the news almost daily, but it had never touched him personally. He lived in a comfortable neighborhood, and his kids went to good schools. He knew and liked their friends, most of whom were kids who had lived in the same ward with his own children most of their lives. His practice consisted mostly of happily married women and an occasional teenager who tried to grow up too fast. He thought Susan probably saw a lot of gang violence in Emergency.

"I thought the bleeding was stopped, but about nine-thirty he began hemorrhaging again and I rushed him back to OR. Noel was just starting anesthesia when the kid suddenly looked right at me and grinned. 'Mama,' he said," Susan choked out the words. "He called me mama, then died. Just like that." She withdrew her hand from Brad's, and wrapping both arms around herself tightly, she rocked back and forth.

"He probably didn't even see you." Brad kept his voice gentle. "He did have a mother for five years, and it's possible she came for him."

She shook her head as if to deny his suggestion. "There's always paperwork when someone dies. I hate it, so I get my part over with as fast as possible. It was right there in black and white on that stupid chart." She clamped her teeth together and her chin betrayed a slight quiver.

"I don't understand." Brad reached toward her once more and abruptly she stood up and took two steps away. Then she turned to face him again.

"I know you don't understand," she spoke in a hoarse whisper. "No one would understand."

"Help me understand," Brad implored. Standing, he swiftly closed the distance between them. His hands gripped Susan's shoulders and suddenly she collapsed against him, her arms circling his waist in a viselike grip. Her body shook as great, heaving sobs tore through her slender frame. Tears wet his shirt. He said nothing, only held her while she cried.

At last she lifted her face to meet his eyes and spoke quietly, as though the storm were spent and she, the exhausted survivor, barely hung on. "That boy was my son."

Brad wasn't sure he'd heard the softly spoken words correctly. He hesitated to ask her to repeat her statement, but Susan went on without prompting.

"I gave birth to a dark-haired baby boy on August 12th fifteen years ago and immediately gave him up for adoption. All I was told about his adoption was that he went to a young couple in Utah. The chart listed Robbie's birth date. He was my son. I let my own son die!"

Two

"IT COULD BE COINCIDENCE. YOU CAN'T BE sure Robbie was your son on the basis of a birth date alone." Brad tried to temper her grief while his mind grappled with her startling confession.

"Don't you think I've told myself that?" She took a step backward and Brad released her. "But there are too many similarities. It's not just the birth date. I gave my baby up for adoption to a Utah couple two days after he was born. Robbie was adopted by a Utah couple shortly after his birth. My baby had dark curly hair and brown eyes. His father was of Mediterranean descent with olive skin and a short, sturdy build just like Robbie."

Brad didn't know what to say. The woman before him was obviously hurting—both from the old pain of giving up her baby and this new trauma of possibly presiding at his death. Losing a patient was difficult enough, but facing the possibility the patient might have been your own child was almost incomprehensible.

Offering counsel and comfort had been a part of him since boyhood, an ability that had been enhanced through the years by both his profession and his Church service. Although Susan MacKendrick was not his patient nor did she even remotely fall under his priesthood jurisdiction, he felt an aching need to help her.

"Nothing to say?" Susan's voice suddenly turned harsh and accusing as she misinterpreted his silence. "Surely in your line of work you've run across unwed mothers who gave up their babies for adoption before. It's the fact I'm a doctor that shocks you, isn't it? We're supposed to know better. Well, I wasn't a doctor then, and if I'd kept my baby I wouldn't be a doctor today." She whirled around and took several steps before Brad managed to stop her.

"Don't mistake surprise for judgement," he warned. "In my experience, it's always the most caring, unselfish young women who want mature, two-parent homes for their babies. You're an intelligent woman, and I don't doubt that fifteen years ago you were an intelligent teenager who made the choice you believed best for both you and your baby."

She blinked back the moisture in her eyes, took a deep breath, then faced him squarely. "I'm not sure I thought about the baby's future at all, beyond knowing I wouldn't wish growing up in my father's house on any child. My major concern was getting myself out of there."

"Weren't your parents willing to help you?"

She laughed bitterly. "Oh yes, my father had it all worked out. I'd quit school and stay with his sister until the baby was born, then he and Mom would adopt it, and I would come home and work for him. I was supposed to forget college—boys, too—and devote myself to repentance for the rest of my life."

"Ah, banished to a convent." Brad gave her a sympathetic smile.

"It does sound medieval," she acknowledged wryly. "Only there's an element of truth in it. Perhaps that's what I deserved–my father certainly thought so—but I'd just turned seventeen, and I couldn't accept that my life was over. I thought if I devoted my life to helping others I could atone for the wrong I'd done. Obviously, I was wrong. If I'd obeyed my father, my son would still be alive."

"You can't be sure of that. You can't even be sure that boy was your son."

"I was so certain I was right and my father was wrong. I thought the worst thing that could ever happen would be not being able to leave."

"Did you consider marriage?" Brad wasn't being snoopy. Susan had evidently buried her wounds rather than letting them heal and now she was hurting. He thought talking might ease her grief.

"It was never an option. Tony and I had been friends since we were small children. We lived on adjoining farms and our parents were friends—if you could call mutual pig-headedness friendship. Tony and I were never more than friends, though our parents decided we should get married as soon as we graduated from high school.

Starting out, we were to live on his father's farm, then eventually join both farms into the largest farm in the county. Tony had a big fight with his parents about it. He told them he wasn't sure he wanted to get married and that he definitely didn't want to farm. He stormed out of the house and came to see me.

"Ironically I'd been fighting with my father, too. The school counselor had told me an academic scholarship was being offered to me that would pay most of my undergraduate expenses for four years in a good school in another part of the state. I practically floated all the way home to tell my parents. Father punctured my balloon in a hurry. He said I didn't need to waste my time going to school anymore. A high school education was more than enough for a farm wife. Besides, colleges were the devil's cesspools, existing only to lure young people into corruption and immorality." She paused so long he wondered if she couldn't bring herself to speak further of the experience that had scarred her young life. Finally she went on.

"Tony and I went for a drive and stopped beside the river to talk. The more we talked, the angrier we both became. Our parents had always dictated how we dressed, where we went, and who we could see. I was never allowed to date anyone other than Tony, have girl friends, or wear makeup. I'd never even been to a school dance. Father ridiculed my desire to be a doctor. Tony had wanted to play football, but his parents wouldn't allow it because it took away time they felt should be devoted to farmwork. He was considering running away right after graduation to join the Navy.

"Then some kids we knew from school came along with hot dogs and marshmallows and invited us to join their impromptu party. They were funny and friendly, and we were both fed up with the rigid restrictions our parents held us to, so we accepted their invitation and when they offered us beer with our hot dogs, we drank it. Later someone produced something stronger and we shared that, too.

"The others drifted away in pairs and we went back to Tony's truck. Need I say more? Two weeks later Tony was found dead of a gunshot wound. The coroner ruled the death accidental since it appeared he had been trying to cross a fence with his rifle in his hand. But he'd been depressed for weeks and there were rumors of suicide."

"You believe he took his own life?" Brad questioned softly. "You don't blame yourself for his death, do you?"

Susan shook her head. "No, I really don't. I blamed the kids we partied with at first. In time I transferred blame to the Church."

"The Church?" Had he missed something? He didn't see the connection.

"The Church has some pretty rigid standards and Tony's parents made certain he knew the penalty for any deviation from the rules. He couldn't face what we had done or the possibility his parents might some day find out. He told me the day before he died that he knew he was eternally damned because he held the priesthood and he'd failed to honor his parents, he'd gotten drunk, and he'd committed fornication."

"Ah, Susan." Instinctively Brad's arms went around her and he pressed her cheek against his shoulder. "Surely, you know repentance is a hard taskmaster, but forgiveness is possible."

"I thought so," she whispered against his jacket. "I worked hard to put my past behind me and become a doctor. Tony believed God was demanding and exacting, always in a towering rage over the evil of mankind because that's what our parents taught, but somewhere along the way—perhaps it was a CTR teacher in Primary who taught me differently—I came to believe in a gentler God.

"I felt God had forgiven me by giving me a chance to save lives. I found out tonight I was wrong. My father said it was vanity and self-ishness that made me think becoming a doctor was more important than keeping my baby. He swore that one day I'd regret with my entire damned soul that I'd yielded to Satan's temptation and compounded my sin by giving away my child. He was right after all. God showed me tonight that everything I've accomplished was at the expense of my son's life."

Wrenching herself out of his arms, she ran to her car. Brad made no attempt to follow her. She needed more comfort than he could offer her.

Years ago Susan had invested in drapes and blinds for her apartment that were designed to block out light so she could sleep whenever she was off duty, night or day. Tonight they weren't enough. Lying on her back, she stared sightlessly at the tiny green light of the overhead smoke alarm. The only other light in the room came from the large block numerals on her alarm clock. But she could still see the faces of her two young patients—the girl giving birth alone and afraid and the boy calling her Mama as his life blood drained away. She closed her eyes, trying to block out their images, but it did no good.

She'd made a fool of herself earlier tonight, breaking down in front of Dr. Williams and crying all over his jacket. She hadn't even remembered his name when she'd first stepped inside the cubicle where the girl was giving birth, though she remembered seeing him around the hospital before. Like most private practitioners within a radius of several miles around Cottonwood Hospital, he had hospital privileges at the facility, so most of his patients delivered there; but since OB patients didn't generally arrive at the hospital via the trauma center, she'd had little contact with him. When she did recognize him she'd associated him with the dynamic woman who had spearheaded a fund-raising drive to upgrade the ER's communications equipment during Susan's first year at the hospital.

A few years ago that same woman had arrived in her ER with massive head trauma. She'd died without regaining consciousness, leaving her doctor husband the most sighed-over physician at the hospital. Vaguely Susan remembered Brad had been heavier when she'd first met him, though now he was certainly trim enough. At several inches over six feet with broad shoulders and long legs, Brad looked young and athletic, although in her opinion, he could stand to add a few pounds. She'd heard a couple of orderlies call him "Bishop" and recalled talk about him being released from that assignment shortly before his wife had died.

A wave of disgust at her behavior rolled over her. After weeping all over him the way she had, he probably found her as revolting as the silly young nurses who stammered and blushed every time he spoke to one of them. No matter how much stress she'd faced, she found it hard to believe she had succumbed to some mental aberration and told him about her sordid past. She closed her eyes and willed sleep to come, but it hovered just out of reach.

Her exhausted body played tricks with her equally fatigued mind. Instead of the oblivion she sought, her arms grew heavy with the remembered weight of the infant she'd held a few hours earlier. As she lay there, the baby she held was no longer the tiny girl of earlier today, but the chubby little boy she'd given away so many years ago, the baby she'd never held or claimed. A surge of joy passed through her as she gazed into his tiny face and cradled his small body in her arms. Then the baby screamed and drew up his legs in colicky agony. Drawing him closer she struggled to soothe and reassure him even as his cries grew louder. Frantically she struggled to remember all she'd ever heard or read about colic. She was a doctor; she should be able to help him. She was his mother; she should . . .

The crying stopped but before her relief could take shape, she looked down and gasped. The baby was gone and in his place lay a young boy writhing in silent agony. "Help me, Mom," he pleaded. As she stared horror-struck, unable to move, the boy's face darkened in contempt for her. "You never wanted me. You don't care what happens to me."

"I do care. I always cared, but I couldn't take care of you. You needed two parents. I couldn't bear to turn you over to my father." She was crying as she reached out to the boy.

Harshly he slapped away her hand and the words that came from his mouth were vile and full of hate.

"Oh, please understand," she sobbed.

Silently he turned his face toward the wall. Her hand gripped his shoulder, but it was too late. She was too late. Her son was dead.

A strangled gasp brought her awake. Feeling completely disoriented, she glanced first at her clock and then at the empty space beside her on the bed.

Grief and guilt vied for dominance in her confused brain. She'd been so certain she was doing the right thing when she'd given up her baby. Tony had taken care of any ideas she might have had about marriage, and at seventeen, there was no way she could support a child. She couldn't go back home. No, *wouldn't* was more like it.

Moving like a robot, she shoved back the quilt and plodded toward the bathroom. A shower would wake her up, get her moving again. Minutes later she stood under the needle-sharp spray with her face turned toward the stinging stream of water. Gradually her body shook off its fatigue, leaving only her mind floundering. She'd be useless to her patients if she didn't snap out of this. During her long struggle to finish medical school and complete her residency, she'd learned to shut down her fears and turn off fatigue in order to survive. Slowly, deliberately, she cleared her mind.

No matter what demons haunted her mind during the night, the clear light of day reminded her there was no going back. The unwise decisions in her past were just that—in the past. Her life had no room for memories of a baby who had never been hers. Recalling her father's dictatorial demands, her mother's weak acquiescence, and a boy who died too soon were a waste of time. Letting her thoughts dwell on a certain doctor whose broad shoulders and blue eyes were too good to be real was another waste of time.

Briskly she pulled on a plain pair of slacks and reached for her Nikes. She'd grab a roll and a glass of milk at the hospital. She'd wasted enough time.

It was eleven o'clock before she made it to the cafeteria for that roll and milk. Figuring she wouldn't bother with lunch at all, she added a banana to her tray before making her way to a table in the corner. As was her habit, she quickly spread a sheaf of reports out on the table to peruse while she ate. She'd learned long ago that studying while she ate both saved time and discouraged others from joining her.

To her annoyance a foursome of nurses settled at a table near her and were soon joined by an orderly from her own department. Vainly she struggled to block out their noisy chatter and sudden bursts of laughter. A persistent ache had lodged between her eyes several hours ago, providing the motivation that finally sent her to the cafeteria for something to eat. She concluded that not eating last night and this morning were the sole reason for the pain in her head. She would never accept that the supreme effort required to block out memories of the past, the frantic pace she'd set for herself and her staff this morning, and her lack of sleep had anything to do with it.

"'Doc Attitude's sure on one today," the orderly groused as he picked up his sandwich. "She's got everyone jumping like she expected Armageddon by two this afternoon and all the casualties are to be shipped our way."

"She can't be that bad. You're just lazy. You'd resent anyone who tried to get a little work out of you," one nurse laughed.

"I expect any minute to have her hand me a toothbrush and a bed pan and tell me to scrub." He continued his complaint and an appreciative titter made its way around the table.

"I heard she lost a patient last night," another nurse spoke up. "She might be upset about that."

"Are you kidding?" the orderly scoffed. "The Doc ain't human. She doesn't get emotional about things like that, especially over some dirty little gutter brat who got his in a gang shoot-out."

"I heard no one's claimed the body," the second nurse went on. "His aunt claims she's too poor to pay for a funeral and he hasn't got anyone else. Can you imagine being so alone there wouldn't be anyone to claim your body when you're dead?" She gave an exaggerated shudder.

Susan froze. She knew about the nickname and it didn't bother her. She also knew her staff chronically complained that she overworked them, and she didn't mind that either. But to learn that the boy was as neglected in death as he'd been in life broke through her defenses in a torrent of pain and grief. All her efforts to block out the past crumbled before her eyes. She'd carried that small body inside her own for nine months, and she'd wanted something better for him than what she and his father had been given. It hadn't been the easy, selfish decision she'd implied to Dr. Williams it had been. She'd been afraid to hold her baby, even once, for fear she'd lose her courage and decide to keep him. She had already picked out a good family for him. The attorney had shown her letters written by a dozen couples who all wanted to adopt her baby. One letter had stood out and she'd known the couple would give her son the joy and laughter she and Tony had been denied.

With a violent shove she pushed her chair back and stood up, knocking her tray to the floor. Barely aware of the remains of her lunch scattered on the floor or the shocked faces turned her way, she ran from the room. She'd turned her back on her child while he was alive, but she wouldn't ignore his death. She'd claim his body, and he'd have the best and biggest funeral this town had ever seen.

Her mind registered a solid object looming in the doorway too late for her to avoid a head-on crash. Her cheekbone collided with a chin, and air whooshed from her lungs as she broadsided a decidedly solid masculine chest.

"You okay?" Two large hands settled around her upper arms, lending her support as she gasped for breath, and she found herself staring into the same blue eyes that had haunted her sleep the night before.

She nodded her head in response to his question and slowly pulled a mantle of composure over her shattered senses. "I'm okay. There's something I have to do, and in my hurry I didn't look where I was going. I'm sorry." She moved to go past him, but he didn't release her as she expected. Her eyes moved questioningly to his face.

"Medical emergency?" he asked, meeting her eyes with a question of his own. She considered lying, then slowly shook her head.

"No, it's personal."

"I'm free for a couple of hours. I'll go along with you," he said firmly.

Not knowing quite how it happened, she found herself moving along the corridor beside him. She knew she ought to protest, but she didn't.

Brad insisted on driving the short distance to the mortuary where the body had been taken. Appearing half asleep he had lounged in a chair while she dealt with the legalities of transferring responsibility for the boy's body from his aunt to herself. As she was making arrangements for Robbie's burial, Brad disappeared for a few minutes, then reappeared at the doorway when Susan stood to leave. Taking her arm, he led her to his car. They'd traveled several miles before she realized they were headed away from the hospital.

"I've been gone more than an hour. I have to get back," she reminded Brad.

"I checked us both out for the rest of the afternoon," Brad responded blandly as he signaled to enter a freeway ramp.

"You what?" she gasped. "You had no right. I have responsibilities—"

"Your first responsibility is to yourself. You're an emotional powder keg at the moment, and the last thing you or your patients need is for you to set foot in that inferno you've dedicated your life to."

"Are you saying you think I'm incompetent to do my job?" Susan reeled from the insult. Medicine was her life. She'd worked harder and studied longer than any other student in her classes. She'd graduated at the top of her class and chosen trauma as her specialty because it was fast-paced and demanding. She'd volunteered for jobs no one else wanted and devoted more hours than anyone else at the hospital. She was good at her job, she was a good doctor, and she thought all the old biases about women being too emotionally delicate to be doctors had been left behind in medical school.

"Take me back to the hospital right now." She infused a note of icy command into her voice.

"Incompetent certainly isn't the word I would have chosen," Brad spoke in an easy drawl as though he had no clue the woman beside him was boiling with fury. "You need some back-off-and-get-it-in-perspective time. No, don't interrupt." He cut her off before she could tell him what he could do with his armchair psychology. "I know what I'm talking about. Three years ago my wife battled cancer with the kind of courage and grace most of us can't even fathom. Then after all she went through, she was struck and killed by a drunk driver. In my mind people who drink then get behind the wheel of a car are in the same league of social irresponsibility as teens and young adults who join gangs and think they can gain power and importance with guns.

"When Cathy died I felt all the guilt and helpless rage you're feeling now. It's gotten better, but it hasn't gone away altogether. When the anger starts pressing in on me, I have to get away for a few hours or a few days. A long hike in the mountains, a few hours of classical music alone in my den, or a fast game of basketball on the court at the park aren't cure-alls, but those things help me put my life back in focus."

"Long walks and music aren't going to help me." She made no attempt to conceal her opinion of his suggestions. "That's one thing I've learned my father was right about. Hard work is the best antidote for self-pity or anger."

"Work helps. Yes, I agree with that." Brad spoke affably as he turned onto a long tree-lined street. "But work alone tends to form a scab over the wound without digging out the poison underneath. It may fester and spread to vital organs." He pulled into a driveway and turned off the engine.

"Where are we?" Susan glanced around suspiciously at the obviously residential neighborhood.

"My house." He flipped a switch to unlock the car doors.

"I'm not going in there." She couldn't hide the panic that edged her voice. She remembered only too well the casual invitations of fellow med students to study-sessions in their rooms or apartments,

occasions that always ended in wrestling matches. She felt a stab of
disappointment in Dr. Williams as she thought of the nurses who
sighed and giggled over him. There had been more than a few snide
cracks about the good doctor always being surrounded by women,
and plenty of juicy speculations about his live-in housekeeper. She
berated herself for naively accepting his help. At her age she should
have known better.

"You're wrong, you know." A flicker of amusement glinted in his
eyes. Evidently he could read her face a little too well. "My housekeeper is inside and my daughters will be home from school in a few
minutes. You'll be perfectly safe."

Her eyes met his and she wondered if she could trust him. She
wanted to. A smile slowly began to surface and she reached for the
door handle. Brad quickly exited the driver's side and hurried around
the car to hold her door.

Together they proceeded up the driveway toward the house. A
sudden noise drew their attention to the garage door. It rumbled
upward and Susan stared in shock and dismay at the beautiful young
woman who stepped out of the garage. Even in her concealing work
overalls, she appeared to be in her early to mid-twenties.

"Brad! I was hoping you'd be home early today." The woman
reached for a zipper at the front of the one-piece garment she wore
and drew it steadily downward as she talked. "I want to take the car
out for a little test run next Saturday. Kelly asked to go with me, but I
wanted to check with you first."

"It looks like you're going to have it done in time for Dad's
birthday." Brad grinned appreciatively and the woman nodded smugly.

"It'll be ready in time," she affirmed, smiling happily, seemingly
unaware that her hands were black with grime and a smudge dusted
one cheek.

Susan's eyes widened as the young woman casually stepped out of
the encompassing suit and tossed it aside, revealing a figure in slim
jeans and a teeshirt as classic as her patrician facial features. Just then
a little face topped with a mop of red curls peered around one jeans-
clad leg to smile impishly up at Brad. Black smudges covered her face.

"Hi, Daddy," the little urchin giggled. She hid her hands behind
her back, but not before Susan saw that they were as filthy as those of

the young woman she half hid behind.

"Don't you have a hug for Daddy?" Brad held out his arms.

The little girl giggled again. "Mrs. Mack said I need a bath and I better not ruin any more of your doctor shirts."

Brad glanced down at his white shirt and laughed. "Well, you'd better head straight for the tub then, because I don't plan to wait all night for my hug." The little girl dashed toward a door leading from the garage to the house. Before she reached it the young woman caught her.

"I think we'd both better do a little washing up at the sink out here before going inside," she called over her shoulder to Brad.

"The car looks great," Brad complimented before the grimy pair disappeared behind a large van. He then wandered slowly around a vintage car Susan recognized vaguely as some kind of antique. Black and maroon, the car appeared to have a great deal more shiny chrome than its original owner had ever seen. It was high and boxy and sported a rumble seat, too. A million questions—mostly about the gorgeous brunette who was obviously very much at ease in Brad's home and with his children—popped into her mind.

"Is she your housekeeper?" Susan asked in a small voice.

"Uh, no. She's a mechanic."

"A mechanic who makes house calls?" She couldn't help the snide tone that crept into her voice. "Women who look like that don't become mechanics."

"Now, now, doctor," Brad grinned impishly. "Your bias is showing. There's no reason why a woman, even a drop-dead gorgeous one, can't be a mechanic."

With an exaggerated wave of his hand, he ushered Susan toward the front door. Stifling her irritation, she stepped past the door he held open for her.

Three

SUSAN STOOD IN THE ENTRYWAY AND LET HER eyes roam warily around the large room. She didn't know what she had expected, but she had to admit the room was pleasant. Solid, comfortable furniture appeared designed for comfort while the pillows on the sofas and chairs showed signs of being well used. Books, lamps, and a piano declared the room to be a place where family or guests might choose to linger. A wide staircase led to the floor above and though the carpeted treads looked a mite worn, the oak rails gleamed from a recent polishing. Gradually her fingers relaxed, releasing her tightly clenched fists.

An unexpected sound drew her attention to a child's playpen nearly hidden by a large, over-stuffed chair. Inside, a small boy banged a plastic wrench against a larger toy and smiled toothlessly in her direction.

"Well, hello, Dutch," Brad's voice came from behind her. The baby immediately pulled himself upright on wobbly legs and held out his arms.

"Da, da," the baby giggled and waved his arms until Brad reached him and casually lifted him into his arms.

Stunned, Susan stood motionless, uncertain what to do or say as Brad buried his face in the baby's fat neck, and childish laughter filled the room. Grasping Brad's hair in his chubby fists, the little boy shouted, "Da! Da!" with growing exuberance. But Brad's wife had died three years ago, and this baby looked to be somewhere around a year old. He couldn't be Brad's child. Well, he could, but who . . . ?

"He calls everyone 'Da da.' Even me." Susan started in surprise at the voice. She looked down to find a slightly older version of the moppet she'd met in the garage. Instead of grease, however, this one had a generous smear of peanut butter across her face.

"Goodness, is that baby awake already?" An older woman bustled into the room. "Did you wake him up?" she asked, directing a scowl at Brad. While he denied the charge, three more girls with flaming red hair burst into the room, clamoring to hold Dutch. The pair from the garage soon arrived, accompanied by a puppy that wove between the girls' legs, barking with excitement.

"Girls!" Brad raised his voice enough to be heard over the commotion. Gradually the noise dimmed and he held out his hand to Susan. Nervously she accepted the gesture as a lifeline thrown her way.

"I want you all to meet a friend of mine," Brad introduced her. "This is Susan MacKendrick. She's a doctor and sometimes we work together at the hospital."

"Do you help babies get borned, too?" the youngest girl asked in obvious awe.

"No, I'm a trauma physician." The child obviously didn't understand her answer, but what did she know about explaining the various medical specialties to a five-year-old? She generally delegated pediatric cases to other doctors.

"Doctor MacKendrick fixes people up when they get hurt," Brad explained for her. "She fixes lots of broken legs, banged heads, and big cuts." He turned back to Susan. "This curious little grease monkey is Kelly. The peanut butter kid beside you is Heidi. This tall young lady," he pointed to his oldest daughter, "is Bobbi. Ashley is holding the baby, and Michelle is hanging over her shoulder. Our housekeeper, Mrs. Mack," he pointed to the older woman. "I believe you've already met the family mechanic, Holland James." He flashed a roguish grin toward the stunning brunette. "And last, but far from the least," he said, walking toward the little boy on his daughter's lap and hefting him into his arms again, "this is Harrington Jesperson James, whom his mother—that's Holland—planned to call 'Little Hank' in honor of her father, but who ended up being "Dutch" instead."

The little girl beside Susan nudged her elbow. "Uncle Allen—he's Dutch's daddy—says it's kind of like a joke, but I don't get it. He named Dutch's puppy Amsterdam, but that's really dumb. Nobody wants to say, 'Here, Amsterdam. Here Amsterdam,' so we just call him, 'Puppy.' Sometimes Uncle Allen is really weird."

"Not too weird," Holland laughed. "He just likes to play with my name. My father was from the Netherlands," she explained to Susan, "and my mother's family always called him 'that stubborn Dutchman.' My mother dreamed of going to Holland to see the tulip fields, so she named me Holland after both my father and her dream. But speaking of Allen, Dutch and I better get moving or he'll growl at us for ruining dinner. It was nice to meet you, Susan. Persuade Brad to bring you up to our house some night. We love to show off our spectacular view of the valley. People like Brad think all the great views are here on the East bench, but you haven't seen anything until you see the view from the Oquirrh side of the valley."

With a flurry of hugs and kisses from all of the girls and admonitions from Mrs. Mack to keep Dutch bundled up so he wouldn't catch cold, Holland transferred her son and his puppy along with a bag of diapers and toys to a gleaming 4x4 parked at the curb.

As Susan stood at the window, she watched the small truck pull away, pondering why the revelation that the "mechanic" was married to "Uncle Allen" had lifted her spirits. It shouldn't matter at all.

"I'm sorry if seeing Dutch caused you pain." She turned at the sound of Brad's voice.

"No, it's all right. I gave away my baby a long time ago. I may have related to that unwed mother a few days ago, but I don't see my baby in every child I meet. Besides, I'm too busy for regrets," she lied, and believed she told the truth.

A steady thumping noise turned their attention to the hallway. Susan turned to see Bobbi framed in the doorway. The girl looked past her to speak to her father. "You promised you'd play one game with me."

"Will you be all right?" Brad asked Susan softly. She nodded her head and Brad left with his daughter. The other girls didn't immediately return to the house after seeing Dutch and Holland off; instead, they chased each other across the lawn. Her attention drifted to the driveway where Brad and Bobbi dribbled and feinted, then took turns smoothly dropping a basketball through a slightly crooked hoop. A lump rose in her throat. This is what she'd wanted fifteen years ago for her baby. Giving him up had nearly rent her soul in two. Only the belief that she was giving him a chance at the love and laughter she and Tony had missed had made signing that paper possible.

"Oh God," she whispered against the window pane. "Please help him to know I truly loved him. I tried so hard to do what I thought was best for him—and for me. Help him to forgive me."

Closing her eyes, she remembered a long-ago summer day when Tony had led her into the woods to see a bird's nest he had discovered. Once again she saw the awe and excitement in his eyes as a tiny chip appeared in one of the eggs. Together they'd withdrawn to a nearby hill so the mother bird would return to her nest to greet her emerging baby, but Tony had frequently sneaked back to peek at the nest with its growing occupants.

Susan leaned her forehead against the cool glass and felt a calmness that had evaded her for years. Perhaps their baby hadn't been entirely alone all those years.

"Would you like to leave now?" She hadn't heard Brad reenter the house. She turned to face him.

"Yes. I think it's time."

Leaves crunched beneath his feet as Brad hurried down the walk. He liked the crisp sound. Inhaling deeply, he looked around in sheepish surprise and experienced a sense of delight as bright colors caught his eye. When had the foliage turned to brilliant reds and vibrant golds? He'd always liked fall, but this one had crept up on him, catching him unaware. Actually he had only vague memories of summer. All the seasons had receded into a uniform grayness in recent years.

He frowned as he tried to recall the last time he'd taken time to appreciate the seasonal changes. Probably not since Cathy's death. Just thinking about her brought sadness to his heart, but this time the pain dimmed as he remembered how much Cathy loved color. In fact, fall had been her favorite season. A memory of her standing beside their cabin near Park City in the midst of hundreds of trees whose brightness matched the flaming red of her wind-tossed curls brought a smile to his lips. Cathy had lived every minute to the fullest. He missed their long autumn hikes with color all around them and leaves crunching beneath their feet. He felt a twinge of guilt as it occurred to him that Cathy would probably be disappointed in him if she knew he'd allowed all of her lovely seasons to blur together into a dreary sameness. He ought to take a drive through the nearby mountains—maybe American Fork Canyon, or better yet, the Nebo loop. No, it wouldn't be the same without Cathy—although the girls would probably enjoy it.

Up ahead he spotted the mortuary and slowed his steps. He couldn't remember at the moment why he'd decided it was important to attend this funeral. He didn't like funerals; they reminded him too acutely of his own loss. Perhaps it wasn't too late to turn around and go back to his office. At the front of the mortuary he could see a slender figure tugging at the heavy glass doors of the building and he continued walking. Susan MacKendrick shouldn't have to face this alone.

Brad's first thought on entering the small chapel was that the boy had evidently had more friends than he had expected. The small room was overflowing with floral tributes. But gazing around the room, Brad saw only a middle-aged, shabbily dressed couple, probably the boy's aunt and uncle, and two rows of scruffy teenagers in baggy clothes and bulky jackets. Well, that was something. The gang showed more loyalty than Brad would have assumed they were capable of. Maybe there was more hope for those kids than most people recognized. After all, anyone capable of love and loyalty couldn't be all bad.

At the front of the room two men sat behind a small podium and an elegantly dressed gentleman sat at the organ, softly playing Brahms. A woman in a long black dress—a soloist, he guessed—sat nearby. Susan MacKendrick sat alone on the front row opposite the aunt and uncle. The flowers, no doubt, were from Susan. He squared his shoulders and made his way to the front to sit beside her.

She looked up, startled, as he sat down, but unless he was way off base, there was gratitude and relief in her eyes as well. It hadn't really surprised him she had taken responsibility for the boy's funeral. The kid's death had devastated her and brought to the forefront a lot of unresolved emotional issues in her life. He wished she would seek counseling, but he knew she wouldn't appreciate the suggestion. Doctors were notoriously reluctant to seek medical help for themselves no matter how badly they needed it, and he'd be surprised if Doctor Susan MacKendrick was an exception to the rule.

Later he couldn't recall when he reached over and took her hand, but it was probably while the soloist's clear alto almost whispered, "Lead me, guide me, walk beside me. Help me find the way . . ." When the rag-tag gang members stepped forward to escort their fallen comrade's casket to the hearse, Susan followed with faltering steps and Brad clamped his arm about her shoulder. He left it there until the graveside service was finished, and the small crowd dispersed, leaving the two of them standing alone beside the flower-strewn grave.

"Would you like to go somewhere for hot chocolate?" For all the brilliant sun filtering through the trees, there was a sharpness in the air that hinted of winter.

"I'm all right. I should get back to the hospital . . ."

"No, you're not going straight back to the hospital," Brad spoke sternly. "Doctor's orders. There used to be a little place near here that made wonderful chili and I think we ought to see if it's still there." Ignoring her protest, he tucked her arm through his and began a leisurely stroll across the leaf-dotted grass. Wherever the leaves lay thickest, he shuffled his feet to enhance their crinkling sound.

As they walked beneath a low hanging branch, he lifted it slightly with one hand and a shower of gold filtered around them. He was enjoying himself, he realized with a bit of a start. It had been a long time since he'd taken pleasure in a simple walk through autumn leaves. He stopped and watched in awe as a single red maple leaf fluttered before them, flirted for just a moment with a fickle draft of wind, then settled briefly on Susan's shoulder before the errant breeze carried it away. A picture of Cathy flashed through his mind and he felt a moment's guilt, quickly followed by a peaceful assurance that Cathy wouldn't mind that he'd taken time to offer Susan a small distraction from her grief.

She shouldn't have let Brad manipulate her into having lunch with him, Susan thought. Glancing quickly around the small restaurant, she noticed that almost every table was full. One table near the window was surrounded with men from a nearby construction site, but the others seemed to be occupied by families. Hearing the shrieks and laughter of children, she closed her eyes. Regret filled her heart. Not once had she wiped up her son's spills, not once had she heard him laugh, nor had she been there when loneliness had driven him to find care and acceptance with a street gang.

"Susan, come on, give it a try." Brad indicated her untouched chili and the soft taco he'd ordered for her. She eyed the bowl skeptically. Her mother's cooking had been of the plain meat-and-potatoes variety, and her limited social life had kept her from tasting spicy foods in the homes of friends. Her few forays into international cuisine via the microwave during her college years had left her unimpressed. But she didn't want to disappoint Brad. He'd shown great consideration toward her, and it had helped more than he'd ever know to have his support through the funeral service. Cautiously she raised her spoon to her mouth.

It wasn't bad. It burned a little going down, but it wasn't as fiery as she had anticipated. Brad smiled encouragement and she took another taste.

"How do you feel about John Gunther being reappointed to the hospital board?" Brad asked before taking a huge bite of his taco.

"I don't have a problem with Gunther," she answered. "He opposed my appointment, but a lot of men of his generation are still skeptical of women doctors, let alone allowing one to be a department head. I do my job and I haven't heard any complaints from him." She picked up her taco and eyed it warily. Tentatively she nibbled at the edge of it. Cheese and shredded lettuce dropped to her lap. Embarrassed, she hastily returned the taco to her plate and reached for a napkin.

"It's no big deal," Brad laughed at her embarrassed confusion. "That's part of the fun of eating a taco."

"Dumping the filling all over yourself is fun?" She stared at him, wondering if he'd lost his mind.

"No, it's the challenge to see if you can get more in you than on you."

"Have you considered seeing a psychiatrist?" She surprised herself with the teasing question.

"But of course, I have zee appointment with Doktor Nutzenheimer theez afternoon."

Susan laughed. "Speaking of psychiatrists," she went on, "Dr.

Richards is transferring to a teaching hospital in California."

"I wonder who will take his place," Brad mused, then suggested a few preferences. The two settled into a discussion of hospital personnel then drifted to equipment they hoped the hospital would eventually acquire.

"I keep thinking there must be some diagnostic tool available that monitors internal bleeding better." Susan's earnest comment brought them both back to the tragedy that had brought them together.

Brad reached across the table to cover her hand. "Abdominal wounds have always been tricky, Susan. You did everything you could to save that boy."

"It wasn't enough."

"Perhaps it was," Brad went on. "That boy was in trouble and headed for bigger trouble, yet there was a spark of something good in him, something that recalled those early years when he had a mother who loved him. The Lord has promised us we won't be tried beyond what we have the strength to handle. Perhaps Robbie had reached his limit; further trials may have pushed him into actually killing someone. His physical death may have saved him from the more serious consequences of spiritual death."

Brad wasn't being flippant, nor was he offering a salve for her conscience. She could see that. She was saved from having to respond by Brad's pager. She realized that Brad must have left his car at the mortuary since he rode in the limousine with her. And they had dismissed the limo at the cemetery.

"Look," he slammed a couple of bills and a handful of change on the table. "There are two phones in the back. I'll call my office and you get us a cab."

It was late and the office should have been dark when Brad slipped his key into the lock. He'd spent the entire afternoon with Missie Madison. She had panicked when she'd noticed a little spotting and felt a few twinges. She didn't appear to be in immediate danger of losing her baby, but he'd decided to keep her in the hospital at least overnight. With her history, her condition could turn nasty very quickly. Something he'd read in a recent medical journal kept nagging at his mind and he'd decided to go to his office to hunt up the article. If there was any possibility that the technique he'd read about might help Missie carry her baby even one more month, he wanted to try it.

Brad's partner sat in the receptionist's chair with a mound of papers before him. Jack was a great doctor, but paperwork overwhelmed him.

"I thought you'd be gone long before now, Jack," Brad greeted him. "Rachel's going to kill you when she sees this mess." Their ultra-efficient office nurse kept up a running battle with Jack over his sloppy ways.

"I should have. This is a waste of time anyway," Jack said glumly as he waved a helpless hand over the papers.

"What are you looking for?" Brad moved over to stand behind his partner.

Jack hesitated, looking sheepish, then admitted, "The combination to Dad's safe."

"What safe?" Brad was puzzled. He and Jack had been partners for ten years, ever since Jack's father had died and Jack had found his practice too much for one doctor. Brad knew every inch of the office suite and he didn't recall ever seeing a safe. While the drug cabinet in the lab was as secure as a safe, it wasn't really a safe. Besides, it required a key, not a combination.

"Oh, not here." Jack carefully thumbed through the papers in his hand. "At home."

"Ah," Brad nodded, understanding now. Jack's parents had been killed in a private plane crash and he had inherited not only his father's practice but the family home in the Avenues, an established residential neighborhood not far from downtown Salt Lake City.

Shuffling through the stack of papers, Jack muttered, "Dad told me if I ever needed the combination I could find it in his personal file here at the office. I'm beginning to think I must have boxed it up with his patient files I put in storage."

"You mean in the ten years since your father died, you haven't opened that safe?" Brad asked incredulously.

"What? Oh." Jack shrugged his shoulders. "There aren't any valuables stored in there—no jewelry or money or anything like that. Dad just kept some of his more sensitive files in his safe. He used to handle quite a few private adoptions."

"Why the sudden interest?" Brad asked casually, not wanting to betray his own sudden interest.

"This came today." Jack handed him an official-looking envelope. "It's a court order demanding my cooperation in locating the birth parents of a kid who is going to die if he doesn't get a bone marrow transplant. The attorney who handled the adoption claims the birth mother was one of Dad's patients. I'm supposed to contact her and see if she's willing to come forward to be tested as a potential donor. Unfortunately I can't remember the combination and I can't find the paper Dad wrote it on."

"No one can force her to cooperate, can they?"

"No, the mother's privacy is protected. I contact her discreetly, then the choice is hers . . . So what are you doing back here, anyway? I thought you'd be spending the night at the hospital with that patient who came in bleeding this afternoon."

"She's stable at the moment, but I expect she'll have a few more scares. Then she'll probably go into premature labor for real unless I can figure out a way to stop her. I remembered a procedure I read about recently; I thought I'd check it out." Brad moved toward the door to his office, but his mind was still on Jack's explanation. He stopped and looked questioningly at his partner. "Have you handled any private adoptions yourself?"

"Not really," Jack answered almost absently. "I've referred a few women to social agencies that handle adoptions, but I don't have an arrangement with an attorney like Dad had. I have a patient right now who has been trying for eight years to get pregnant without any luck. She's finally given up and wants to adopt. If I had a patient wanting to give up a child now, I'd be really tempted to see what I could work out."

"How hard is it to find information about a child like the ones your dad placed?"

"Pretty hard right now. That stupid combination's got to be here someplace."

"That's not what I mean, Jack."

"Yeah, I know. Some doctors and attorneys protect their files more zealously than agencies do, especially if there's anything the least bit questionable about the adoption. However, most consider it a matter of ethics to protect their client's interests. A few are a bit careless or have staff that can be bribed."

"How about that court order? How hard is it to obtain one?" He might have a talk with his dad. Although he was retired from the bench, he might know a way to find out whether Robbie was really Susan's child.

"I should have cleared out this stuff years ago," Jack muttered as he dropped one stack of papers and picked up another. "So why all the interest in old adoptions? I know for a fact none of your girls are adopted. You don't have an earlier indiscretion hidden away somewhere, do you?" He grinned wickedly at Brad before resuming his search.

Brad laughed. "Not me, but you never know what might pop up in your murky past."

As he reached for his doorknob, a piece of paper lying on the floor between his office and Jack's caught his eye. He picked it up and a slow grin spread across his face.

"Hey, Jack!" He walked back to the front office. "Is this what you're looking for?" He dropped the index card in his partner's lap. "If you'd straighten up your office enough, you could work at your desk and you wouldn't be dropping things on your way out here to Rachel's desk."

Jack picked up the card and let out a whoop. "You found it! Now I won't have to pull Dad's records out of storage and hire a team to dig through them, or face contempt-of-court charges. Thanks, old buddy. I owe you one."

A peaceful feeling spread through Brad's body. He felt like he'd done something really great when all he'd really done was pick up a piece of paper. But that piece of paper had given him an idea.

Four

SUSAN TIPPED BACK HER CHAIR TO MORE EASILY prop her feet on the only other chair in her small cramped office. She never missed a chance to get her feet up. With one hand she scooped her keyboard off the desk and into her lap where she tapped a series of letters with two fingers. She could type after a fashion if she wished to, though it certainly didn't rank high on her list of desired activities. Usually she used a dictaphone, but hers had developed a short and was out for repairs. No one else seemed to have one she could borrow at the moment.

When memories of Brad striding through autumn leaves intruded on her thoughts, she resolutely shoved the picture away. Nor would she allow herself to think about newborn babies or a boy dying on an operating table. For a week she had banished all thoughts of the past, and she had avoided any occasion where she might bump into Brad. She reminded herself that she had chosen to make medicine her life, and the only way to be her most effective self was to eliminate all emotions and memories.

A tap sounded at her open door. She looked up to see a young nurse glance at her quickly then lower her eyes. "Dr. MacKendrick, Dr. Gines asked if you'd take a look at the X-rays on that football injury that came in an hour ago."

Susan swung her feet to the floor and tossed the keyboard onto the desk. Blocking out the past was easier when dealing with patients than while doing paperwork, and she welcomed the interruption. Striding past the nurse, Susan felt rather than saw her flinch, and she frowned. It never ceased to annoy her the way some of her staff acted as though they were scared to death of her, and she had to fight the temptation to utter a few sharp words.

Inside the examination room, four X-rays hung on light panels. A burly teenage boy, bigger than most grown men, lay on a gurney, yelling threats and obscenities against anyone who dared touch him while Dr. Gines stared without expression at the photographic images on the wall, his back toward the youth. The boy was obviously incapable of moving or he'd be gone by now, Susan thought. Without any acknowledgment of the other occupants of the room, Susan carefully reviewed the shots of the boy's left hip.

"Well, there's no question it's broken," her voice revealed a tinge of sarcasm since it was obvious what needed to be done, and Dr. Gines should have been able to call up an orthopedic surgeon and set up the procedure on his own.

A string of curses burst from the boy. Susan ignored him to concentrate on Dr. Gines.

"I know it's broken," Gines spoke with some irritation. "I also know it has to be pinned, but Junior here won't consent to surgery."

"Won't consent! He's a minor, isn't he? Where are his parents?"

"His mother is out in the hall wringing her hands. She won't do anything Junior doesn't want her to do."

"Oh, for crying out loud!" Susan snatched the clipboard from Dr. Gines and marched out into the hall. A tiny, frail woman sat with her face in her hands, weeping. When Susan approached, she looked up to ask, "Can Junior go now?"

"Certainly not!" Susan snapped, then took a deep breath, reminding herself to deal as patiently as possible with this woman. "Your son has a fractured hip. It needs to be set by an orthopedic surgeon. Dr. Alston is on call and he's very good. He'll place metal pins in the hip to keep the bones from moving while they heal. Junior will be on crutches for about two months, then he'll be as good as new."

"Oh, no," the woman gasped. "Junior says it's just a pulled groin muscle and he'll be fine in a couple of days."

"Did Dr. Gines show you Junior's X-rays?" Susan asked.

"Yes, but they don't make any sense to me."

"His hip is broken. Those pictures show very clearly that a serious fracture has occurred. A few days' rest *won't* heal a fracture." Susan's exasperation with the woman was beginning to show. "You need to sign this consent form so we can get on with the surgery."

"Oh, no." The woman shied away from the clipboard Susan offered her. "Junior would be very angry if I signed that. The state play-offs begin next week. He said he'd be fine by then."

"He won't be fine," Susan retorted. "If that hip isn't set correctly, he'll never walk normally again, and he certainly won't play football."

"Junior says . . ." A fresh bout of tears rendered the woman incapable of speech.

"How old is Junior?" Susan demanded.

"Sixteen." Junior's mother stammered. "But he's—"

"Don't tell me he's practically an adult because I won't believe you," Susan interrupted. "Right now he's in there throwing a tantrum in the best two-year-old fashion. He's a minor, you're his mother. It's up to you, not him, to make decisions concerning his medical care. So what's it going to be? Are you going to give him a chance to grow up with a normal body, or are you going to let him decide to become a cripple?"

"If Junior wants me to . . ." Her voice trailed off in a whimper.

"Go talk to your son." Susan whirled around in disgust and pointed to the examination room where the boy continued to shout. She didn't want to hear one more word about what Junior wanted.

Several crude words greeted the woman as she entered the room. These were followed by a string of threats if she signed the consent papers. Susan's eyes dropped to the papers in her hand and she smiled grimly. The boy hadn't come in on his own, and his wimpy mother hadn't brought him in. She'd be willing to bet the boy's coach dragged him to the hospital. She set off determinedly for the waiting room.

Five minutes later, after carefully explaining the situation to Coach Tia'afu, she led the former college linebacker into the small room where Junior thrashed about, demanding to be released.

"You're suspended!" the big man roared the moment he saw Junior. "Now apologize to your mamma and these doctors."

"Suspended? But, Coach . . . It's just a little groin pull. It'll be all right by next week."

"You're not only a smart mouth, but now you're a doctor, too?" The coach glared at the kid. "There are the pictures," he waved at the X-rays. "No more football this season."

"But, Coach . . ." When it became obvious he couldn't change his coach's mind, Junior swore in disgust.

"Enough!" Tia'afu roared. "Shut your mouth and tell your mamma to sign the doctor's paper. No surgery, no more football— ever. Permanent suspension! Understand?"

Susan extended the clipboard toward the frightened little woman, who glanced nervously at her son and waited for him to nod his head before she signed.

Susan clamped her mouth shut and stepped back out into the hall. Dr. Gines could make the arrangements from this point. If she hung around she'd be tempted to tell the woman what she thought of her parenting skills. She'd never understand how some parents lost track of who was the adult and who was the child in their relationships with their children.

An ear-splitting scream stopped her before she'd taken two steps. She glanced up to see a tall young man with a screaming child in his arms and a distraught woman fluttering around him.

An orderly reached the group before she did, and Corbett directed them to an empty cubicle. As the father carefully set the sobbing little girl on the examination table, Susan shook her head in disbelief. The child had a doll attached to her head, and a lock of the girl's long blond hair disappeared inside the doll's mouth. *When did dolls start eating?* she wondered. The last association she'd had with a doll, it only drank from a little bottle, then promptly wet its diaper.

"My poor baby," the mother crooned as she popped a piece of candy into her daughter's mouth. She looked up at Susan. "Please hurry," she implored. "Taylor is so scared."

"Does it hurt?" Susan asked the child as she leaned forward to examine her scalp where the doll appeared to have halted its voracious journey. The girl would have a small bald spot, which might be a little sore for a day or two, but there was no serious damage. Most of the lock of hair appeared still firmly attached to the girl's head.

Susan reached for a pair of scissors and the child screamed, "Go away! I hate you."

"I won't cut you, just a little piece of your hair," Susan attempted to calm the child.

"No!"

"Don't cut her hair!" both parents shouted in unison.

Were they serious? Susan looked from one parent to the other. Just how did they propose to free their daughter from the toy's viselike grip without cutting her hair? And why hadn't they performed the simple procedure at home rather than drag her to a trauma center?

"Please don't cut it," the mother sobbed. "I couldn't bear it if Taylor lost her beautiful hair."

With a sigh Susan picked up the phone to call for maintenance. If she couldn't cut the doll free, obviously the doll would have to be dismantled. Ten minutes later she left the cubicle shaking her head as an unhappy maintenance man attempted to take the doll apart and an unhappy little girl ordered him not to hurt her baby. Attempting to soothe the child, both parents promised in unison to buy her a new doll just like the one she'd received that day for her birthday.

"Not another one that eats hair," Susan muttered under her breath. The problem was apparent to her. Couldn't toy manufacturers and parents see that a child who received a doll that could "eat" rubber french fries would also try to feed the doll other things, like hair? Children put everything imaginable in their own mouths; of course they would do the same with a doll who was designed to eat any object placed in its mouth. A person didn't have to be a parent to know that.

As she reached her office, Susan stopped just outside the door to think. If she'd raised her child, would she have fussed over him and spoiled him, giving in to his wants even when common sense told her a toy was dangerous? In trying to avoid the dictatorial control both Tony's parents and her own had exerted over them, would she have allowed her son to become a tyrant like Junior? She'd never know what kind of parent she might have been—because she would never be a parent. The thought left a heaviness in her heart.

She entered her office and sank down in her chair, her mind still on the two children she'd seen in the past hour. *Classic examples of poor parenting skills,* she affirmed to her own silent satisfaction. *I'll bet Brad doesn't let his girls get away with that kind of nonsense.*

"Oh, no," she groaned aloud, realizing where her thoughts had returned.

"Oh, no, what?" A voice came from the doorway. Susan's head

jerked up and she found herself staring into a familiar pair of blue eyes. For a moment she wondered if her thoughts had conjured him up, then she tightened her lips in annoyance. Being fanciful wasn't her style. Brad was real, much too real, and he was standing in her office.

"Nothing important," Susan answered breezily as she picked up a pen and attempted to look busy. She made notations on several papers without looking up, but Brad was hard to ignore. Physically, he was a large man, as were a number of other doctors who occasionally visited her office. But somehow the other doctors didn't leave her feeling like the room had shrunk, and her reaction to the man annoyed her. Perhaps if he thought she had urgent paperwork to do he'd go away.

"Do you have a few minutes?" Brad asked.

"Well, I really have to finish this . . ." She let her voice trail off. She felt uncomfortable with the subterfuge. It really wasn't her style.

"It won't take long."

"Perhaps later . . ." She attempted to put him off indefinitely without being rude.

"Okay," Brad agreed. "Corbett said you're working a double, which means you're off at eleven. I'll pick you up then. We can talk over dinner."

He was gone before Susan could rally her senses. Why hadn't she let him say whatever he'd come to say? She didn't want to have dinner with him, and she certainly didn't want to start the kind of gossip that would spread like wildfire through the hospital if anyone saw them leave together. She picked up the telephone. A quick call to his office would enable her to cancel without having to actually speak to him. She hesitated, then slowly returned the phone to its cradle. Perhaps she should find out what Brad wanted to talk to her about.

Mrs. Mack looked pointedly at Brad's plate. "Aren't you feeling well, doctor? You've hardly eaten a thing."

Brad refolded his napkin and hastened to reassure her. "I'm fine. I just don't want to eat much right now because I'll be going out to dinner in a little while."

"Are we going?" Heidi looked up in hopeful anticipation.

"No, honey," Brad winked at her. "Not this time. I'm having

dinner with Dr. MacKendrick, but she can't leave the hospital until eleven o'clock, way after your bedtime."

"Why are you having dinner with her?" Ashley wanted to know.

"I need to talk to her." Brad didn't want to go into detailed explanations. What he had to tell Susan didn't concern anyone other than her.

"Can't you call her on the phone?" Ashley continued to question him.

"No, I don't think that would do," Brad laughed. "She's been working at the hospital since seven this morning. I think she deserves to eat a good dinner while we talk."

Ashley shrugged and resumed eating her dinner. He caught a doubtful expression on Michelle's face, but she didn't say anything.

"Is Holland going to tend me?" Kelly asked eagerly.

"I thought maybe Mrs. Mack would listen for you." He turned a questioning eye toward the housekeeper. "You should all be in bed and asleep long before I leave."

Brad rose from the table and moved toward his den. He was surprised when a small voice spoke behind him.

"Dad, I think we should talk."

Brad turned to see his oldest daughter standing in the doorway. Bobbi's cheeks appeared flushed, and she was giving a spot on the rug more attention than it deserved. Brad's spirits took a nose dive and he found himself wishing Cathy were here.

"All right, Bobbi. Come on in and close the door." He'd be calm, even professional if need be. He didn't want to antagonize his daughter or leave her unwilling to talk to him, but if his suspicions were correct about the nature of the "talk" ahead of him, he suspected she'd be disappointed in his answer. What could he say to make her understand that he wasn't just being difficult and that their church leaders weren't just a bunch of old fogies who wanted to spoil her fun? There really are sound emotional reasons for putting off dating until sixteen, he wanted to tell her.

Slumping into the chair by his desk, Bobbi stared down at her long braid and picked at the band securing the end of it.

"Go ahead," Brad encouraged her.

"Dad!" Suddenly the words exploded from her in an almost incoherent rush. "Do you think somebody should date somebody if that somebody doesn't like the first somebody's family?"

Brad blinked in astonishment. It wasn't exactly the question he'd expected. Right topic, wrong question. "Are you saying," he began carefully, "you know someone who doesn't like me or your sisters and that leaves you with divided loyalties?"

"No, Dad. Not exactly. I guess this person likes you."

"Likes me, but not your sisters?"

Bobbi slowly nodded her head, and Brad rubbed two fingers across his eyebrow as he tried to formulate a response to his daughter's concern. Finally he spoke. "Family loyalty is important and a person shouldn't let someone else say mean, negative things about family members. Maybe you should tell this person good things about your sisters and help them to get to know each other better, and the person's feelings might change."

"I don't think so." Bobbi looked at him dubiously. "May I ask you something else?"

"Certainly." Brad stared at his daughter, perplexed by her odd formality.

"Well, do you think two people should go on dates if there's no chance they'll get married?"

"Honey, very few people these days marry the only person they've ever dated. Sometimes a person seems like someone you might want to marry, but after a few dates, you know it won't work out, so you break up and look for someone else."

"Did you date other ladies before you married Mom?"

"Uh . . . yes." Brad wasn't sure where Bobbi's questions were leading.

"How many?"

"I don't know," Brad laughed. "A few."

"Did you think you might marry all of them?"

"No, not all. There were a few I dated because they asked me and I thought it would be rude to turn them down. There were a couple I dated because they were popular and pretty, and I guess I wanted to show off a little bit by being seen with them. But most of them were the kind of ladies I might have married, except I didn't fall in love with any of them except your mother."

"Are you going to get married to— to somebody else?"

A sharp pain gripped his heart. Brad couldn't believe he'd heard his daughter right. Was she worrying that he might remarry and she and her sisters wouldn't be as important to him? Or did she perhaps want him to remarry because it was too awful having him be their only parent? What did this conversation have to do with him anyway?

"No, Bobbi, I don't think so. I can't promise I won't ever want to get married again, but right now I can't even imagine being married to anyone but your mother." He could tell his words didn't reassure his daughter.

"Then don't do it, Daddy. My Young Women president said we shouldn't date until we're ready to consider that the relationship might result in marriage. And we shouldn't lead someone on, letting them think we're interested in marriage when we're really not. She said sixteen is the minimum age for dating, but waiting longer is okay because if we fall in love too soon we might not get to do other things like go to college. Really, Daddy, I think there should be a maximum age, too, and you shouldn't date Dr. MacKendrick because she doesn't like kids, and you're too old anyway," she finished breathlessly.

"Whoa, wait a minute, Bobbi. When did we start talking about me? And what makes you think I'm dating Dr. MacKendrick?"

"You're taking her to dinner tonight, aren't you?" Bobbi met his eyes and he recognized a familiar stubborn glint.

"Yes, we're going to dinner together, but it's not a date," Brad defended himself.

"Is it a business meeting?" Bobbi continued to grill him.

"No, it's personal. But it's not a date."

"Dad, you said when a boy and a girl who aren't children anymore go places together and it isn't business or a group activity, it's a date."

Brad did a double take as his daughter threw his words back at him. Was having dinner with Susan a date? Certainly not, he assured himself. Dates had romantic overtones and romance was no part of his friendship with Susan. He was simply helping her gain some information she seemed to need. His daughter's set face reminded him she was waiting for an explanation. He was a thirty-seven-year-old adult; he didn't *have* to justify his actions to a fourteen-year-old child! *Maybe he did,* a voice somewhere inside his head argued. If he expected candor from Bobbi when she began dating in a few years, he'd better be candid with her now.

"Susan MacKendrick has gone through an emotionally painful experience, and I would like to help her. I learned something today that might help her feel happier, and I think I should tell her about it someplace away from work."

"What—?"

"I can't tell you about it because I don't have Susan's permission to talk about it," Brad cut his daughter off before she could voice her question.

"I don't know, Dad. I still don't think you should go," Bobbi voiced her reluctance to accept his argument.

"It'll be okay, honey," he promised, and rose from his chair to give her a hug.

As she left the room she made one last parting shot. "If Mom were still alive you wouldn't be going to dinner with Dr. MacKendrick, so it is too a date!"

Two hours later Brad smiled as he remembered the look of astonishment on Susan's face when he told her he'd pick her up for dinner. She needed someone to shake her out of her rut, and he had to admit he enjoyed doing just that. Briefly he wondered if she'd slip out of the hospital and be gone before he arrived. No, that wasn't her style. She might want to, but she wouldn't. Susan MacKendrick didn't take easy outs.

Leaving a small light burning in the kitchen, Brad shrugged into his jacket and made his way to the garage. His thoughts continued to dwell on Susan. How could one person have so many facets to her personality? he wondered. In the past few weeks he'd revised his perception of her as a stern perfectionist, and he no longer saw her as a strictly no-nonsense career woman either, though he acknowledged both her dedication to her career and her commitment to excellence in medical care. Over and over his mind returned to the frightened teenager whose one act of rebellion had ended in disaster. Now he saw a softer, vulnerable woman struggling with guilt and loneliness.

Backing out of the driveway, he noticed the light was still on in Bobbi's bedroom. She should be asleep, but he wasn't surprised she was still awake. When he had told the children he'd be going out after they were all in bed, she had been the only one to object. Uneasily he replayed their conversation and wondered why she objected so strongly to his spending time with Susan. Would she feel the same way about his spending time with any woman, or had she taken a dislike specifically to Susan?

Bobbi's parting words lingered in his mind, and he acknowledged he wouldn't be having dinner with Susan tonight if Cathy were still alive. But that didn't mean he and Susan were going on a date, did it?

He hadn't dated another woman since the day he'd literally bumped into Cathy on his way into the Harold B. Lee Library at BYU more than fifteen years ago, and he'd never had any desire to date another woman since that long-ago day.

What about now? the voice in the back of his head persisted. *You've been looking forward most of the day to being with Susan tonight.*

Brad shifted in his seat uneasily, suddenly wondering if Cathy would consider his having dinner with Susan a date.

Five

BRAD WATCHED AS SUSAN ATE HER CAKE WITH obvious enjoyment, and something warm unfurled deep inside him. He wondered how he could have forgotten how enjoyable it was to share dinner with a woman after a long hard day. He'd been right to ignore his daughter's reservations about him taking Susan to dinner. Bobbi was too young and too newly aware of male/female relationships to understand that sometimes friendship was enough. Having dinner together wasn't necessarily a date.

Left to her own devices, Susan would probably have settled for a microwave meal or something out of a can. He knew that much about her. He also knew she hadn't really wanted to go to dinner with him, but once they reached the restaurant and placed their orders, she'd relaxed and seemed to enjoy their conversation as much as he had. She'd enjoyed her food, too, he thought in wry amusement. She was hungry and she didn't pretend otherwise. He remembered from his own stint in trauma as a young resident how much energy the frantic pace in a busy emergency room required and how voracious his appetite had been when his shift ended. A twinge of guilt surfaced, reminding him of all the candy bars he'd eaten on the way home from the hospital those nights, even when he'd known Cathy would have a nutritious meal waiting. She'd never understood how he could eat several chocolate bars and still have room for dinner. A doctor, of all people, with a sweet tooth had been beyond her comprehension.

With the back of her fork Susan captured the last crumbs of dark chocolate cake on her plate and as she lifted them to her mouth she noticed him watching her. A soft flush tinted her cheeks, quickly followed by an expression of defiance. He felt a grin spread across his face.

"Want some more?" he asked.

"No." She shook her head. "I've already eaten too much."

"Not too much," Brad contradicted. "Working the way you do burns a lot of fuel. Besides, I've always held a deep appreciation for good food myself." Glancing down he noted his own plate was empty and he'd managed to eat a piece of the rich chocolate cake as well. He'd enjoyed his dinner a great deal, and he honestly couldn't remember the last time he had really enjoyed eating. That pleasure had evaded him since those awful months when Cathy had struggled with every bite that entered her mouth and promptly lost, courtesy of her chemotherapy-induced nausea.

"Your own appetite has been less than normal since your wife died, hasn't it?" Susan seemed to be reading his thoughts, or perhaps she remembered his less-than-svelte figure from a few years ago.

Brad nodded. "Food seemed to lose its importance after Cathy died. She was committed to living a healthy lifestyle, and my eating habits caused her a lot of concern. For years we kept up a good-natured, quasi-serious running battle over her attempts to feed me health foods and my weakness for sweets, especially chocolate. After she died, sneaking a candy bar lost its appeal." He shrugged his shoulders in a self-deprecating way.

"You still miss her, don't you?"

"Yeah, I do." He picked up his water glass and ran a thumb carefully around the rim. He kept his eyes lowered, not meeting hers. "Cathy carried around with her so much light and vitality that even when she was ill, I felt she was somehow illuminating my life. When she died, it was as though someone had turned off the light and left me struggling in the dark. I've even gone so far as to question why God took her and not me when I've always known I needed her far more than she needed me. She would have managed alone far better than I am doing."

Susan frowned, trying to understand. "That doesn't make sense. She didn't have a career so supporting your family would have been much more difficult for her."

"I don't mean financial support." He set his glass down and rubbed his chin with one hand. He wondered how this conversation had come about. He'd never really talked about his relationship with his wife other than to reminisce over shared experiences with close family and friends, and he wasn't sure why he felt compelled to do so now.

"And I'm not implying I'm some emotional weakling or dependant, but I think some people have a greater capacity than others to give emotional support. Cathy was one of those. She was a builder, a giver, requiring little in return. That's not to say I didn't give her emotional support. I did and she accepted it, but she didn't *need* it. When she faced cancer she did just that, *she* faced it. I admit I felt shut out by her self-sufficiency. I wanted desperately to take care of her and she knew that. She understood my need to be needed, so she leaned on me, allowing my need to be filled."

Susan was quiet for several minutes, appearing deep in thought. When she spoke, an element of wistfulness colored her words. "You were fortunate to be loved so much, and I suspect you underestimate how much your wife needed and relied on you. When I was a little girl I imagined that someday someone would really need me; that's partly why I went into medicine. And my skills as a doctor have been needed, but no one has ever needed *me* except my baby—and I let him down."

"That isn't true. You didn't let your baby down, and you didn't let that boy you think was your son down either," Brad spoke earnestly. "That's what I wanted to talk to you about. I think I know a way we can find out if Robbie really was the child you gave up."

"I told you—"

"Yes, you told me about the birth and adoption dates and the similarity between the boy's appearance and your baby's father. But that isn't conclusive proof," Brad warmed to his subject. "One night last week I found my partner searching for medical records connected to an adoption his father arranged a long time ago, and I learned that a family medical history is provided to adoptive parents. It can also be accessed by the child when he reaches eighteen or by his guardian if his adoptive parents die while he's still a minor."

"So?"

"Do you remember filling out such a form?"

"No. Maybe. I don't know. I sort of remember answering a lot of questions about whether anyone in my family had ever had cancer or heart disease or anything like that. I couldn't fill in much information about Tony's family. His parents came from Italy as teenage newly-weds and converts to the Church. They never talked about their previous life or families."

"If we can get our hands on a copy of that medical record, wouldn't you recognize if the information is the same?" Brad leaned forward in his eagerness to share his plan.

"I might, but how do we get a copy?" Susan wrinkled her brows. "I've already checked with the various records departments and been told that even though he's dead, his adoption records remain sealed."

Brad grinned. "I took the liberty of calling Robbie's aunt. She didn't want to talk to me at first, but when I assured her I wasn't a cop and that she couldn't be held responsible for anything the boy did, she agreed to talk to me."

"Does she have a copy of Robbie's family medical history?" Susan went straight to the point.

"I don't know. She said she has a box of papers that belonged to her sister. It might be in there."

"Will she let us see the papers?" Susan asked anxiously.

"See them!" Brad laughed. "She said we can have them if we want them. To her they're just trash she should have burned before now. If you're interested we can go get them tomorrow."

"Any time you say." A smile lit her face and Brad reached across the table to lay his hand on top of hers. He meant the gesture as one of understanding, but as his hand covered her long, capable fingers he discovered her hand felt uncannily right in his and he wondered if perhaps this was a date after all. No, he shrugged off the question. He was simply sharing a quiet evening and a moment of hope with a friend.

To say Maria Hererra invited them into her home the next day wouldn't be entirely accurate; her sullen gesture that they should enter was anything but welcoming. Maria indicated they should sit on the sofa, so they picked their way across the room to where two deep impressions on that piece of furniture revealed the only uncluttered surface available. As Maria shuffled off to retrieve the box of papers, Susan looked around in dismay, picturing a small boy dwelling in the gloom and clutter of that small house. Schooling her face not to reveal her distaste, she stared blandly past the remnants of several meals adorning the coffee table before her and waited for Maria's return.

A movement across the room caught her eye and she muffled a gasp as a small gray mouse scuttled beneath a ragged chair piled high with numerous years' accumulation of magazines. Brad's hand settled around her forearm, and he whispered, "You're not afraid of a little mouse, are you?"

"Of course not," she whispered back. "I just feel sick to think Robbie ever lived in this house."

"He wasn't here long," Brad answered grimly. "If I remember right, his aunt said he was too much work and bother. He wouldn't mind her, so she turned him over to the county."

Susan shuddered. This wasn't what she'd wanted for her child. She looked up to see Maria making her way back into the room. She was carrying a cardboard boot box, which she shoved unceremoniously toward Brad.

"There's nothing worth anything in there. We looked, but that fancy-pants lawyer already told us Don only owned a little farm and it wasn't even paid for. When we sold it there wasn't enough to raise no kid."

"No insurance?" Brad asked in a sympathetic voice, though Susan could read something else behind his innocent question.

"Buryin' money. That's all." Maria's scowl deepened.

"I don't suppose there's any of that left?" Susan asked sweetly, too sweetly. Brad squeezed her arm and she silently acknowledged his warning. It would be foolish to let her rising anger at the sloppy, greedy woman before her jeopardize their mission. She wanted that box.

"It cost an awful lot to bury Rosa and Don," Maria said defensively and her scowl turned to wary suspicion.

"I'm sure you did your best for your sister and her family," Brad spoke in conciliatory tones as he rose to his feet and pulled Susan up beside him. "We're really grateful for your help with our research project," he continued to speak amiably as he moved toward the door. Seething, Susan followed his lead. She couldn't wait to get out of this house where laziness and greed had left no room for a small boy.

"Just a minute . . ." Maria moved toward them.

"I really want to thank you," Brad held out a hand and eagerly clasped Maria's. Susan's eyes widened. Was she imagining things or had Brad slipped something inside Maria's hand? Was he actually giving that horrid woman money?

"We've got to be going now," he said. "We really do appreciate your letting us have Rosa's box."

Maria withdrew her hand from Brad's grasp and slowly backed up. She appeared to be contemplating a weighty problem and Susan found herself holding her breath. If Maria backed out now, would she ever know about her son?

"It's just worthless junk," the older woman muttered. She made no attempt to detain them as Brad reached for the door and Susan hurried through ahead of him.

Susan waited until they were settled in Brad's car before saying anything. She kept her eyes trained on his profile as he pulled smoothly into traffic. The words came slowly. "You bribed her, didn't you? Or did you buy the box?"

Brad shifted uneasily, but he never took his eyes off the road. "I guess it was a bribe."

"I can't believe straight-arrow Dr. Bradley Williams actually resorted to paying a bribe."

"I can't either." He flashed her a boyish grin. "I've seen it work on T.V. Some crook starts to renege on a deal, so the hero slips him a little cash, and just like that, the deal is on again. I can't believe it actually worked."

"I can't believe you actually did it," Susan repeated dryly. "What would all those people who still call you bishop think if they knew you bribed someone?"

"I don't know. I guess it wasn't too ethical to give her money, but all I could think about was how much you need to know whether Robbie was your son. She looked like she was about to snatch the box back," he defended himself. "Besides I was getting a pretty strong message that no matter what I said, money was the only language she understood. Do you suppose we might consider the money a tip rather than a bribe?"

Susan laughed. "I guess that's between you and your conscience. Your ethics might be questionable, but I'm glad you got the box for me. And that makes it my debt. How much did you give her?"

"You're offering to pay me back?" The incredulity in Brad's voice was obviously false. "No way. I'd really question my ethical integrity if I allowed you to become an accessory to the crime."

"I'm already an accessory." She tried to keep her voice steady and emotionless in spite of the giggle threatening to spill from her throat. The mere thought of giggling was enough to sober her. She hadn't giggled since she was a child, if then.

In her apartment they sat cross-legged on the carpet with the box between them. Susan took a deep breath and Brad noticed a slight tremor in her hand as she reached for the lid of the box. Even though the lid was dented and battered, Susan carefully placed it on the floor behind her before turning back to the box. Her hand stilled and several seconds passed before she reached for the first paper. It was torn and stained as though a cup had been picked up and set down on it numerous times.

"It's Rosa's will," Susan spoke softly. "Evidently she had a few good pieces of jewelry she wanted to go to the young lady who would someday marry Robbie. I can guess who got those," she added cynically.

"Don't." Brad touched her arm. "Bitterness won't help Robbie, only hurt you."

"I know," she acknowledged. "But it's so hard not to feel bitter both for Robbie's sake and my own. I feel like we were both betrayed."

"Maybe this is too much for you. If you like I'll take the box and go through it for you," Brad offered, though he knew what her response would be before she spoke.

"No, this is something I have to do myself."

"But not alone." Brad smiled encouragingly. "The box is a shambles. Maria and her husband doubtless dug through it many times before they concluded it was worthless. I'll sort personal letters into one pile, documents into another, and anything unusual into a third pile. Perhaps if everything is organized it will be easier to find what we're looking for."

"I think Rosa must have organized the papers at one time," Susan observed. "See the narrow satin ribbons scattered through the box? I think she used them to tie similar materials together."

"You're probably right." He reached for the top paper and turned it over. "This is Don's will. I'll start the document stack right here beside you." He set the paper where she could easily reach it and returned to the box. For several minutes he sorted while she read, then as his fingers closed around a sheaf of papers, several photographs slipped to the floor. He picked them up and examined them briefly before handing them to Susan.

"I think you should look at these," he urged her to interrupt her careful perusal of the paper in her hand.

He watched her face as she examined the photograph of a couple standing in front of a small, but attractive house with a long driveway bordered by a profusion of colorful flowers. The woman was laughing up into the face of the man who stood beside her holding a toddler in his arms. The man and the child appeared to be laughing, too. All three were dressed neatly in jeans and long-sleeved denim shirts.

Slowly Susan turned to the next picture. It was Christmas morning and a slightly older pajama-clad boy knelt amid an array of wrapping paper and toys before a tree to connect the cars of a brightly colored circus train. The woman sat beside him, one hand on his shoulder.

The last picture showed the boy astride a pony while the man stood beside the small horse with one hand on the horse's bridle and the other circling the child's waist.

"He really was loved for a little while, wasn't he?" Susan's voice held a little catch.

"Yes, he was. I think he would have grown up just fine if his parents hadn't died so young."

"But they did die and look what happened!"

"Susan, life is unpredictable. You know that. If you'd kept your child there are no guarantees he would have been any better off. You wouldn't have been able to earn the income you do now and who knows what poverty may have driven you both to. And what if you'd been the one to die? Who would have raised him?"

Susan shuddered. Would her parents have raised her son to be the son they'd always wished she had been? Would they have loved him more because he was a male? Or would they have rejected and hated him because she had disappointed them? She'd never know, but she could speculate.

The stacks of paper on the floor grew deeper as Brad pulled them from the box. When he finished he clasped his hands behind his neck and leaned back against the sofa, watching her as she meticulously worked her way through the documents and a few more photographs. In minutes he appeared to be asleep.

Susan worked her way through the first stack. She found adoption papers along with the couple's marriage license and birth certificates. There was even an amended birth certificate for Robbie, but no medical information other than a tiny blue book in which all of his childhood inoculations had been listed. Disappointed, she began on the letters.

"Want some help?" Brad's eyes were still closed.

"I can do it. There aren't very many."

"It'll be faster if I help." Brad sat up and reached for a stack of envelopes. Quickly he thumbed through them. "Most of these seem to be from Rosa and Maria's mother," he commented.

"The two I just read were from her, too. She seems to think Rosa did some great disservice to Maria and that if she doesn't return what she took from her sister, God will punish her."

"Don't tell me Maria was the poor, picked-on child while Rosa got all the breaks! I don't think I can buy that story," Brad laughed as he pulled a sheet of paper from an envelope and began to read. "Ah, here's one from Maria."

A long, low whistle escaped Brad's lips and Susan looked up from the letter she held.

"Listen to this." He shook his head and began to read, "You cheated me. You said you didn't have no more money, but Mama says Don bought a farm. Farms cost lots of money, so you lied. That lawyer says there's nothing I can do and the papers are all signed. He says you're going to put Mama in one of them old folks places and I should pay my share and the government gets her house. I ain't paying nothing. She was fine in her house and you shouldn't of signed away her house cause it was my inheritance. Them places cost lots of money too so I know you got some stashed away. You better pay me another $5000 or you'll be real sorry."

"Nice lady," Susan said sarcastically. "Why on earth did Rosa leave her child to her sister when obviously there was no love lost between them?"

"Good question." Brad picked up Don's will to see if the answer lay there. A few minutes later he spoke thoughtfully, "According to this, Rosa's mother should have become Robbie's guardian, but this will is dated two years before the letter I just read. The will was drawn up shortly after Robbie was adopted, leaving everything to him, with his grandmother to have control of whatever assets the couple might have until the boy reached eighteen. Two years later, according to Maria's letter, her mother was admitted to a nursing home. She may have died before Robbie was orphaned or been too incapacitated to care for him. At any rate, when Rosa died Maria stepped in claiming to be next of kin."

"Until the money ran out," Susan added.

"Until the money ran out," Brad agreed. "I wonder what the two sisters were feuding over." Susan could see Brad already had a theory what the feud was about. In the far reaches of her mind, the same suspicion was surfacing in her thoughts. Was it possible?

"I wonder if . . . what if Robbie was actually Maria's child?" Brad voiced his thoughts aloud while watching Susan's face closely.

"Maria sold her baby to her sister?" Susan's face showed her distaste for the idea.

"Not directly. In a private adoption the adopting couple simply agrees to pay exorbitant maternity costs and legal fees. Even if Rosa did adopt Maria's child and Maria wanted more money later, it's still not babyselling. It's extortion."

Susan lowered her lashes in a vain attempt to hide her emotions. She should be glad of the possibility Robbie wasn't her child. Instead she felt as though once more she was giving up her baby, losing her child.

Six

"HOW DO WE FIND OUT?"

Oddly it pleased him that she said "we." "I suppose we could ask Maria."

"Do you think she'll tell us the truth?" Susan asked skeptically.

"I don't know, but I think we should give it a try, or rather I should."

"I'm the one who needs to know," Susan argued.

Brad paused, thinking. He didn't want to offend Susan but Maria's antagonism and suspicion toward Susan had been obvious. And to some extent, it was reciprocated by Susan. "I don't think Maria quite took to you," he said carefully.

"You're probably right," Susan sighed. "There's something about that woman that sets my teeth on edge. But . . ."

"No buts," Brad placed a finger across her lips. "You're accustomed to handling your own problems, taking care of yourself, and asking no favors. You didn't ask; I volunteered. And it's way past time you started letting someone do something for you once in a while. That's what friends are for, to share the load when the going gets tough."

She turned away to stare silently out the window for several minutes. He saw her throat move as she swallowed once. Without turning to face him, she spoke softly to his reflection in the glass. "I've never really had a friend except Tony. I don't know what friends do."

"Come here." He held out his hand to her and waited, wondering if she would accept his invitation. He knew she could see him in the glass, but she might choose to pretend she didn't. Slowly, almost as though she expected to be burned, she turned and placed her hand in his. Gently he led her to the sofa and sat down beside her without releasing her hand.

"I know a lot about friendship," he spoke softly. "As a young boy I once saw some other children teasing and picking on a smaller boy on the school playground. It upset me and I ran over to help him. Another boy did the same thing. After we chased away the bullies we took Allen—that was his name—to the boys' bathroom to clean up his bloody nose. The three of us have been close friends ever since. We grew up together—fishing, mountain climbing, playing sports, dating. We even share ownership of a mountain cabin. When Allen's parents ignored him, Doug's family and mine found room for him. When Doug's wife disappeared, Allen found her and watched over her and her son until he could find a way to reunite them. They shared my pain when Cathy was ill and grieved with me when she died. Friends care, and they do what they see needs to be done without being asked."

"Tony was the only child ever allowed to visit me and all of our chores had to be finished before we could play. Tony's parents let him go to scout camp once, but mine said Beehive camp was a foolish waste of time and money. I resented my parents limiting my choice of friends, but even if they'd allowed me to participate in activities like camp, I wouldn't have gone anyway." She lifted her chin as though she expected his disapproval.

"Why not?" Brad asked gently.

"I didn't fit in. The other girls made fun of my hair and the way I dressed."

"Was it so bad?"

"Terrible!" She shuddered in remembered horror. "I wasn't permitted to wear pants, and my mother made my dresses that were always some dark color with long sleeves and a hem almost to my ankles. My father insisted I wear heavy oxfords and keep my hair braided. I never even owned a tube of lip gloss until my sophomore year in college."

"Where did you grow up? Shortcreek?" Brad raised one eyebrow in a pseudo gesture of shock.

"No. My parents found much to admire in some of the ultra-conservative fundamentalist groups, but they drew the line at polygamy or turning their farm over to any self-professed united order group. In all fairness, I think they knew the gospel to be true. But my father fervently believed some aspects of the gospel were more true than others, and that he had the right to decide which were the most true. Whatever Father decreed was right, Mother and I were expected to conform to."

"Did he punish you if you didn't agree with him?" Brad asked. Something in his voice told her he wasn't asking from idle curiosity.

"He never hit me, if that's what you mean."

"Punishment takes a lot of forms other than physical," he reminded her gently.

"I didn't have the courage to disobey very often, but the few times I did, he yelled at me and belittled me. He never forgot my mistakes nor missed an opportunity to remind me how lazy, irresponsible, and stupid I was."

"That's one form of abuse, a form with long-lasting side effects. Sometimes it takes years of counseling to overcome the sense of worthlessness that kind of treatment leaves on a child." Brad's sympathetic voice touched some barren spot deep in her heart, telling her his concern was genuine. But it touched a nerve, too, making her speak defensively.

"I took the same mental health classes you did on my way to an M.D. I recognized all the signs of a psychologically abused child in myself when I was two-thirds of the way through medical school. Only there was a difference. Somewhere along the line I received a testimony that my Savior loves me. That made all the difference."

Susan remembered only too well that painful time of her life. As she let her mind wander, she could see herself that day on campus rushing to an appointment with Dr. Schoefelt. Her heart hammered in fright as she tapped on his door two minutes after the appointed time. She didn't know why he wanted to see her. She'd turned in her paper on time and she'd worked especially hard on it.

"Come in, Ms. MacKendrick." He indicated she should be seated. Nervously she twisted her hands as he leaned back against his desk until he was almost sitting on the edge. He picked up a paper, rolled it into a loose cylinder, and tapped it against the palm of one hand. Finally he spoke, "You'll receive a failing grade in my class, and

I'm recommending to the department chair that you be dismissed from the surgical program."

"Why?" she gasped. "My grades . . ."

"I can only assume you got the high grades presently on your transcript by cheating as you did on this paper." He unrolled the paper in his hand and handed it to her.

Puzzled, she examined the paper. It was hers, but she couldn't see why he thought she'd cheated. Raising her eyes, she stammered, "What—what is wrong with it?"

"Nothing," he snapped, his eyes cold. "It's almost perfect—but you didn't write it. Didn't you think I would notice how similar all your reports are to those of Mr. Clint King? This time you went too far; you copied his paper word for word."

"I did not!" she shouted with sudden fury, seeing in a blinding flash why Clint had invited her to study with him, allowed her to use his computer, and always walked beside her during hospital rounds. "Clint must have copied *my* paper."

"Miss MacKendrick, Mr. King is one of the best pupils in my class. He is nearly always first with the right answers, while you never know the answers to anything."

Susan had a sudden picture of herself next to Clint, muttering the answers she was too shy to speak aloud. Foolishly she'd felt a thrill of pride each time he voiced her answers aloud and received the professor's approval. But how could she convince Dr. Schoefelt she wasn't the one who was cheating? Her shoulders slumped as she recognized there was nothing she could do. No one would accept her word over that of bright, clever Clint.

She left Dr. Schoefelt's office in tears, not knowing where to go or what to do. She'd wandered around the city for hours until she came to a wooden footbridge spanning a small stream. At the center of the bridge she braced her arms against the wooden rail and stared down into the water at her own reflection. Behind her reflection was that of a simple ward house steeple reminding her of the simple faith that had helped her through her lonely childhood. She closed her eyes and began to pray.

As she prayed, peace seeped into her heart and a calm voice promised, "I am with you always." She opened her eyes and knew what she must do.

She'd returned to campus and asked for a meeting with her program counselor. Though she wasn't certain he believed her, he arranged for probation rather than dismissal from school.

"No one will ever trust a surgeon who doesn't believe in herself," the counselor cautioned. "Fighting dismissal is only the first step."

Susan had worked hard and avoided Clint for the rest of the quarter. Pushing herself to speak up in class and on hospital tours was difficult, but she made herself do it, and each night she'd knelt beside her bed and felt reassured that she wasn't alone. At the end of the quarter, probation was dropped, and Clint quietly disappeared from school.

Without embarrassment she realized that she'd shared her painful memories with Brad. Softly she concluded, "I know that to my Elder Brother I have great worth. When I had no other friends, he was my friend."

"I'm glad, because leaning on God can help us over a lot of tough spots. But it puzzles me why you felt the Lord was your only friend when you're a bright, attractive woman and must have been a lovely girl. You said you attended church. Weren't there any girls in your Young Women classes you could have gotten to know better?" He reached for her hand and tugged gently until she sat back down on the carpeted floor beside him.

She wrapped her arms around her legs and spoke wryly, "Teenage girls are so busy beating back their own insecurities, very few can risk befriending the dorkiest kid in town. In all honesty I never blamed those girls for ostracizing me. If any of them had tried to be friendly, my pride would have rejected them anyway. When I was alone in the fields or woods, it didn't matter how I looked or that I didn't know how to talk to other kids, but at church and school my appearance embarrassed me. I would have sooner died than become the other girls' pity project."

"Well, you certainly don't look like anyone's pity project now," Brad grinned at her. Tall, slender, and perfectly groomed, she looked more like the fantasy woman projected by the classier fashion magazines in his office waiting room. Slowly she returned his smile.

"I'd better not. Between what I pay my hair stylist and the amount of money I spend at Nordstrom's, I certainly shouldn't look like a charity case."

Brad laughed. "Believe me, there's nothing pitiful about the way you look now." The words surprised him almost as much as they did Susan, and he suspected a red tide was sweeping up his neck to match the crimson blush coloring her cheeks.

"Well, then, since we've settled that issue, how about it? Are we friends? And will you let your friend do a little snooping into Maria's family secrets?" he asked.

"Yes, I think I'd like to be your friend." The words emerged in a husky whisper. "And about Maria, thank you."

"Good." He mentally kicked himself for not being able to think of anything more witty to say. "I, uh, need to check in with my answering service and I'd like to be home for dinner with my family, so I guess I'd better be going." He stood as he said the words, but found himself reluctant to leave Susan's apartment. "Call me if you find anything interesting in that stuff." He waved vaguely toward the pile of papers on the floor.

"I will," Susan promised. She reached for the door just as he did and his hand closed around hers. Startled, they both drew back, glanced quickly at each other, then away. Noting Susan's flare of bright color lessened Brad's own sense of awkwardness, and he chided himself for his adolescent reaction to a simple touch of hands. The rosy tint to her cheeks heightened his awareness of her basic inno- cence. She may have given birth to a child and be a medical specialist, but her personal experience was sorely limited. He wanted to hold her in his arms and assure her . . . of what? He had no idea. He only knew he felt an overwhelming urge to touch her, to form a physical link, no matter how tenuous, with this woman.

Briefly his fingers brushed hers as he bid her a hasty farewell, and he knew it wasn't enough. That knowledge plagued him as he drove away.

Thoughts of Susan never strayed far from his mind as he stopped at the hospital to check on Missie, then drove home. Not even the noise and confusion of a house full of children completely distracted him. When the lights were off and he was settled in bed, her face crowded out all other thoughts.

Was he beginning to care for Susan? Surely not. No other woman had stirred his interest in a personal way since he had met Cathy.

Then why couldn't he stop thinking about Susan? Why did he find himself wanting to hold her? The answer might be very simple. He'd been a married man for almost fourteen years, and during that time he'd enjoyed a healthy, intimate relationship with his wife. Was his attraction to Susan simply his body's way of telling him it missed that physical expression?

It felt wrong to want a closer relationship with Susan. He'd made vows to Cathy and surely it couldn't be right to find himself drawn to another woman. He believed in eternal marriage; he could wait until he and Cathy were together again. He shouldn't feel this bleakness in his soul because he'd have to end his friendship with Susan. But continuing had to be wrong. What if she began to care for him? Guilt swamped his thoughts as he recognized his own reluctance to end the escalating friendship that was growing between Susan and himself. He wondered if his thoughts might be a kind of infidelity.

Unable to sleep, he turned on the bedside lamp and reached for his scriptures. His eyes fell on Cathy's scriptures where they still rested beside his own. Slowly he reached for hers.

It wasn't the first time he'd leafed through Cathy's scriptures. His books were liberally highlighted by a marker pen, but hers were a journey of discovery. Favorite passages were not only highlighted, but personal observations had been penned in the margins, pictures were sketched over favorite passages, and small mementos were sprinkled through the pages. He found some note cards from a talk she gave to a group of Young Women tucked in Isaiah, a columbine from near the cabin in Psalms, and a tiny, silver foil angel in Luke. A small purple pansy he'd plucked from her landlady's garden the first night he'd walked her home was pressed between the pages of Ruth.

Near the back of the book he discovered a piece of newspaper he hadn't seen before. When he straightened the yellowed piece of print, he saw that the clipping was an obituary notice. He stared at it curiously, struggling to recall the name. Finally he concluded he didn't know the woman; neither her picture nor her name were familiar. Puzzled, he began to read of a woman who had penned her own obituary before dying of breast cancer and concluded by requesting that those she loved remember her by planting a pink tulip. He smiled, remembering the huge bag of pink tulip bulbs his wife had brought home shortly before her own death. Holland had insisted on planting them a few weeks after Cathy's death in a huge circular bed beneath his bedroom window. They'd been a gentle haze of pink each spring since that time.

Faint pencil markings at the bottom of the notice caught his attention, and he moved closer to the lamp to read Cathy's penciled note: *Please add a red one for me.*

Brad wiped a tear from his eye and wished he'd found the clipping three years ago. He'd go out tomorrow and buy red tulips to mingle with the pink.

Slowly he leaned back against the headboard of the bed, remembering Cathy's love of vibrant color. She'd filled his life with color, and if he'd ever stopped to think, he would have wondered at her choice of pale pink tulips. Now he knew they weren't for her; they were for all the women who shared her sisterhood through fighting a common enemy. But for herself, she chose brilliant red. Red for life and love, for valor and excitement.

Peace and warmth crept into his heart and he sensed his wife was near. Closing his eyes he relaxed, savoring her presence, recalling the sweet way she'd always been there for him when he felt troubled or overwhelmed. He marveled at the calmness and peace he felt. Cathy hadn't been a quiet, soothing person; she was a mover, a shaker, a motivator. She inspired confidence and urged him to excel. She never let him forget that both she and God expected his best. He smiled again, remembering the joy and excitement she radiated and shared with him at every milestone in their lives.

He willed himself to see her flaming red hair and beautiful face, but it wasn't Cathy's image he saw before him. Instead it was a tall, lithe shape with honey-blond hair that filled his mind. Troubled, he tried to shut out Susan and concentrate on Cathy. Eventually he succeeded, but he drifted to sleep with a lingering sense that Cathy wasn't pleased with him.

He awoke troubled the next morning and nicked himself shaving. Grabbing a piece of tissue paper, he attempted to staunch the trickle of blood that threatened to drip from his chin to his white shirt. While holding the small piece of tissue against the cut, he caught sight of himself in the mirror. It was like seeing a stranger. The soft roundness of his features that had earned him the nickname "baby face" during his football years had disappeared, replaced by angles and planes. His hair had receded slightly on top and his sideburns had turned silver. Small grooves outlined his mouth and fanned the outer corners of his eyes. His eyes had changed, too; they had aged more than the rest of him.

The mirror reflected back a framed photograph from the bedroom behind him. Impulsively he took the few steps necessary to retrieve the picture. It was his wedding picture, his and Cathy's, taken in front of the Salt Lake Temple. He held it up and studied the face of the young man he had been fifteen years ago. That young man had been happy and confident, and very much in love with the girl beside him dressed in yards and yards of white ruffles and lace. A fleeting sadness reminded him of the hopes and dreams they'd shared. Theirs was a now-and-forever kind of love, but they hadn't anticipated their *now* would end so soon. His gaze lingered on the laughing young bride and he wondered if she had changed as much as he had since death had parted them more than three years ago. His eyes returned to the image of his own, much younger face, and he knew that the man he'd been on their wedding day was as completely gone as Cathy.

Soberly he resumed dressing. As he straightened his tie and slipped on his shoes, he thought of the ten years his friend Doug had been separated from his wife before finding her again. In all that time Doug had never dated or shown any interest in another woman. Then there was Allen, who hadn't married until he was thirty-four. He'd dated dozens of women, including fashion models, an actress or two, even a lovely young heiress, but once he discovered Holland he suddenly forgot other women even existed. Brad made a mental note to call Doug and Allen to see if they were available to go to lunch.

Allen was already at the table Brad had reserved in a quiet hotel dining room. Faint piano music was playing in the background as the two men shook hands. When Doug arrived, they gave their orders to the waiter, then Doug and Allen turned to Brad expectantly.

The words he'd carefully rehearsed flew out of his head. How could he ask their advice about anything so personal even if they'd been closer than brothers all their lives?

When he remained unable to speak, Allen broke the silence for him. With a teasing grin he asked, "Could this have anything to do with a certain lady doctor I hear you've been seeing?"

"You're dating someone?" Doug looked startled.

"We aren't exactly dating, but I've been thinking about it," Brad admitted. He rubbed his open palm across his mouth and took a deep breath. "I find myself thinking about Susan a lot. I started out helping her with a problem she was having difficulty dealing with, but now I find I enjoy her company and I want to be with her for personal reasons."

"What's the problem?" Allen chuckled. "Doesn't she want to go out with you?"

"I think she likes being with me," Brad answered quietly.

"The problem is Bobbi, isn't it?" Doug ventured an astute guess. "I played basketball with her and Jason last night, and it's obvious something's bothering her."

"Bobbi is only part of the problem," Brad admitted. "I don't know why she dislikes Susan. Susan's a strong, take-charge, perfectionist kind of doctor. Her staff calls her 'Doc Attitude' behind her back and considers her a slave driver, but socially she's a scared little girl. Around the girls, Susan scarcely opens her mouth; she acts like she's afraid of them. But the real problem is Cathy—or rather, me. I don't want to care about any woman other than Cathy, but I can't get Susan out of my head. I've asked myself over and over if I'm just lonely and miss having a woman to talk and laugh with. If I'm simply tired of crawling into an empty bed at night. But in all honesty, I don't think that's my problem. I don't just miss Cathy. I want to be with Susan."

"Brad, you gave me some good advice when I needed it, but I'm not sure I possess the wisdom to give you the same quality advice now," Doug started thoughtfully. "Cathy has been gone for three years now. There's nothing wrong with wanting a new relationship with another woman."

"No, I know there's nothing morally wrong with dating or even remarrying, but Cathy and I were so close. I feel disloyal to have the thoughts I do about Susan."

"Cathy had strong feelings about marriage," Allen added. "She never approved of my single lifestyle. I suspect she'd be the first to want you to enjoy a second happy marriage, and knowing her, if there's any way she can do it, she's probably doing a little matchmaking."

Doug chuckled and even Brad smiled, remembering how hard Cathy had worked to get Allen and Holland together.

"If Megan died, you wouldn't even consider remarriage, would you?" Brad challenged Doug.

"No, I don't suppose I would," Doug admitted. "I've known since the day I found Megan, the day she turned sixteen, that there would only ever be one woman for me. But you aren't me and Megan isn't Cathy. What's right for us isn't necessarily what's right for you."

"You didn't ask me," Allen added. "But I'm going to answer anyway. I can't even imagine going on living without Holland, but if I lost her as you lost Cathy, I believe I would remarry. I've been happier in my marriage than I've ever been before in my life. I think I would try to recapture that happiness."

"When I was wallowing in despair and it looked as though I'd lost Megan forever, you told me to get down on my knees and ask the only one who could really help me," Doug spoke from his own hard-earned well of faith. "I think it's time to take your own advice."

Brad nodded mutely and only half listened as his friends went on to make plans to spend a Saturday at the cabin snowmobiling. As he mulled over all they'd said, he realized Doug was right; he had yet to really lay his problem before the Lord.

When he returned to his office and found that his first appointment had canceled, he asked Rachel to hold all his calls and to not disturb him for half an hour. He spent that time on his knees beside his old-fashioned oak desk. The words didn't come easily, and when at last, he rose to his feet, he felt dissatisfied. The communication he'd experienced in the past had evaded him.

When Rachel's voice came over the intercom telling him he had a patient in room two, he put his own problem aside and concentrated on his work.

On the way home from work that day, he stopped at four different stores. November was a little late to be buying tulip bulbs and the selections were severely picked over, but he eventually found a small bag with a picture of bright red tulips on the front.

When he got home Kelly came running to meet him and

together they set out to plant the bulbs. He dug small holes and Kelly carefully placed a bulb in each one, then together they patted the dirt back into place.

"These are for Mama," he explained as he tamped the last of the soil over a bulb.

"Can Mama see them all the way from heaven?" Kelly asked.

"I think she can," Brad answered.

"Does Mama like red flowers best?" she turned her face up to ask.

"Your mama liked all kinds of flowers, and she always liked bright, pretty colors the best," he assured her.

"Maybe you should go to the flower place and buy her a big bunch of red roses. Uncle Allen gives Holland lots of roses with see-through paper around them."

Brad knelt in front of his daughter to speak to her at eye level. "I used to buy your mama flowers like that once in a while, probably not often enough, though. But last night I read a little note she wrote a long time ago and I learned she wanted a red tulip flower to remind us she loved us."

"Daddy," she scrunched her face with worry lines. "Seeds take a long time to grow. I think we better go to the flower place and buy one that's already growed."

"No, honey, I think this is the way your mama wants us to get her red tulip." He scooped Kelly into his arms and walked to the porch steps where he settled with the little girl in his lap.

"Your mama likes tulips because after they're through growing and being pretty, the leaves and the flower die and all that's left is a big brown seed. The seed isn't really dead, but it has to have a long rest. It sleeps all winter under the snow, then when spring comes and the days start getting warmer, the seed starts to grow and becomes a beautiful flower again."

"And we can see it?"

"Yes, we can see it and touch it." He smiled at her.

"And smell it?"

"Sure, we can smell it, too."

"Is it the same flower as last time?" Kelly scrunched her face as she struggled to understand.

Brad shook his head. "No, it's not the exact same flower. It's a new one from the old seed."

"Daddy, I think when flowers die they go to heaven just like

Mama. There's lots of flowers in heaven helping Mama to be happy. I think she wanted us to plant red flowers for us so we'd be happy, too."

A sudden burning filled Brad's heart. Could that be the essence of Cathy's message last night and of his prayers this afternoon? Did she wish him to plant a red tulip, not to turn his thoughts to her, but to remind him to be happy, to seek new life? Strangely he'd never once thought of Cathy being unhappy in her new life, but he'd viewed his own future as one of waiting and enduring until they could be together again. The thought had occurred to him before that Cathy wouldn't be pleased to know he'd let the changing of the seasons pass without noticing or caring. With deep certainty he knew she didn't approve of the way he divided his life between work and parenting, using these dual demands as excuses for limiting church service and spending time with friends.

And Susan? Would Cathy approve of his friendship with her? A picture came to mind of walking across the cemetery with Susan and watching a brilliant red leaf flutter in the air before briefly tangling in her honey-blond hair. Perhaps he was seeking a sign where only coincidence existed, but the gentle peace stealing into his heart told him his premise was not wrong. Cathy could not only accept another woman in his life, but she loved him enough to encourage him to seek once more all the love and color they had once shared together.

Last night he'd experienced a moment when he'd felt his wife was near, then sensed her disapproval when his thoughts turned to Susan. Had Cathy been disappointed because of his increasing interest in another woman, or had she disapproved of his determined rejection of Susan?

Seven

SUSAN GAVE HER HAIR AN EXTRA SPRITZ THEN paused to gaze at the stranger in her mirror. The woman reflected back had a ridge of color at the top of her cheeks that owed nothing to makeup and her eyes sparkled as Susan's never did. Her mouth turned up slightly at the corners. She wore jeans and a tailored cotton shirt, not the usual attire seen on Susan Adele MacKendrick, M.D. She looked happy, but even as Susan watched, the sparkle dimmed and she wondered if she had the right to feel so lighthearted.

What had possessed her to accept Brad's invitation to spend the day at his cabin? As if he'd seen her initial reluctance, he had quickly assured her they wouldn't be alone. His children would be there and the two friends who shared ownership of the cabin and their wives and children would be there, too. It was exactly the kind of situation she usually avoided.

But Brad had asked and she'd accepted. It had been that simple. The doubts had crept in later. Brad had told her Doug taught at the university and his wife, Megan, was the co-anchor of an in-depth television news show. They had two children, a fifteen-year-old son, Jason, and a three-year-old daughter, Mary Kate. Allen James was widely recognized as a landscape and wildlife photo artist, and she'd already met Holland, who billed herself as a part-time student with a yen for tearing engines apart and putting them back together. She'd also met their small son. How could she talk to these people? She'd never learned to converse on any topic other than medicine.

She felt tongue-tied and ill-at-ease around Brad's children, and she sensed his older daughters didn't like her. They'd probably resent her inclusion in their outing with their father.

She shouldn't go. But for some inexplicable reason, she wanted to. She hadn't seen Brad for nearly a week and she missed him. Of course, if anyone had suggested she might miss Brad or any other man, she would have hotly denied it. She didn't need a man in her life. Nevertheless, thoughts of the tall, broad-shouldered doctor had intruded more often than she cared to admit during the past week. But only because she was anxious to hear if he'd been in contact with Maria, she assured herself.

A navy-blue and white cable-knit sweater lay on the bed, and she reached for it just as her doorbell rang. Thoughts of Maria were not uppermost in her mind as she opened the door to find Brad dressed in denim jeans, a matching long-sleeved shirt, and a fleece-lined vest. He smiled and a strange flutter started just beneath her breastbone as she met his deep blue eyes, leaving her suddenly breathless.

"Ready?"

She nodded her head and gathered up her parka. He took her arm and together they left her apartment building.

The drive to the cabin was beautiful. The snow that had fallen in the mountains earlier that week provided a glittering backdrop to the dark pines. She hadn't grown up near the mountains, and her only experience with them had been from the window of a car or plane. As a child she'd wanted to visit the mountains, but her father had never had time for trips or vacations so she'd never gone. She wondered if Brad's daughters knew how lucky they were to have a father who took them places and laughed and joked with them.

In the sixteen years since she'd left home she could have camped and hiked, especially since coming to Salt Lake where mountains surrounded the city and were easily accessible. Why hadn't she? She could imagine Brad saying she hadn't because she was on some kind of guilt trip. He'd say she was still punishing herself for the mistakes she'd made as a teenager. Denial sprang instantly to mind. She *had* been busy, she argued silently; her career had demanded her full attention. Nevertheless, her innate honesty recognized a core of truth.

She took her eyes from the magnificent scenery to look at Brad. As she watched, she noticed a slight frown turn down one corner of his mouth and several times he glanced in the rearview mirror.

Curious to see what had garnered Brad's displeasure, she turned to look over her shoulder, expecting to see some vehicle tailgating behind them. Instead she saw five heads of red hair huddled together as Brad's daughters carried on a whispered conversation. Michelle shook her head as though disagreeing with her sisters, but was apparently quickly overruled. Bobbi lifted her head and her eyes met Susan's for an instant. Something flashed in the back of the girl's eyes, and Susan felt chilled. Slowly she turned back to the front, feeling as though a cloud had obscured the sun.

Had she imagined the animosity in Bobbi's eyes? She didn't think so. But what had she done to cause the girl to dislike her so much? On the few occasions she'd seen the girl, Susan had made an effort to be polite, but her efforts hadn't been reciprocated. Did Bobbi dislike her personally, or would she dislike any woman in whom her father showed interest?

Startled, Susan wondered if Brad's daughters thought she was trying to take their mother's place. The idea was ludicrous. Susan had no intention of taking Cathy's place. She couldn't if she wanted to. She had no ambition to run a household as large as the Williams'. Cooking, cleaning, and gardening had never held any particular interest for her, and she certainly didn't know the first thing about being a mother. Besides, Cathy had been beautiful, accomplished, friendly, and deeply involved in church and community affairs. She was a woman loved and admired by all who knew her. There was no way that an overly tall, plain woman with next to no social skills and a murky past could begin to take her place. Even if she wanted to. And she didn't want to; she only wanted to be a doctor. But even as she affirmed her commitment to her career, a traitorous little voice in the back of her head questioned if that was all she really wanted. Rather than examine too closely what she did or didn't want, she decided to stop thinking about it and concentrate on the scenery instead. This one day she would simply enjoy the beauty around her.

Meanwhile Brad continued to frown as he watched the girls in the mirror. They were up to something, he suspected. They'd been abnormally quiet ever since he'd picked up Susan. He didn't get it. Why were they so set against Susan? Granted, she was quiet and didn't seem to have much to say to them, but he remembered how incapable of speech Holland had been when she first arrived. The girls had nevertheless taken to her immediately. He'd been surprised Bobbi hadn't challenged Susan to a basketball game. Bobbi had taken one look at Holland and had immediately seen her in terms of a basketball star, and Susan was even taller than Holland. Bobbi's antagonism didn't make sense.

He knew Susan had a formidable side that brooked no nonsense when it came to medical care, but she'd never displayed that side of her personality around the girls. Instead, if he were risking a diagnosis, he'd say Susan appeared a bit intimidated by his daughters.

Could it be they sensed his interest was more than friendly toward Susan? He scoffed at the idea that they might be exhibiting some form of jealousy. After all, Michelle and Ashley had both tried their hands at a little matchmaking not too long ago and been disappointed when he didn't share their enthusiasm for either Ashley's fifth-grade teacher or Allen's new office manager. Both "Miss Lewis" and Kaitlyn Bronwell were attractive women, but neither one had inspired him to pursue their acquaintance.

Brad watched Susan from the corner of his eye as the Explorer started the long climb toward the cabin. She seemed to withdraw deeper inside herself with each mile. He knew she'd had few opportunities in her life to have fun and was needlessly worrying about interacting with his friends. He'd like to reassure her, but he sensed words would be useless. If there were some way he could guarantee that she would enjoy this trip, he'd grab it, but another peek in the mirror left him suspecting it wouldn't be easy.

When they arrived at the cabin, the snowmobiles were ready to go. Susan eyed the small tractor-like machines dubiously. She'd never ridden on one before and her memories of driving a tractor weren't even remotely close to a recreational activity.

"Where's Dutch?" Kelly called as she ran to Holland.

Holland scooped her up for a hug as she answered, "He's with Mary Kate's grandma. She volunteered to keep both of the little ones today." Mary Kate was Doug and Megan's young daughter.

"I wanted to play with him," Kelly pouted.

"He's too little for snowmobiling," Holland laughed.

"Then can I ride with you?" Kelly brightened.

"Sure." Holland gave her another squeeze and set her on her feet. "But you have to keep your hat and goggles on. If you take them off, I'll take you right back to the cabin."

As introductions were made, Susan felt relief at the warm greetings the other adults gave her. Holland invited her inside the cabin, where she urged Susan to wear one of her waterproof snowmobile suits. It was a little tight and a little short, but it would do.

The children were soon each paired with one of the adults except for Bobbi and Jason, who rode together after a vigorous argument over which one got to drive first. Susan settled on the back of the seat behind Brad and decided it wasn't too different from straddling a horse. She wondered if she'd be as stiff tomorrow as if she'd actually ridden a horse.

"Hold on tight," Brad grinned as he turned to draw her arms snugly around his waist. Oddly enough, she liked the feel of her arms around him, but she was glad he was preoccupied with starting the machine.

Sun glinted on the broad expanse of snow and Susan felt a smile tug at her lips. The whole world looked like a magical wonderland. The snow frosting the pines provided a glittering contrast to their deep green, and the meadow appeared to be a marvelous swirl of brush strokes in every shade of white and pale blue. She pressed her cheek against Brad's broad back and realized with a start that she was enjoying herself. She couldn't remember the last time, or even if there was a previous time, when she'd felt so lighthearted and happy.

The small engine roared to life and Susan tightened her grip on Brad as the snowmobile began to move. At first she kept her head down to avoid the wind and concentrated on maintaining her hold on Brad. Gradually she relaxed enough to raise her head. When she did, she gasped at the splendor all around her. She'd always enjoyed pictures of the mountains in summer splendor, but other than a few ski posters, she'd never thought much about how they would look covered by snow. Suddenly she understood the almost mystic lure that drew skiers to the slopes in spite of the cold and the broken limbs she'd become familiar with as a doctor in a Utah hospital.

Brad turned to flash her a wide grin before returning his focus to the trail ahead, and she knew he understood. He loved these mountains and was pleased by her emotional response to the beauty around them.

Nearly an hour passed before Doug, who was in the lead, pulled off in a small clearing that overlooked the valley. The others followed and one by one their engines stilled. A slight breeze whistled through the tree tops, and a tiny avalanche of snow whispered soundlessly from a trembling branch overhead to the ground below. Susan didn't move. It was all too achingly beautiful.

Brad's gloved hands moved to cover hers where they clasped his waist and he turned until his eyes met hers. Something in their depths touched her soul. She wanted to cry—or laugh.

"Daddy!" A girlish shriek shattered the moment and Susan hastily withdrew her arms from around Brad. She looked up to see Heidi hurling herself toward her father, chattering as she ran. It seemed she wanted to go somewhere with Bobbi and Jason to see some deer.

"We'll all go," Brad laughed as he swooped his daughter up in his arms. "There's a place near here where we nearly always find a small herd of deer in the winter," Brad explained to Susan. "We can't get any closer with the snowmobiles without frightening them away. It's not far and the hike isn't difficult because the herd has already cut a trail through the snow."

Heidi squirmed to be released and when he let her go, she hurried back to Jason's side where she confidently took his hand. Kelly loudly informed everyone they had to be quiet so they wouldn't scare the deer. Susan watched as the two older children with Heidi between them started down the path, and Ashley and Michelle quickly followed them. Allen reached into a small compartment on his machine and withdrew a camera and a small leather pouch before joining Holland and Kelly. Kelly anxiously tugged Holland toward the trail where the others had disappeared into the trees.

Susan was surprised when Brad removed one glove, then reached for her hand. Slowly he withdrew one of her mittens, folded it, and slid it into her pocket. Then he squeezed her fingers and tucked their clasped hands into his parka pocket. She felt a strange lurch in her chest and glanced up to see an enigmatic smile on Megan's face before she and Doug turned to follow the trail. Without saying a word Brad pulled her closer and they followed the others.

From a vantage point above a small sheltered valley, Susan could see a cluster of brown forms moving slowly across a meadow. Brad handed her a pair of binoculars, and she watched the dainty animals with a sense of awe. She gazed for several minutes before handing the glasses back to Brad.

"How could anyone shoot anything so lovely?" she whispered.

Brad chuckled. "I couldn't, but I understand the many generations of men who kept their families alive by providing them with venison, and I can understand the farmers who occasionally see them as pests that destroy crops and haystacks."

"I guess that's true, but I think I'd have to be awfully hungry before I could kill a deer and eat it," she sighed.

"My grandmother hated venison." Brad's eyes sparkled as he told the story. "Some of my uncles used to go deer hunting every fall, and she'd tell them they were plain stupid and that God made cattle for human consumption; deer were meant for coyotes and cougars. She grew up on venison and she swore that when she married it would be to a man who could afford beef. Grandpa was always rather proud that Grandma never had to eat venison once in the fifty-one years they were married, though he admitted there were a lot of meals they had to settle for chicken. And he never told her that he occasionally raided one of his daughter-in-law's kitchens for a slice of venison to stick between two slices of bread."

Susan laughed with Brad, then was suddenly still as he wrapped his arms around her and drew her close. His hand cupped her chin while his eyes searched hers for endless seconds. Thoughts and feelings careened through her mind at too dizzy a pace to sort or analyze. She was a rabbit, trembling with fear, mesmerized by his eyes. She was a child, wanting all the magic of a storybook Christmas, but afraid to hope. Then she was a woman responding to the warmth and desire of one special man. His lips parted in a brief smile before they closed over hers. It was all the magic she'd been denied all her life. His kiss awakened a hunger she'd never known, and without conscious thought she moved closer to the source of the warmth and wonder surrounding her.

When he released her, she clung for just a moment before the world intruded once more. Mortified, she glanced around and was surprised to find they were alone. The others had all gone. In the distance she heard the roar of an engine. She flushed with embarrassment, knowing she'd been conscious only of Brad. What must the others think?! Brad's daughters would really hate her now for monopolizing their father. With their constant exuberance how could she have totally forgotten their presence? And what if they'd seen their father kissing her? She could feel the tide of red climbing up her face. Glancing self-consciously at Brad she learned he didn't share her embarrassment. A satisfied grin spread across his face.

Ducking her head, she mumbled, "We'd better go back."

"Yes," he responded, but didn't make a move toward the trail. She knew he was watching her, but she couldn't meet his eyes.

"Should I apologize?" he asked softly. Before she could answer he went on, "I won't. I'm not at all sorry I kissed you. And I think you liked it, too."

She turned her face away, her eyes seeking a distant line of snow-laden pines. She couldn't speak. She couldn't even understand her jumble of emotions. She couldn't deny she'd liked his kiss. In fact, "liked" was a pretty tame word for the way it had made her feel, but she didn't want to like it. She hadn't wanted him to kiss her, but she couldn't deny that she'd been a willing, even eager, participant. Tony hadn't made her feel like this. Of course, her mind had been too befuddled by alcohol that night to really know what she'd felt. The few men she'd allowed to kiss her while she was going to college hadn't touched the woman inside her. They'd left her convinced that kissing was a highly overrated activity, something she could easily do without.

Anger replaced her confused emotions. She hadn't wanted to remember that somewhere inside her was a woman's feelings, a woman's needs. She didn't want to be a woman; she only wanted to be a doctor. Brad was to blame. He'd awakened this awful ache, made her see with a blinding clarity all she was missing. She had a horrible suspicion her life would never return to the peace and purpose she'd known before Brad intruded in her life. But she would try. If it took every ounce of strength in her body, she would eliminate from her mind the feelings Brad had aroused. She shivered, slowly becoming aware that clouds had drifted across the sky and a cold wind whistled across the ridge where they stood.

Deliberately she turned to face him, and gathering all the strength and poise she'd mastered in the chaos of trauma medicine, she pushed aside what had just passed between them. "Did you ever find out about Maria?" she asked coolly.

Brad cocked his head to one side and watched her for several minutes before answering. "I asked Doug and Allen to give us a few minutes alone so I could tell you. I didn't maneuver to get you alone for any other reason, though I'll repeat, I'm not sorry I kissed you."

"I don't want—"

"I know. You weren't ready." A sad little smile played across his lips. When she realized she was staring at his mouth, she forced herself to look away, angrily chiding herself for her thoughts. She took a couple of steps away, deliberately creating more space between them.

Brad's jaw clenched and his lips tightened. "I won't pounce on you, you know. The next time I kiss you, I'll make certain it's what you want, too." He reached in his pocket and very deliberately pulled his glove back on. "As for Maria, our suspicions were correct. She gave birth to Robbie, then handed him over to her sister for a hefty amount of money. Then she convinced their mother that coercion had been involved."

Susan stood rooted to the spot where she stood. The sun no longer sent its sparkling light across the snow. She felt cold and empty. For one insane moment she longed to throw herself in Brad's arms and feel his comforting warmth. She wouldn't do it. She didn't need Brad, she reminded herself. Her arms ached as they had once before. The day she'd walked away from that hospital without her baby, she thought she would die of the pain. She was older now. She knew she wouldn't die, but this time she wouldn't walk away with nothing. A steely determination she hadn't been capable of at seventeen settled in her heart. This time she wouldn't blindly trust that she'd done the best thing for her baby. It wasn't too late. She wouldn't let it be too late!

"I'll find him," she whispered, unaware she spoke aloud.

"Susan, don't." Brad closed the distance between them and clasped her shoulders. "Let it go."

"I have to know," she whispered hoarsely, slipping out of his grasp.

"You can't compare your son to Robbie," Brad reasoned. "There's no reason to think your baby didn't go to a good home. You placed him through a reputable agency, and, believe me, those places do thorough home studies before they trust an infant to a couple. It wouldn't be fair to suddenly appear in his life now. Robbie's adoption was highly irregular; there was no home study, and no provision for his care after his adoptive parents' deaths."

"I have to find my son," Susan insisted. "I can't go any longer not knowing if he's happy, if he has enough to eat, or if he's even alive."

"And what will you do when you find him?" Brad spoke, resignation in his voice.

"I don't know," Susan whispered from a deep well of pain.

"All right, I'll help you." Brad's shoulders slumped and he looked as dejected as she felt. Susan started to speak and Brad cut her off. "Don't argue. I didn't ask if you wanted my help. You're getting it whether you want it or not." He ushered her toward the path. No further words were exchanged as they moved back through the forest toward their snowmobile.

Brad threw his leg over the saddle and motioned for Susan to climb on behind him. The temperature had dropped and the air tasted of snow. He wanted to get back to the cabin before the storm hit.

When Susan settled behind him, leaving a gap of several inches and gingerly wrapping her arms around his waist, he berated himself for rushing her back there at the lookout. He'd known from the start that he wasn't the only one facing guilt and reservations in their relationship. Just because he'd finally come to terms with the possibility of another woman in his life, he should have remembered Susan still had a lot of unfinished business she had to face before she could consider allowing him or any other man into hers.

As he twisted the ignition key, the engine sputtered, then died. Opening the throttle a little wider, he tried again, but the small snow vehicle failed to start. Brad noticed a strong aroma of gasoline coming from a puddle near his feet. Frowning, he tried to think what to do. Only the roar of the wind reached his ears. He dismounted and indicated for Susan to step off of the snowmobile as well. Opening the engine compartment, Brad could see immediately that the drive belt was broken, and that fuel was dripping from a broken hose. On closer inspection he could see that neither the belt nor the hose had simply broken. They had been cut, or hacked, in two with a sharp blade. Someone had deliberately sabotaged the machine. A quick check revealed that his spare belt was missing. He and his friends had pulled pranks on each other when they were boys, but instinctively he knew neither Doug nor Allen was responsible for the damaged belt. But if they didn't do it, who . . . ? His mouth tightened to a grim line and he turned to face Susan.

"I can't fix it," he said bluntly. "We're stuck here until the others become concerned about our absence and someone comes back for us."

"How long will that be?" she asked, casting a glance toward the darkening sky. Brad frowned at the snowflakes lazily floating between them on the rapidly escalating wind. Even as he watched, the snowflakes' tempo increased, alerting him that a full-scale storm was beginning.

"I don't know, an hour maybe. If this storm hits the way I think it will, the others won't be able to come back for us for several hours. We'll need to find shelter."

"All right. Any suggestions?" He felt a surge of pride that she neither complained nor appeared to be scared. Her immediate acceptance of his estimation of the situation renewed his hope that something positive might come of the feelings growing in his heart.

"We have a few supplies on the snowmobile—tarp, matches, a survival kit. I'll get them, then we'll head for that pile of rocks." He pointed to a jumble of boulders near a solid rockface they'd passed earlier on their way to see the deer.

By the time they reached the rocks they could barely see each other through the curtain of snow. Susan caught on quickly as Brad moved several fallen tree limbs across the tops of two large rocks and spread the tarp over them. She helped him, then tossed out the smaller rocks that littered the space beneath the tarp. Working together, they created a small cave approximately six feet wide and four high, where they'd be able to sit fairly comfortably with their backs against the cliff.

Brad gathered as much wood as he could find before the snow obliterated his ability to tell wood from rocks. After several attempts he managed to start a small fire at the open end of their shelter and settled back against the rock beside Susan. They said little as daylight faded and the snow continued to fall. Brad produced a thermos of hot chocolate he'd placed on the snowmobile hours ago while Susan changed into one of Holland's snowsuits and they ate granola bars from the survival kit. It wasn't exactly dinner, but they'd both worked on slimmer rations before during various medical crises. At intervals one or the other would add a log to the fire. Their suits had kept them dry so far, but the night would be long and cold.

Doug pulled a small square packet from the survival kit and handed it to Susan. "Here, wrap this around you."

She turned it over several times in her hands, then smiled. Opening the insulated foil blanket, she looked at Doug. "Unless you have another one of these, we'll share," she informed him in a no-nonsense voice.

"I need to stay awake to keep the fire going." His protest was feeble and she knew it.

"Something tells me neither one of us is going to get much sleep." She pulled the blanket around his shoulders, and he shifted to place his arm around hers and pull her close enough for the blanket to cocoon them both.

Oddly they seemed to take turns sleeping, waking only when the other rose to add wood to the fire. Brad found there was something inviting and intimate about returning to Susan's side to huddle under the blanket after feeding the fire. As he stared past the flame, he pondered the feeling. Susan relaxed against his side and he adjusted his position enough to accommodate her head against his shoulder. It had been more than three years since he'd held a sleeping woman in his arms, and he had to admit it felt good to hold one now. He was glad she wasn't just any woman; it made all the difference that she was Susan. Deep in his soul he knew he'd like to hold her every night for the rest of his life. He shied away from that line of thinking; he wasn't sure he was ready to think in those terms and he knew Susan certainly wasn't ready.

His thoughts turned to his family. They would be worried and Bobbi would be eaten up with guilt. He didn't doubt she'd used the big scout knife she kept at the cabin for summer fishing expeditions to cut the belt, which meant she'd planned on marooning them. What was there about his relationship with Susan that caused his daughter to react so aggressively? Bobbi wasn't a destructive child. Like her mother, she was warm and giving, exhibiting the temper commonly attributed to her hair color only in the face of some injustice. She was highly competitive in sports, but meticulously fair. There was nothing fair in this attack. It was time he and his daughter had a long talk.

Eight

TOWARD DAWN THE STORM DECREASED TO A gentle flutter of falling snow. Soon that too ceased, and a thin sliver of light pierced the clouds. Brad sat with his arms wrapped around his drawn-up knees watching as shades of pink and gold chased away the stark black and white of the night. He was aware of Susan beside him in the narrow opening of their shelter, but he didn't turn or acknowledge her presence until she spoke in a hushed whisper.

"I never knew snow could be so beautiful."

"It always amazes me." Brad's tone matched hers. "In the city I see snow in terms of accidents, winter flu and colds, pneumonia, a driveway to shovel, and being wet and cold. Here I see a majesty and feel a reverence I can't explain other than to compare it to the quiet and peace I experience in the temple."

"I've never been inside the temple, but I think I know what you mean. After I gave up my baby I went immediately to the small private college that had offered me a scholarship. It was a couple of weeks before school was to start and the campus was almost deserted. As I wandered around I found myself in a little chapel with wooden pews and incredible stained glass windows. I sat down and looked around in awe. The faintly colored light from those windows seemed to set that room apart from the world outside the chapel. It wasn't the beauty as much as the sense of peace and quiet in that room that touched me."

Brad smiled into her eyes, encouraging her to go on. He needed to know more about this woman who touched him in a way he cherished, but didn't quite understand. Susan looked away, seeming to focus on something in the distance.

"I felt an overwhelming need to pray, and I did. Slowly the peace of that room stole over me, and I felt God wanted me to pursue an education and become the best doctor I could be. I promised him that day I would devote my life to saving lives to atone for the life I'd given away."

"Susan, listen to me," Brad said, turning her face toward him so that she had no choice but to meet his eyes. "I don't think God was displeased with your decision to give up your baby. Your choice was the answer to another woman's prayers. I'm certain you have fulfilled the promise you made that day many times over, but it's important that you realize that God didn't require any such promise of you. He only asked for a broken heart and a contrite spirit. That you've given, too. I have no doubt that he has forgiven you. Now it's time to forgive yourself."

"I thought I had—until Robbie died in my operating room." Susan's voice was filled with sadness. "Now I feel cut adrift; my life out of focus. There's this compelling need to know that my child is not lost before I can give my work my full attention again."

"You're an extremely talented doctor, Susan, but I don't believe for one minute that God expects or even wants you to devote your entire life to medicine. Perhaps what has happened is his way of letting you know you need to re-examine your priorities and remember there is more to life than your career."

"It's all I know," she responded sadly.

"You mean it's all you've allowed yourself," Brad countered. "I've seen your CD collection and suspect you enjoy classical music a great deal. Do you ever take the time to attend a concert? Your apartment, your clothes, your reaction to this landscape tells me you have an eye for beauty. This whole business about Robbie has convinced me you have a sensitive soul. You should love—and be loved."

"I'm not sure love really exists," she spoke wryly. "Anyway, it doesn't for me. My parents never loved me, and I certainly don't entertain any tender feelings toward them. I didn't love Tony and he didn't love me. We were simply two lonely kids with nowhere else to turn."

"Your parents may have loved you more than you knew," Brad argued. "It wasn't necessarily a lack of love that prevented them from seeing you as an individual with rights and needs of your own."

"Don't try to defend them to me. And if your next step is to tell me I should forgive them, forget it. They don't want my forgiveness. They consider themselves the wronged party. Just before I finished medical school, I wrote to them, apologized for disappointing them, and told them I was willing to put behind me all the hurt of the past. I even invited them to attend my graduation and asked if I could go home for a few days before beginning my new job." She laughed bitterly. "The only answer I received was a terse one-sentence note. 'We have no daughter.'"

"And you've had no contact with them since?" Brad asked.

"I send them a Christmas card and write them a short letter every Christmas, but they never write back or call."

Brad didn't know what to say. Her family was incomprehensible to him. He'd known an abundance of love all his life, first from his parents and siblings, close friends, then Cathy and their children. He remembered his whole family's hurt and disappointment when one of his brothers announced he wouldn't be going on a mission and that he and his girlfriend were planning a hasty wedding. His mother had cried, but it hadn't prevented her from showing great compassion for her son's situation and doing everything possible to make him and his young wife feel they were loved and wanted members of the family.

"Did you ever consider that the best way to put your dysfunctional family behind you might be to become part of a new family?" he asked.

Susan looked at him skeptically. "Are you suggesting that a husband and children would suddenly make everything all right?"

"If you put it that way, no." Brad scratched his head. "I just meant it doesn't seem right for you to miss out on all the happiness of being part of a family just because your parents screwed up."

"Brad, you amaze me. Just because you come from a large, close family, and you and your wife started the same kind of family, you think that's the answer for everyone. I assure you, it is not. Plenty of people never marry and not everyone who marries has or wants children. Besides, it wasn't my parents who screwed up. It was me." Once again she gazed off over the winter landscape before them.

Brad studied her profile for several minutes before he spoke. "Susan, I admire people who have the maturity and honesty to admit their mistakes, but you're wrong if you believe you were the only one to screw up. Some children make terrible choices in spite of the best possible parents, but some parents must share the responsibility for their children's mistakes. I believe your parents fall in this latter category, and even if they don't, they'll have a lot to answer for in refusing to accept your request for forgiveness. And if you tell me you're one of those people who never wanted a child, I'll call you a liar. The penance you've prescribed for yourself didn't come about because you didn't care about your child, but because you cared so terribly much. You can't close that chapter of your life even now because you gave your heart to that child in the brief time you had him. Like all good, loving mothers since the beginning of time, you can't ignore the possibility he might need you."

"Yet you suggest I marry and have other children to relegate him to the past where you think he belongs." A slight edge tinged Susan's words with sharpness.

Brad suddenly felt weary. "No, I don't believe love works like that. You could have a dozen children and love each one dearly, but you'll never forget your first child. I know that, and I even believe that's the way it's meant to be. Each child holds its own unique position in a parent's heart. I love each of my daughters in a different way. That's not to say I care more for one than another. The heart has an endless capacity to love, and each child claims its own share. If one is gone, another doesn't take its place. That child's place stays his or hers forever while the new child claims virgin territory all its own."

She didn't respond or turn toward him, but as he watched, a silver tear slid down her cheek. With one gloved finger he reached to brush it away. Suddenly she turned with a look of anguish on her face and cried, "Brad, I—" then she crumpled against him with her face buried against his coat. He wrapped his arms around her, rocking and consoling, as he held her close.

Too soon a sound reached his ears and he lifted his head. Off in the distance he heard the growl of snowmobiles. His friends were returning for them, and though he knew he should be looking forward to the cabin's warmth and a good hot meal, he experienced a modicum of regret. Being snowbound with Susan hadn't been unpleasant; if anything it had reinforced his growing feelings for her.

With the arrival of Allen and Doug, she would withdraw from him again and he would have to face Bobbi.

The snowmobiles first appeared as two wavering black dots, but as they drew closer, Susan made out the shapes of Doug and Holland. By the time the rescuers reached the abandoned snowmobile, Brad and Susan had broken camp and waded through the knee-deep snow to meet them.

"Are you all right?" Holland exclaimed as she drew to a stop in front of the nearly buried machine.

"We're fine," Brad assured her. "But unless you brought a new drive belt, even a hotshot mechanic like you isn't going to get this thing moving." He swiped away a layer of snow for emphasis.

"We brought one." Holland and Doug exchanged a grim look. "Plus a few other things."

"I assume the culprit confessed." Brad's voice held a strange note, and Susan turned to stare at him. His shoulders slumped and his eyes held a strange mixture of hurt and sadness. Her heart went out to him as she grasped the meaning behind his words. One of his daughters had cut the drive belt, leaving them to face a winter blizzard with very limited resources. She had never once questioned why the snowmobile malfunctioned. Knowing it had been a deliberate act brought a stab of pain. She hurt for Brad and once more she hurt for the little girl she had been, the one no one seemed to want.

"She didn't act alone," Doug spoke for the first time, a note of apology in his voice. "All but Kelly returned from the lookout ahead of us. The girls sabotaged your snowmobile without us suspecting a thing. We knew Bobbi and Jason were fighting about something when we stepped into the clearing and Jason took off on his snowmobile with Michelle instead of Bobbi. Back at the cabin Bobbi and Jason continued sniping at each other, and Michelle and Ashley kept up a whispered argument while Heidi cried.

"When the storm hit and you weren't back, Michelle became upset and confessed everything. She insists she and Jason tried to talk the others out of it."

"They did it because of me," Susan gasped. It had been her fault. If not for her, Brad would have enjoyed a beautiful day with his family, and there would have been no risk of frost bite, hypothermia, or a long, sleepless, cold night.

"Don't blame yourself," Brad said as though he could read her mind. Through clenched teeth, he continued, "This was Bobbi's idea and she's the one who needs to understand the consequences of her actions."

"Jason will be punished, too." Doug made his feelings on the matter clear. "He has to understand that loyalty to his friends ends where lives are endangered. He should have told me immediately what happened."

From the corner of her eye, Susan saw Holland stand up and swing one leg over the seat. She took a couple of steps then seemed to stagger.

Noting her pallor, Susan stumbled through the snow to the other woman's side. "Is something wrong?" she asked.

"I stood up too fast, that's all." Holland gestured the others back and bent over the stalled machine. "I'm fine."

As Susan watched, Holland pulled a small hose from her pocket to replace the damaged fuel line. A thin stream of fuel trickled across one glove as she worked.

Susan was surprised that Holland didn't protest when Doug and Brad insisted on fitting the drive belt into place themselves. When they finished, Holland revved the engine a few times then made a few adjustments. Stepping back, she brushed a stray lock of hair beneath her knit cap and started to smile, then suddenly made a dive for the back of a snowy bush.

Brad was the first to respond when the sound of violent retching reached their ears. By the time Susan reached the obviously sick woman, Brad was wiping her face and gently assuring her he would tear a strip off Allen for allowing her to come up the mountain this morning whether anyone needed rescuing or not.

Doug took one look at Holland. "He doesn't know, does he?"

"Is that true?" Brad's voice raised and he looked angry enough to throttle Holland.

"Stop badgering her," Susan added her shouts to the men's. She didn't understand why the men were suddenly so angry. "Can't you see she's sick?"

Holland grinned weakly at Susan. "I'm not sick. I'm pregnant. And no, I haven't told Allen yet, but now I'll have to tell him before these two beat me to it."

"Darn right!" Doug growled.

"You should have sent Allen up here while you waited back at the cabin with Megan," Brad added.

"Megan isn't at the cabin and Allen wouldn't know the first thing about repairing this machine. We decided to have Megan and Allen take the kids back to Salt Lake. In case another storm front moves through, we thought it best to take advantage of the break and get them home. Dutch has never been away from both Allen and me overnight before, so I thought his Daddy, at least, should get back as soon as possible. Besides," she winked. "It seemed like a good idea to allow Brad a little time to cool down before he confronts his kids."

"Why didn't you go with them, instead of your husband?" Susan asked, puzzled.

Holland laughed. "You never saw three men in your life with less mechanical skill than these three. Allen is hopeless, and Brad is only marginally better. Doug actually knows quite a bit, but he has to make three mechanical drawings before he can change a spark plug."

Both men glared at her, but she only laughed harder.

"But why don't you want your husband to know you're pregnant?" Susan pursued the puzzle. Allen seemed to dote on Dutch and he'd probably be just as enthusiastic about a second child, even if the two babies were a little close.

"Morning sickness," Holland answered nonchalantly.

"Morning sickness? But don't most women experience a little nausea during the first trimester?" She directed her question to Brad.

"Yes, most do. But when Holland was expecting Dutch, she became seriously ill and had to be hospitalized to prevent dehydration. The nausea cleared right up while she was in the hospital, but as soon as she went home, it returned. We all about went out of our minds with worry until Allen discovered a link between her illness and garage smells."

"Gasoline fumes aren't good for anyone, and they're much too dangerous for a pregnant woman," Susan frowned at Holland. "Didn't your doctor caution you to stay away from things like that?"

"He warned me about paint, but he didn't say anything about gas or oil," Holland defended herself. "Anyway, as soon as I knew what was wrong, I took care to always work outside. But Allen decided that wasn't good enough, so he locked up my tools." She gave a resigned sigh. "He'll lock them up for sure now."

"I'm sure he will," Brad drawled, "And if he doesn't, I will."

Seeing the dejected look on Holland's face, Susan found herself sympathizing with the younger woman. She knew how difficult it would be for her to give up her work for seven or eight months even for a cause as worthy as a healthy baby. In an odd way she found herself envying Holland. Even though her husband and friends were being annoyingly bossy, they were doing it because they cared about her. Here was a woman with superior skills in a traditionally mascu-line field and instead of resenting her, the men in her life appeared to be inordinately proud of her ability. Being a great mechanic didn't make her less of a woman in their eyes. Too bad their masculine protective instincts didn't extend beyond telling her what not to do, Susan thought, looking at Brad and Doug.

As she shifted her gaze to Holland, Susan recalled an emergency training clinic she'd attended a few years back. All of the participants had been fitted with small, lightweight gas masks for use during a simulated chemical explosion. When she returned to Salt Lake, she decided, she would contact the team of doctors who led the exercise. One of those gas masks might be the answer to Holland's problem. She'd discuss the particulars with Brad at the first opportunity. Then again, why should she discuss it with Brad? She'd find out Holland's obstetrician's name and talk to him—or her.

A kind of depression settled on Susan's shoulders. She really did want to help Holland, but part of her enthusiasm for the project revolved around the anticipation of working with Brad. Sternly, she reminded herself she didn't work with Brad and never would. Their specialties seldom called for any contact between them. She needed to put such thoughts out of her head. She didn't have time for Brad in her life. If she allowed herself to care about him she'd only get hurt when he faced reality one day. In time he would understand that she could never be like Cathy and that his children hated her.

"Is everyone ready to go?" Doug asked, sounding impatient to be on their way. One look at the dark clouds building again to the west convinced everyone to hurry. Susan took a couple of steps toward Holland, and Brad stopped her.

"You're riding with me. Holland will fare better without anyone holding on to her."

"I agree," Susan answered smoothly. "I'll be ready to go as soon as she trades gloves with me."

Holland glanced at her gloves in surprise, then wrinkled her nose as the odor of gasoline wafted toward her. A grin spread across her face as she quickly pulled the gloves free. "Thanks," she whispered as the two women made a hasty trade.

After dropping Susan off at her apartment, Brad hurried back to his Explorer. Snow was falling lightly again and he knew they were lucky to have made it out of the mountains before the main storm hit. Yet a part of him wished he and Susan were back on the mountain in their snow cave, safe from all of the problems and demands of everyday life.

Seated behind the steering wheel, Brad pounded a fist against it in frustration. Just as he expected, Susan had distanced herself from him again on the ride back to Salt Lake. Several times she'd seemed about to say something, then had remained silent. He was glad she hadn't actually said what he knew she was thinking. Nevertheless, he thoroughly expected the next week would find her much too busy to see him even for lunch.

She might have been simply respecting his own disinclination to talk, but he doubted it. He'd been somewhat distracted as he pondered what he would say to Bobbi when he reached home, and he guessed Susan was worrying about the same thing. He'd really wanted Susan and his daughters to have an enjoyable day and get to know each other better. His kids were generally pretty well-behaved and he'd been proud of the consideration they usually exhibited toward others. He couldn't imagine what had prompted them to commit an act of vandalism that had endangered his and Susan's lives. He honestly couldn't blame Susan if she washed her hands of him and his family.

He'd tried to convince her to let him stop somewhere for breakfast before taking her home, but she'd insisted on going straight to her place. He felt reluctant to leave her, knowing she needed him whether she thought so or not. He knew that leaving her now, before they could talk out all that had happened to them, would cost him considerable ground.

Taking her to his home instead was an option he'd considered and discarded. He had to get to the bottom of Bobbi's antagonism before subjecting Susan to any further such incidents. On one hand, he believed Susan needed him and he wanted to be with her. On the other, Bobbi needed him now, too. Something about his relationship with Susan was hurting his daughter, causing her to act out in an uncharacteristic way.

When he pulled into his garage and shut off the motor, he sat for a minute reminding himself he mustn't lose his temper. No matter what Bobbi had done, she was his daughter, and he loved her. He had a sudden memory of the squalling infant a nurse had placed in his arms. She'd been fiery red from head to toe, both skin and hair. She'd opened one eye as if taking his measure and promptly stopped screaming. He'd lost his heart then and there.

Despite the faint sounds of the stereo playing somewhere in the house, an unusual stillness filled the house when he stepped through the door. Mrs. Mack met him in the kitchen with a look of sympathy and suggested he shower while she fixed him a hot breakfast. He quickly agreed, relieved to postpone confronting his children a little bit longer.

Brad was soon warm, dressed in clean, dry clothes, his stomach pleasantly full. Delaying wouldn't be to anyone's benefit. Mrs. Mack gave him an encouraging nod and he slowly pushed away from the table to climb the stairs. He found Heidi sitting on the bottom step. When he crouched down beside her, she burst into tears and threw herself into his arms.

"I'm sorry, Daddy. I didn't know you would have to sleep in the snow and be all wet and cold in the dark."

Picking up the little girl, he settled on the top step with her on his lap. "I'm fine now," he assured her. "But a little while ago I was wet and cold and it certainly was dark. But the worst part was learning it was my own little girls who did that to me."

"We didn't mean to and when Uncle Allen told us nobody could go get you because there was too much snow, I ran upstairs and asked Heavenly Father to save you."

"Asking Heavenly Father's help was the right thing to do, but you forgot one of our family rules. Remember we never break each other's things. I wouldn't have been in any danger if you girls hadn't broken my snowmobile. And there's something else. I'm always nice to your friends when they come to see you or they go places with us, but none of you were very nice to my friend."

"Is Dr. MacKendrick your friend, Daddy?" Heidi twisted her head so she could see his face.

"Yes, Susan MacKendrick is my friend and I was hoping you'd be her friend, too."

"I didn't know she was your friend, Daddy. Bobbi said she was a bad lady and we should make her go away. If she's your friend, maybe she isn't bad. But I don't think she wants to be my friend. She doesn't talk to me, and Bobbi said she doesn't like kids." Heidi was clearly confused.

"Bobbi doesn't know what Susan likes or dislikes."

"Ashley said Dr. MacKendrick wants to get married to you, then she'd be our wicked stepmother and she'd make us all go away." She started sobbing again. "I don't want to go away, Daddy. I want to live in our house with you 'til I'm all grown up, then I'll marry Jason and we'll live on a farm with lots of black and white cows."

Brad didn't know whether to laugh or cry. Mostly he felt angry that Heidi's older sisters had given her so much misinformation. Gently he rocked her in his arms and hushed her tears.

"Daddy," Michelle's voice came from behind him. "I tried to stop them, but no one would listen to me. Jason tried, too. Uncle Doug said we took the coward's way out when we kept quiet and just left instead of telling. I'm really sorry."

"I am, too." Ashley's voice was almost a whisper. "It seemed like something someone in one of my books would do. Sort of a brave, exciting adventure. Bobbi said you'd be stranded for just a little while, then she'd go back and rescue you. She said we wouldn't be hurting you. We'd really be saving you from the clutches of a wicked woman, because Dr. MacKendrick would be so mad she'd just go away."

"That does it!" Brad placed Heidi on her feet as he stood. Hearing Susan maligned was the fuse that triggered his temper. "All of you go to your rooms. I'm going to have a little talk with Bobbi." His long legs carried him down the hall with quick, angry strides. He paused in front of his oldest daughter's room.

Nine

BRAD KNOCKED ON THE DOOR, BUT DIDN'T wait for an invitation to step into his daughter's room. Bobbi sat against the headboard of her bed with her arms wrapped around her updrawn knees. Her hair had come loose from its braid, leaving a thick tumble of waves that obscured her face. She didn't move or in any way acknowledge his presence. Her stereo was playing so loudly, she might not even have heard him enter the room.

Slowly his anger dissipated, leaving him unsure how to proceed. As Brad stood facing Bobbi for several long seconds, he wished Cathy were here to help him. She'd always seemed to know just what to say or do where the girls were concerned. He'd always thought his own relationship with his children was a strong, positive one; he'd considered the bond between himself and his oldest daughter to be especially close, but now he wasn't so sure.

Since the moment he'd learned Bobbi was responsible for leaving him and Susan stranded in a winter storm, he'd felt painful disappointment. That she would deliberately damage something belonging to him and recklessly disregard his and Susan's safety was out of character for the daughter he thought he knew. But that she had also encouraged her younger sisters to dislike Susan tore at his heart.

He turned off the stereo, then spoke her name softly and waited.

Finally she swept her hair back and glared up at him. "I can't believe you'd take her side."

"I'm not taking sides; there are no sides involved," Brad responded more sharply than he intended. "I'm asking for an explanation of why you deliberately destroyed that drive belt, leaving two people stranded in a blizzard, and why you've filled your sisters' heads with a lot of nonsense about Susan."

"I planned to go back for you, but Doug wouldn't let me," she answered sullenly.

"It's a good thing he stopped you or your life could have been in danger, too."

"You wouldn't have cared," she muttered under her breath but Brad heard her. He sighed in exasperation.

"I would care. You know that. I'll always care what happens to you."

He walked toward the bed and sat down, reaching one hand forward to brush Bobbi's red curls back from her face as he'd done thousands of times before. She jerked away from his touch.

"I used to think you loved our family more than anything else in the world." She choked on the words. "I thought you really cared about us."

"What has happened to change your mind?" Brad asked, genuinely puzzled.

"You care more about Dr. MacKendrick than you do about us," Bobbi accused.

Is that what this is all about? he wondered. Could it be so simple as jealousy?

"No, you're wrong about that. I'll admit I'm beginning to care a great deal about Susan. We've become very good friends. But how I feel about her in no way changes my love for you and your sisters," Brad tried to reassure her.

"It does," Bobbi argued fiercely. "If you really cared about us you'd stop seeing her."

"You're being unreasonable, Bobbi. You don't know Susan. You haven't even tried to get to know her. For a sportswoman who talks a great deal about fair play, I expected better of you."

"Are you going to marry her?" Bobbi demanded bluntly.

Marriage? He'd shied away from thinking where his relationship with Susan might be headed. But his heart told him he couldn't rule out that possibility. He couldn't pretend even to himself that Susan MacKendrick was just a good friend. Somewhere along the way his feelings had deepened. But before he could even contemplate remarrying he had a lot of work cut out for him. Susan wasn't ready to consider the possibility, and obviously, neither were his children.

"I don't know," he answered as honestly as he could. "We haven't talked about it. But even if I do ask Susan to marry me someday, would that be so terrible? Would you really object if I remarried?"

"But Mom—"

"Bobbi, this isn't about your mother," Brad cut her off. "I believe your mother wants me to find happiness in marriage again. You mustn't ever doubt my love for your mother nor hers for me. Nothing and no one will ever replace her, but loving your mother doesn't preclude the possibility I might find a different love with a different woman."

"Do you love *her* as much as you love Mom?" Bobbi's voice quavered and he could see a hint of tears in her eyes.

"You can't compare love," he spoke as gently as he could. "Your mother and I fell in love when we were very young. We had almost thirteen years of marriage, a lot of shared dreams, and five children, which built and added to the love we started with. My feelings for Susan are new and not fully developed. I'm only sure I like being with her. It's exhilarating to talk or work with her. I miss her when we're apart and often find myself thinking of her. I admire her greatly and want her to be happy."

"Will you marry her even if—if I don't want you to?" Bobbi appeared to be holding her breath, waiting for his answer. How could he answer such a question?

"Bobbi," he reached for her hand as he struggled to keep communication uppermost in his mind. "It would be easy to answer your question by reminding you that I'm the adult here and if I choose to marry, it's my choice. But that isn't completely true because any choice I make will affect you and your sisters. I want you to be happy and if marrying Susan would cause you real grief, then no, I wouldn't bring her into our home."

"Really, Daddy, you won't marry her?" Bobbi started to smile.

"I didn't say that." He struggled to keep his own temper and hurt in check. "I'm saying I won't do anything I know will make you unhappy, but at the same time I expect the same consideration. Giving up Susan would cause me a great deal of unhappiness. Is that what you want?"

"No, Daddy, but . . . you told me I should choose my friends wisely. You said if my friends had low standards and behaved immorally, I would be more tempted to do bad things than if I chose friends who shared my standards. You said when I started dating I should be especially careful to only date boys who keep themselves morally clean. Don't those rules matter anymore when you're all grown up and you've already been married?"

"Of course they still matter." Stunned, Brad stared at his daughter. Did she think he was having an affair, or whatever it was fourteen-year-olds called it these days? "Honey, I'm not sure what you're implying," he spoke carefully. "But I swear there is nothing immoral about the relationship between Susan and me."

Bobbi burst into tears. Between sobs she gasped, "I didn't mean you, Daddy. I know you have a testimony and you honor your priesthood and all that. But you said good people are tempted, too, and if they don't avoid evil companions, even the righteous may fall."

"This is ridiculous," Brad snapped. He couldn't believe it. His daughter was preaching to *him*. He rose to his feet and paced across the room. "We're right back to the accusations you've made about Susan being wicked or evil," he ground out. "She's a good person and doesn't deserve this kind of slander. You have no idea how many lives she's saved, how committed she is to the same gospel that has always been the center of our lives, how—"

"But Daddy," Bobbi was on her feet shouting now. "She is wicked! She had a baby when she wasn't married, and she hates kids so much she gave her baby away." She stared at her father defiantly as though daring him to contradict her.

"Where did you hear this?" He suddenly felt tired and defeated.

"I didn't listen on purpose." Bobbi stood her ground, obviously unwilling to apologize for any breach of etiquette. "When you brought her here that day I was going to ask both of you to play basketball with me, but when I walked into the living room you were talking and I heard her say it. It's true, isn't it?"

Suddenly Brad found himself praying for help to explain a story that wasn't his to tell. He couldn't allow Bobbi's version of Susan's past to stand unchallenged, but neither could he lie to her. How much could he tell Bobbi without betraying Susan's confidence?

"Sit back down, Bobbi." It was more order than request, but the girl complied. He didn't know what he would have done had she refused. "I have no right to tell you personal details about Susan's past. I hope she'll forgive me for what I am going to tell you, and I hope I'm not mistaken in trusting you to keep what I tell you confidential. When Susan was just a little older than you are now she made a mistake that she immediately regretted. She didn't have loving parents who would help her and she didn't have enough education to support herself and a baby. She couldn't marry her baby's father because he died before he even knew about the baby. She loved that baby more than anything, but she couldn't take care of him, so she gave him the best gift she could. She gave him up to a young LDS couple who couldn't have children any other way, so that he would have two parents to love him, support him, and raise him in the Church.

"Now young lady, I want you to understand a couple of points." Bobbi dropped her eyes and looked anywhere except at her father. "You've made a lot of assumptions on the basis of a few overheard sentences. You influenced your sisters to share your bias, then through your actions endangered both Susan's life and mine. I'm not comparing your thoughtless actions to Susan's mistake, but perhaps you should think about that. I am going to point out that Susan repented of her action and has devoted her life ever since to gaining forgiveness and helping others. She has repented and I believe God has forgiven her, but that is between them. It is not for me or you to judge her."

"You wouldn't want me to have a friend who slept with her boyfriend and had a baby," Bobbi mumbled, sounding uncertain of the point she was trying to make.

"If one of your friends made such a sad mistake I would expect you to show compassion toward her. If she continued making the same mistake and believed there was nothing wrong with what she was doing, then I'd expect you to end the association and look for a friend who shares your values."

"But Daddy, you're an obstetrician. You've told me over and over that you love delivering babies, that babies are special, and there's nothing else like that moment when one of your patients holds her baby in her arms for the first time. And you used to tell me a bedtime story about the first time you held me. If you love babies so much, how can you love a woman who gave away her baby?"

"Bobbi, your personal experience with babies has been with babies like Mary Kate and Dutch. But you're old enough to know from the news, movies, and social studies classes at school that there's a big difference between homes where two mature adults with a reasonable income—like our friends the James and Beckwiths–have a child, and homes where single teenage girls with no job skills and no decent place to live are trying to raise their babies alone. Without good jobs and insurance, they often condemn their babies to poverty and living in poor neighborhoods. Their babies grow up without the support and advantages fathers can give them. Single mothers cut themselves off from friends and college, and all those opportunities most teenagers dream about. Too often they end up neglecting and resenting their children because of all they miss out on. I suspect that a young girl who thinks she loves her baby too much to give it up, or thinks there's something romantic and noble about raising her baby alone, in reality knows little about real mother love. I mean the kind of love where a woman will make any sacrifice necessary to give her child the best chance in life she possibly can, including a stable home with two mature parents."

"You're a single parent and we get along just fine," Bobbi continued to argue.

"I'm not so sure about that after this weekend," Brad retorted. "Anyway, I'm not a teenager with no job skills and you had eleven years with the best mother a girl could ever want. You're smart enough to figure out the difference. I also think you're smart enough to recognize that what you did was wrong. So now the question is what are you going to do about it?"

"I'm sorry, Daddy." She hung her head. "I didn't mean for you to have to stay there all night. I really was going to go back for you. The snow wasn't my fault."

"No, you didn't cause the snowstorm," Brad conceded. "But you should have considered the possibility."

"Are you going to punish me?" Bobbi eyed him warily though her eyes still showed a touch of defiance.

"Bobbi, you know how I feel on that score. I'm far more concerned with repentance than punishment." He and Cathy had agreed from the start that it was more important for their children to understand what they had done wrong and to help them devise a plan for correcting their errors than for them as parents to simply mete out punishment.

"Do I have to apologize to Dr. MacKendrick?" Bobbi worried her bottom lip with her teeth.

"Not until you're ready to do so. A have-to apology is never particularly sincere. If you can't say it and mean it, your apology would be worthless."

"Then what do you want me to do?" Bobbi spoke somewhere between perplexity and anger.

"First, I think you should be completely honest with yourself. Think about this awhile; decide in your own mind whether your actions were right or wrong. And remember the only actions that need concern you are yours, not mine, and not Susan's. Then get down on your knees and ask your Heavenly Father for understanding. If your faith is as strong as I think it is, he'll help you know what you should do."

Silently he vowed to take his own advice. He, too, needed to know what to do about his feelings for Susan. And he needed to know whether or not bringing her into his family would help or hurt his children. Or would Susan be the one to be hurt?

Susan sank into her recliner chair with a groan. Wearily she unlaced her shoes and slipped them from her feet. She'd worked double shifts all week, and now she was paying for it with an exhaustion that went beyond mere fatigue. She'd been so sure she could use work to block memories of Brad and their time alone on the mountain. Only it hadn't worked as well as she'd thought it would. Brad's face, his words, even the feel of his arm around her as they huddled together wrapped in a foil emergency blanket, intruded on her thoughts at inopportune moments. It didn't help that every time she entered her office or walked inside her apartment, his voice was on her answering machine. The only reason she'd left the hospital early tonight was because she knew he would be there most of the night. She'd heard him paged to delivery and since the ER was adequately covered, she'd opted for a good night's sleep.

Slowly she flexed her toes against the carpet and told herself to get undressed and climb into bed. She would in just a moment. Sitting felt so good; she hadn't done much of that all week. She leaned back and the footrest gently lifted her feet. Her eyes closed, and the sleeping woman failed to protest when her dreams carried her where, awake, she refused to allow memory to go. She sighed and snuggled closer when Brad's arms pulled her near and his lips touched hers.

A persistent ringing jerked her awake. Momentary confusion left her wondering why Brad was kissing her in the doctors' lounge. Shaking her head to clear away the cobwebs of sleep, she realized she was in her own front room and the ringing was her doorbell. She glanced at her watch as she stood and to her dismay discovered two hours had passed since she'd arrived home and she was still wearing her coat.

Uneasily she wondered if Brad had given up leaving messages and was now at her door. She didn't have many callers—just home teachers and visiting teachers—but with her schedule, they always made appointments before arriving. She warily peered out the tiny security window.

At first she didn't see anyone, but as her gaze dropped lower she saw a small face crowned by a mop of red curls peering up toward her. What was the child doing here, she questioned even as she hurried to release the door.

"May I come in?" the girl asked hesitantly.

"Oh, yes. Come in." Susan looked beyond the girl to search the hallway. "Surely you didn't come alone?" she asked.

"I came with Jana and Stephanie, but they've gone to a movie, so I'm by myself now." The girl stepped inside and immediately peeled off her coat. "I'm Ashley, in case you don't remember all our names. Most people get Michelle and me mixed up, but they shouldn't because we're really easy to tell apart. Michelle is twelve and I'm only ten. That's why Bobbi says Michelle will have to start wearing a bra pretty soon. I don't think I ever will."

"Uh, does your father know you're here? Won't he be worried?" Flutters of panic in Susan's stomach reminded her she was out of her depth. She generally avoided children, and a ten-year-old visitor at a quarter to nine at night was far beyond her scope of experience.

"Daddy's delivering a baby and Mrs. Mack thinks I'm staying overnight with Jana, so I'm not worrying anybody," Ashley responded confidently.

Susan frowned. She might not have much experience with children, but the possible ramifications of a child out alone when everyone thought her safe somewhere else terrified her. Her first inclination was to call Mrs. Mack and demand she keep closer watch on Brad's children. She opened her mouth, intending to let Ashley know just how stupid and foolish she was to lie to those responsible for her and how dangerous it was for a child to be out alone on the streets after dark. But something stopped her, perhaps the image of her own father reminding her of her own thoughtless stupidity as she struggled to grow up and understand the world around her.

Ashley hung her head. "I know it wasn't truthful to tell Jana's mom I was going home with Bobbi and Michelle. And they thought I was going back to sit with my friends, but it was the only way."

"The only way for what?" Susan led Ashley toward the sofa.

"To come see you."

"But why did you want to see me and how did you know where I live?" Susan blanched, remembering her apartment complex was four or five blocks from the nearest movie theater.

"Oh, it was easy to find out where you live. Daddy has a rola-something thing on his desk with the names, addresses, and numbers of all his friends, other doctors, and people from our ward. I found your address and checked Daddy's map to see how far I would have to walk. It was easy. I didn't get tired or cold or anything."

Susan wondered if she might still be asleep. She didn't know what to say or do. As it turned out, she didn't have to say anything. Ashley went on.

"I had to come see you because one of us should apologize for being so mean to you, and Bobbi said she wouldn't, and Michelle said she didn't need to because she didn't do anything mean, and Heidi and Kelly are too little. So, I'm sorry." She dramatically clasped her hands together over her heart and meekly bowed her head.

"You're sorry?" Susan gasped. "You came all the way here to say you're sorry? You could have telephoned. Anyway, I don't blame you for anything." She wasn't handling this well. She didn't know anything about talking to a child. Come to think of it, she couldn't remember ever being the recipient of an apology before, either.

"It was a really mean thing to do. Michelle said we shouldn't do it, but she's kind of a scaredy-cat, so I didn't listen to her. I just finished reading a really great story and it had a wicked stepmother in it, so when Bobbi said you and Daddy might get married and you'd be our stepmother, I just thought you would be a really wicked stepmother like in my book. That stepmother banished the princess to a far country where she had to work really hard and never got to see her father again. Only, a really brave prince came along and rescued her. I thought I was being really brave, too, but I wasn't. I just imagined I was like that prince. Michelle says I have too much imagination. She's right, you know. I really do have too much imagination."

Susan's head reeled. She didn't know what to say. She wanted to assure the child she didn't plan to be her stepmother, wicked or otherwise, but before she could find the words to express herself, the child went on.

"It really isn't fair. Princes always get the best parts while the princesses only get to be rescued," Ashley complained.

"I never thought that was fair either," Susan was astonished to hear herself say. "It always seemed to me that a real princess ought to get busy and save herself."

Ashley clapped her hands in glee. "I think that, too. If I were a princess I wouldn't wait for some dumb old prince to save me. I'd slay the dragons and chase away the evil sorcerers myself, and I'd even sail away on my own ship. Michelle says it wouldn't be any fun if I were all by myself, but I think it would. Do you think I would get lonesome?"

"Uh, I don't know. You might." Susan stammered her answer.

"Well, maybe I would. I like people. I like to talk to people almost as much as I like to read and that's a whole lot. It's just boys I don't like. Michelle says I'm too young to understand about boys. She thinks she knows everything because Troy Atkinson wants her to be his girlfriend and he's the most popular boy in the ninth grade and Michelle's only in the seventh grade."

"Michelle is kind of young to have a boyfriend, isn't she?" Susan ventured.

"That's what Bobbi told her, but she just got mad. She said Bobbi doesn't want anybody to be anybody's girlfriend because she doesn't have anybody who wants her to be his girlfriend and that's why she's so mean to you 'cause you're Daddy's girlfriend."

"Me?" Susan gulped. She wasn't anybody's girlfriend, and she didn't want to be anybody's stepmother either. She'd better go call Mrs. Mack and see about getting Ashley back home. She rose to her feet, feeling slightly lightheaded from trying to keep pace with her visitor.

"Why are you wearing your coat?" Ashley sounded puzzled. "It's not at all cold in your apartment, but if you have a mean landlord who turns off the heat when you're not expecting it, I'd understand. I read a story about—"

"No, no. I just forgot to take it off when I got home from work. My landlord isn't at all mean," she hurried to assure her guest. Rapidly she pulled off her coat and hung it in the closet. "I was so tired I forgot about it."

"Goodness, if you just got home from work you must be hungry. Daddy said you're an emergency doctor and you work really hard so you deserve a good dinner when you get off work. I'll fix you a really good dinner." She bustled toward Susan's small kitchen.

"Wait." Susan hurried after her. "You can't cook dinner."

"I can't cook as well as Mrs. Mack, but I can make a perfectly good supper. Besides I owe you dinner because my sisters and I made you miss dinner at the cabin and you had to eat yucky granola bars," Ashley firmly made her point.

"Oh, dear." Now what was she going to do? "I think we'd better call Mrs. Mack so she can come get you."

Ashley leaned her head to one side as though thinking. Finally she shrugged her shoulders and sighed. "I never thought about going home after I apologized. Michelle says I never think far enough ahead. She's right again, of course. Michelle's always right and that's really annoying. All right, you call Mrs. Mack while I fix dinner. She's going to be awfully mad, though."

Susan hid a smile. Ashley might look like her mother, but she certainly possessed her father's straightforward determination. She hoped Brad wouldn't be too angry when he learned about his daughter's escapade.

When she returned to the kitchen she found Ashley was right. She could cook. The table was set for two, and a steaming omelet covered each plate. A tall glass of milk sat beside each plate, and Ashley was placing a plate of buttered toast on the table. Was Ashley old enough to operate a stove? Susan wasn't sure but just because she'd assumed the child had meant to heat up soup in the microwave, that didn't mean she needed to ignore the lovely smells coming from her plate.

"Your sisters are asleep, so Mrs. Mack and I decided it would be best if I drive you home," Susan informed Ashley.

"Is she awfully mad?" Ashley inquired nervously.

"She's upset," Susan acknowledged.

"Now I'll have to apologize to her, too," Ashley sighed mournfully.

Susan paused with her fork halfway to her mouth. Her eyes met Ashley's and for several seconds they stared at one another. Then suddenly they were both laughing. When they finally sobered enough to resume eating, Ashley launched into another story. Susan couldn't remember ever having such an amusing dinner partner.

They finished eating and Susan insisted the dishes could go in the dishwasher. They didn't need to be washed tonight. In her car Susan made certain Ashley fastened her seat belt, and she listened to the girl's chatter as she drove the five miles to the Williams' home.

It was nearly eleven o'clock when they pulled into Brad's driveway. Susan watched from her car as Mrs. Mack hurried from the house to meet Ashley. Ashley turned to Susan with a broad grin and suddenly wrapped her arms around the surprised doctor.

"You can be my new mom, if you want to," she whispered. "You're not at all like Bobbi said." Then she was gone. Susan found herself swallowing a lump in her throat as she backed out of the driveway. If she were interested in being anybody's mother, she'd choose to have a daughter just like Ashley, imagination and all.

Ten

BRAD MADE QUICK NOTES AS CHARLOTTE Frazier talked, then thanked her profusely before hanging up. Minutes later Rachel walked into his office carrying the sheets of paper his genealogist friend had faxed to him. Somewhere between feeling dazed and exultant, he stared at the list. Twenty-two names. Twenty-two little boys had been sealed to their parents in Utah temples in February and March, six months after Susan's baby had been born. Charlotte had warned him the list might not be complete since some files were closed even to professional genealogists, but an inner prompting told him the child he sought was on that list. Just as a week ago he'd awakened from a deep sleep with Charlotte Frazier's name on his lips and a profound impression that she could help him find Susan's baby.

The thought had occurred to Brad that if the adoptive family were LDS they'd want the baby sealed to them as soon as possible. Brad had remembered as well that a great deal of emphasis had been placed on submitting four generations of family records to the genealogy library in the early to mid-1980s. The baby's new family might well have been one of the families who completed this assignment. Computers had made the task of sifting through millions of names, places, and dates a relatively simple matter. And in the hands of a research specialist like Charlotte Frazier, with access not only to the Family History Library but hundreds of private data banks, he'd dared to hope.

Taking his time, he spread out on his desk all of the information he'd found so far; the baby's original birth certificate, Susan's own medical records which she had accessed from the doctor who had attended her, the paper she had signed consenting to the baby's adoption, the name of the agency that had paid for Susan's medical care and arranged the adoption, and Mrs. Frazier's list. Two of the boys on that list had birth dates that matched that of Susan's baby.

"Dr. Williams." Rachel stood in the doorway. "I've closed up the office. Is there anything else before I leave?"

"No, I'll lock up when I go. Your husband will worry if you're late." Brad looked down at the papers before him.

"Not tonight. John's in San Francisco on a business trip, so if I can help you with those papers, I have plenty of time."

"Maybe you can help. You could give me some advice anyway." Brad turned his attention to the woman who had been his partner's father's office nurse, then had continued on to work for Jack and Brad. Not only had she been associated with the medical field longer than he had, she knew more about accessing records than anyone else he knew. He also knew he could trust her to keep confidential anything he told her.

He handed her the list of names. "I need to know which of these children were adopted in Utah, but born in another state. As you know, adoption records are sealed and the agency that handled the adoption will not release any information. The doctor who delivered the baby knows no more than the birth mother does. I've already contacted him."

"If there's a medical reason . . ."

"There isn't—unless you count emotional stress and that only counts when a woman wants to get rid of a baby, not when she wants to find one. So that lets out a court order," he added with a hint of wry cynicism.

Rachel held the paper for several minutes without speaking. Shadows flitted across her face.

"You're wondering about the ethics of what I'm doing." Brad accurately assessed her silence. "You might as well know, I have my own doubts. This adoption was final a long time ago. I don't like to think of the possible damage that could result from a premature confrontation between a teenager and his natural mother. The adoptive family has a right to privacy and freedom from any interference by the biological mother. But I wonder if the birth mother might have a right to know if her child is safe and well, and that the terms of the agreement she signed when she gave up the child have been fulfilled. As a mature responsible adult, she now needs to know if the decision she made as a frightened teenager was the right one."

"This woman is important to you?" Rachel asked softly.

"Yes, she's important to me," he acknowledged.

"And if you find out her child is happy and being cared for properly, you think that will satisfy her. But what if it doesn't?"

"I don't know, Rachel. I just don't know."

Rachel's eyes held a touch of pity as they met his. "Go on home, doctor. Your little girls need you. I'll see what I can do with this and let you know what I find."

When Rachel left the room, Brad bowed his head toward his interlocked hands and asked himself for the thousandth time if what he was trying to do was right. He'd carefully avoided speculating about how Charlotte Frazier had accessed the information she'd given him. Now he wondered if he was using Church records inappropriately. He honestly didn't know. Was using the medical files and connections he and his office held access to betraying medical ethics he'd never before questioned? Again he didn't know. He only knew that he didn't want to delve into those questions too deeply.

Slowly he gathered up the papers on his desk and returned them to his briefcase. The one thing he did know was that it was time to go home. The thought didn't fill him with the joy it once would have. When Cathy died a vital spark had left his house. And he'd only been marking time since. Only recently had he come to realize how dangerously far he'd allowed his family to drift. Little Kelly had turned to Holland for the love and attention he'd been too absorbed in his own grief to give her. He wondered if somewhere along the way she'd become more a part of Allen and Holland's family than his own. Heidi had turned to Megan and in some ways so had Bobbi, though he felt certain it wasn't from Megan that Bobbi had learned to be so judgmental and unforgiving. Ashley had lost herself in a world of books and fantasy while he had no idea where Michelle had turned. But only last night he'd looked across the room and realized Michelle was wearing makeup, her jeans were too tight, and she spent an awful lot of time on the phone with someone called Troy.

He didn't blame Holland or Megan for usurping a parental role in his children's lives. Quite the opposite was true. He'd be forever grateful for the maternal influences they were in his daughters' lives. He didn't know how he or his children could have survived the past three years without their help. But it was time he took a more active role. His daughters needed him. Somehow he must reestablish the closeness they'd once shared–if it wasn't too late.

He was glad Mrs. Mack had asked for a couple of weeks off to spend Christmas with her daughter. Taking some time off from his practice to spend the holidays with his children would be a good start.

And what about Susan? his heart asked. He'd keep the promise he'd made her to find her son, then let her go. Briefly he'd hoped it would all work out. When he learned Ashley had paid Susan a visit to apologize for her part in leaving her stranded in a snow storm, he'd believed it was a positive sign. Then his hopes had been dashed by Bobbi's continued refusal to give Susan a chance and the other girls' indifference. While he had been hurt and annoyed by Susan's deter-mination to avoid him, he could see now it was for the best. As much as he'd come to care for Susan, his children had to come first. Besides, there was no way he would allow Bobbi to hurt Susan again.

Christmas was just a week away and instead of the magical week of fun and excitement he remembered from the past, he felt like he was living in a war zone. Cathy had always baked Christmas cookies with the girls, but when he suggested making cookies with them, Bobbi and Heidi pleaded to be allowed to go ice skating with Jason.

Determined to make the evening a success with his other three daughters, he dragged out a mixing bowl and searched for a recipe.

"Okay, I'll read off the ingredients and you put everything on the counter," he instructed Michelle. Before she could respond, the tele-phone rang and she ran to answer it. Brad frowned when he realized Michelle was talking to Troy again. Who was this boy? He'd better find out and put a stop to whatever was going on. Michelle was much too young for boys.

"Ashley, I need your help," he called. A few minutes passed and he called again. Finally the kitchen door swung open and Ashley appeared in the doorway with her finger marking her place in the book she held.

"Put your book down, honey, and come help us make cookies."

She sighed, but did as he asked.

"Why do we need more cookies?" she asked as she set both the sugar and flour canisters on the counter. "Mrs. Mack made plenty."

"Holland and me made cookies, too," Kelly boasted. "Mine was green. Uncle Allen said it was a green monster just like me." She giggled and Brad felt a stab of jealousy.

"Don't you like to make cookies?" Brad asked.

"It's okay." Ashley glanced longingly toward her book. She took over and swiftly mixed the batter, leaving Brad wondering when she'd become so proficient in the kitchen and what was the big hurry. They had all evening. While the cookies baked, she returned to her book.

Brad gave up and turned to Kelly for help with icing the cookies. At least she seemed to be having a good time, though he suspected she was getting more icing in her than on the cookies. When she finished, she ran for a paper plate and Brad watched as she selected three cookies, added an extra liberal sprinkling of red and green bits of candy trim and proudly announced as she touched each cookie lovingly, "This one is for Dutch, and this one is for Holland, and this one is for Uncle Allen." He noticed she didn't choose a special cookie for Daddy.

"Oh, you've finished," Michelle spoke brightly as she returned to the kitchen. "And look at you," she laughed as she caught sight of Kelly. "It's tub time for you." She gingerly reached for her little sister's hand and tugged her toward the stairs.

He supposed he should be grateful Michelle had taken the initiative to get Kelly cleaned up, but he suspected Michelle acted from some motive other than sisterly kindness.

"I guess it's up to just the two of us to clean up this mess," he said to Ashley, who slumped on a chair beside the table reading her book.

"In a minute, Dad. I just have one more chapter." She didn't lift her eyes from the page. Brad sighed and began loading the dishwasher.

When he had finished wiping the counter tops, he wandered into the family room to wait for Michelle and Kelly to come back downstairs. As he stood beside the Christmas tree, he thought of how Cathy had loved decorating for Christmas, inside and out. She'd covered every available surface with lights. This year there was only the tree and Bobbi had decorated it almost entirely alone. She'd insisted the others didn't know how to do it right.

At a sound, he turned to see Michelle coming down the stairs alone. "Where's Kelly?" he asked.

Michelle looked startled. "She's asleep. I put her to bed."

"Did you help her with her prayer, and what about family prayer?"

"Daddy, it's late and she was tired. I didn't think you would want to bother with prayers tonight anyway since Bobbi and Heidi aren't here, and I have to hurry."

Brad glanced at his watch. It was later than he'd realized. But he didn't like thinking of Kelly going to bed without prayers. Uneasily he thought of how many nights he worked late and wondered how many of those nights his girls went to bed without kneeling beside their beds. A stab of guilt made him wince. When had he become careless about something so important as family prayer?

From the corner of his eye he saw Michelle reach for the door. Surely she wasn't going out now!

"Michelle, it's too late to go anywhere now."

"I'm just going over to Emily's house. I won't be long."

"No, I said it's too late to go out tonight." Something wasn't right.

"But I promised. Everyone is expecting me."

Brad felt a chill and his voice took on a sharp edge. "Who is everyone? And who is Emily? I don't remember any girl in the neighborhood named Emily."

"Emily is a friend from school. She lives a few blocks away," Michelle answered vaguely.

"You were planning to walk several blocks at night in December with no coat and those ridiculous shoes?" His skeptical gaze zeroed in on a pair of chunky platform shoes.

"Well, no," Michelle's voice turned hesitant. "Emily's brother is coming to get me."

"I don't suppose his name would happen to be Troy, would it?" Brad felt a rage such as he'd only experienced a couple of times in his life fill his chest.

"Yes, but—" A car horn sounded from the end of the driveway. "I have to go." She reached once more for the door, but Brad was there first.

"You aren't going anywhere except up those stairs and into your room," he enunciated very carefully.

"But, Daddy . . ." Michelle wailed.

"Go!" Brad roared. "And while you're up there, wash that gunk off your face!"

"I have to tell him—"

"I'll tell him!" He pointed to the stairs and Michelle burst into tears as she ran toward them.

Brad opened the door and stormed toward a pickup truck jacked up on extra-large tires waiting in his driveway. As he approached the vehicle, it suddenly reversed and tires squealed as it tore down the street. But Brad had seen enough. The young punk driving that truck wasn't doing his sister a favor. He was looking to do himself a favor—at Michelle's expense.

Brad seethed with impotent fury. He'd like to smash the kid's cocky grin, let him know that if he ever so much as spoke to his daughter again he'd kill him.

Slowly the cold night air reminded him he needed to return to the house. As he turned he saw Ashley standing in the doorway. Her face was white. Shame replaced the anger one tiny increment at a time. Temper and violence had never been his way. He hadn't meant to scare his children; he'd only meant to protect Michelle. Where had all the rage come from? Deep in his heart he knew it was more than Troy. Once he would have calmly invited the boy into the house and made his position clear without threats or anger.

After Brad did his best to assure Ashley that everything was all right, he suggested she go to his office and read while he talked to Michelle.

"Are you going to yell at her some more?" Ashley asked, worried.

"I'll try not to," he promised.

"Good," Ashley breathed an exaggerated sigh. "Yelling doesn't help a bit. I know, 'cause I already tried it. Bobbi did too, but Michelle says we're just jealous because she's more grown up than we are."

"Michelle isn't more grown up than Bobbi. Michelle is only twelve and Bobbi is fourteen."

"Daddy, age isn't everything." She suddenly sounded old beyond her years. "Michelle has a . . . bosom. I'd say that other word, but you'd probably get mad. She has her period and everything. Bobbi doesn't, so Michelle says that makes her the most grown up."

Brad remembered that Holland's father had raised her as a boy. He'd always suspected there was something strange about a man who had turned a lovely daughter into a rough and tumble son. Now he wondered if the old man might have been a lot smarter than he'd ever given him credit for.

Brad felt a moment of déjà vu as he knocked on Michelle's door, then stepped into his daughter's room. He remembered his talk with Bobbi hadn't accomplished much. He prayed he would fare better with Michelle.

The phone rang just as Susan shut off the shower. Grabbing a towel on the way, she dashed to the bedroom. She wasn't on call tonight, but it was understood that in an emergency she'd go in. Or it might be Brad. Her heart skipped a beat before she remembered he'd finally taken her none-too-subtle hints and stopped trying to contact her more than a week ago.

She took a deep breath and answered in her best professional voice.

"Doctor MacKendrick?" a small voice queried.

"Ashley?" Though she hadn't seen the child since her nocturnal visit, Susan instantly recognized her voice. "Is something wrong? Has someone been hurt?" Her heart constricted as a vision of Brad, broken and bleeding, flashed before her eyes.

"Almost. Troy drove away before Daddy could catch him, so Daddy didn't hit him or anything, but I think he would if he could catch him. He's talking to Michelle now and he promised he wouldn't yell, but I'm scared and I don't have anybody to talk to. Bobbi went ice skating and Mrs. Mack is visiting her daughter because it's Christmas."

Susan nearly gasped with relief as her mind registered that Brad hadn't been in some kind of accident.

"I-I'm glad you called me. You can talk to me as much as you want." Susan's words surprised herself. Then she realized it was true. She liked Ashley. In fact, the child had frequently been in her thoughts lately. Susan had experienced a sense of warmth each time she'd recalled sharing a simple supper with Brad's chatterbox daughter who obviously lived in a dream world one minute and the next was old beyond her years with her feet firmly planted in the practical cares of her real world.

"It's Michelle. She's been doing really dumb things. She wears clothes that are too little and her friends are really mean. She puts on lots of makeup and she got her ears pierced . . ."

"Lots of girls have pierced ears," Susan said, thinking she should try to soothe Ashley a bit.

"Four times!" Ashley sputtered indignantly. "She has four holes in each of her ears. And her boyfriend wears earrings too and has a pony tail. And—and he drives really fast in his truck and he says I'm a stupid bawl baby. He thinks he's so smart, but if he were so smart he wouldn't still be in junior high school. He got held back in the fourth grade."

"Wait a minute, Ashley." Susan suddenly felt sick. "Are you saying your dad is letting Michelle date a boy that much older than she is?"

"No, Daddy didn't let her go. He yelled at her and made her go to her room, then he ran outside and I was scared. Daddy's madder than when we broke his snowmobile." Susan heard a slight sniffle. "Sometimes Daddy doesn't notice things. But he wanted us all to make cookies tonight and Michelle talked on the phone with Troy instead of helping and I think Daddy noticed everything."

Susan couldn't help smiling in spite of her concern. She knew how single-minded Brad could be. She also suspected Brad might be caught in a time warp where his kids were concerned. To him they'd remained the little girls they'd been when his wife died. She felt sorry for Brad, suddenly faced with teenagers.

An old memory surfaced of her own difficult passage into womanhood. Her father had locked her in her room for two days when she found a tube of lipstick and decided to experiment. He'd fired rock salt at the one young man who, on a dare, came to the house to ask her out. And when she began to menstruate she thought she was being punished for some evil she didn't remember committing and would surely die.

"Your father won't hurt Michelle," she promised Ashley and wasn't sure how she knew that was true, but she did. "She might feel angry and embarrassed for a long time. You'll need to be patient with her and help her understand growing up is good, but just looking grownup isn't the same thing as being grown up."

Ashley was silent for several seconds, then she blurted out, "I like to talk to you, Dr. Susan. Is it okay if I call you Dr. Susan? Doctor MacKendrick doesn't sound like we're even friends and we are friends, aren't we? I mean you listen to me, and you don't tell me I talk too much, or I'm just a kid."

"Yes, we're friends. And if you want to call me Susan, that's okay."

"And can I call you again?"

"Yes, you can call me anytime you want to."

Susan held the phone against her damp towel for a long time after Ashley said good-bye. Her throat felt thick and the backs of her eyes burned. There was something about that child. She wished she were there beside her to hold and comfort her. She'd like to give that little girl all the love and reassurance the child Susan had been denied.

Love? She questioned her choice of words, then slowly admitted the truth. She loved Ashley almost as much as she loved Ashley's father.

Slowly she sank to the carpet beside her bed, her head ringing with denial, but her heart refused to listen. She loved Brad and refusing to face the truth wouldn't change her feelings. But love didn't bring the surge of joy it should have. Instead her heart filled with a dull ache. Brad's wife, Cathy, had been everything Susan was not. How could a man who lived a life like Brad's and who loved a woman like Cathy, ever love her? Even if he did care a little bit about her, Brad was too good of a father to allow himself to continue a relationship with a woman his children disliked.

If she avoided Brad as much as possible perhaps the ache would ease, but she sensed that it would never go away entirely. Giving up Brad's friendship would cause her lasting pain, but she would do it. He and his family would be better off without her. She thought of Ashley and a tear trickled down her cheek. Would it be wrong to continue her friendship with the little girl?

Eleven

CHRISTMAS MORNING WASN'T FILLED WITH THE peace and joy Brad had hoped for, but all things considered, he got through it all right. The younger girls seemed pleased enough with their gifts, but Michelle and Bobbi hadn't bothered to hide their disappointment in the gifts he gave them. He should have taken Rachel shopping with him as he had the last couple of years, but he'd wanted to do it alone this time.

Michelle accused him of trying to keep her a baby and reminded him she was going to be thirteen in a couple of weeks. Bobbi muttered that she didn't need any more stupid dresses. What she really wanted was a new pair of Nikes, some Wranglers, and a green sweat suit.

By ten o'clock Kelly was begging to go to Holland's house to show Dutch her new toys and Heidi was in tears because Jason and his family were spending Christmas in St. George at his grand-mother's condo, so he couldn't come play her new game with her. Ashley disappeared into the den to call her "best friend," then reap-peared to curl up in one of the overstuffed chairs with a new book. Michelle and Bobbi spent the morning sniping at each other. Bobbi called Michelle fat and Michelle retaliated by accusing Bobbi of being as flat as a boy.

Brad struggled to hold his temper. He managed fairly well until Bobbi announced she hated her hair and that she wanted to get it cut. Brad was appalled. All five of his daughters had inherited their mother's glorious red mane. He'd loved Cathy's fiery curls from the moment he'd first met her. He loved the way light and fire shimmered through its length. He'd carry with him forever a picture of her hair spread across a white pillow. When the chemotherapy had stolen all Cathy's beautiful hair, he'd secretly wept.

"You're not cutting your hair," he informed Bobbi curtly.

"But, Dad, I'm too old for braids and it's always in the way," she argued.

"You're not cutting it," he repeated.

"It's my hair. Why can't I do what I want with my own hair?"

"Your hair is beautiful the way it is," Brad replied grimly. "You look more like your mother every day," he added more gently.

"Dad, I don't look like Mom. I'm at least six inches taller than she was. I'm taller than every boy in my class except Jason and Charles Linkenhaur. I'm as tall as Holland, probably as tall as Dr. MacKendrick. They have short hair. I bet you don't tell them they shouldn't cut their hair."

"They aren't my daughters." He left the room before she could say she wished *she* weren't his daughter.

He closed his bedroom door and slowly sank to his knees. "Why, Father, have my children turned against me? How can I go on without Cathy?" A picture of Susan slowly formed in his mind as he clutched his head in his hands. Cathy was dead. It could be many years before they were together again. He'd accepted that, but to have to give up Susan, too, seemed more than he could bear. Just hearing Bobbi mention Susan's name had twisted his heart.

Slowly he rose to his feet, feeling discouraged because no answer had come to him, but he'd promised his father to come for dinner by one. It was time to leave. He looked forward to Christmas dinner with his family; he just hoped that around their grandfather and cousins, the girls would behave better.

Fortunately, Michelle had anticipated he'd order her to wash her face before they could leave, and the day did proceed better at the judge's sprawling country home.

Dusk had fallen when he found himself alone with his father in his comfortable library. He looked up as the older man flicked the switch for the table lamp at his side.

"Not in the mood to watch videos, I see." His father stated the obvious as he settled into the matching chair sharing the small circle of light.

"No, I guess not."

"Something troubling you, son?"

Dad knew perfectly well something was troubling him. He wasn't blind to the machinations his father had contrived to send everyone else to watch videos, so he could be alone with Brad. All right, he'd play along. He might as well since he wasn't doing too well on his own.

"Tell me, Dad. How did you do it? How did you go on with your life after Mom died?"

"Work. And more work."

"I've tried that and it's nearly cost me my family," Brad responded with a touch of bitterness.

"I told you what I did. I didn't say it was a good thing." The judge leaned back and chose his words carefully. "When your mother died I thought my life was over. You kids were all grown up. Even our youngest was married. I let the law become my life. It wasn't until my obsession contributed to Megan's fright and sent her fleeing from Doug that I learned I had to let people back into my life."

Brad knew his friends Doug and Megan didn't hold his father responsible for the long, lonely years they'd spent apart. Still, the judge had frightened Megan badly those many years ago by threatening to bring charges against the shy sixteen-year-old if she were part of her stepfather's plan to extort money from Doug.

Brad's father continued, "That experience taught me I had to stop waiting to die so I could be with Sally. I had to start living again."

"Is that what you think I'm doing, just waiting to die?" Brad asked incredulously.

"Seems that way. It's been three and a half years. You should be meeting people, having a little fun."

"You mean women."

"Yes, Brad, you're not the kind of man who should be alone. You should marry again."

"You never remarried."

"I considered it. I even came close once."

Brad sat up straighter and looked at his father, checking to see if he was serious. The older man chuckled. "That surprises you, doesn't it."

"Yes. I'll admit I wasn't aware you ever became interested in someone else after Mom. But if you found another woman you could love, why didn't you marry her?"

"Her children objected, and she decided she couldn't go against their wishes."

"I'm sorry, Dad."

This time it was the judge's turn to look surprised. "You say that as though you really understand," he mused.

"I think I do," Brad admitted. With little prompting, he told his father about Susan and his daughters' refusal to give her a chance. He went on to describe the unhappiness that had descended on his home. When he finished, the judge steepled his fingers and held a contemplative pose for several minutes before commenting.

"I'd like to meet your Susan—" Brad started to interrupt, but the judge refused to yield. "I know, you don't claim she's your Susan. But you'd like her to be. You've been wise enough to recognize that though you feel ready to move on with your relationship, neither she nor your children are ready. That's good because you aren't the only one who counts here, not even you and Susan together. But if I'm reading this right, I'd say Susan and the children may actually be more ready than you are."

"What!" Brad exploded. "I told you I've had an assurance that Cathy would accept Susan. I even admitted I love her."

"Son, you haven't dealt with your anger."

"I don't understand."

"Tell me honestly, do you still feel God has been unfair to you? After all, you served a mission and as a bishop, and you've sincerely tried to be a good person. You even chose a career where you could help others. Still he took away the one thing you loved and valued more than anything else, the only thing you ever really desired for yourself—your wife."

"I don't blame God," Brad denied. "I've even tried with all my heart to forgive the drunk who killed her."

"Tried, that's the key word. You haven't forgiven him and now your anger has spread to your children because you believe they are denying you a chance to regain the home and love you once had. But in the end, it's God you're really angry with because he won't give you back the life you once enjoyed. Face it, Cathy won't be coming back. And even if she could come back, your life would be different today from what it was three years ago. If you were to marry Susan, she wouldn't think or act or look like Cathy. Your little girls won't remain little girls, and some day they'll leave you for a life of their own. You can never have your old life back. And to have a new life, a real life that is, you have to forgive."

Brad didn't respond. He could feel tears running down his cheeks and didn't bother to brush them away. Did he blame God for all that had gone so terribly wrong in his life? Is that why family prayer had become an occasional thing, why his own prayers had become brief, rote repetitions much of the time? He'd stopped going to the temple the second year after Cathy's death. Going alone had been so difficult. Or was that only an excuse? But he had a testimony. He knew the gospel was true, so what was he to do?

"Brad," the judge said, placing his arm around his son's shoulders. "There's no such thing as sitting on the fence. You can't just mark time waiting for the beat to begin again. If you aren't moving forward, you're sliding backward. There's no in-between."

His father's words held a ring of truth that Brad recognized. He'd tried, he'd honestly tried to do what was best for his family. That trying had included keeping everything in their lives as familiar and normal as possible. He'd learned in medical school and had seen the concept reinforced during his years as a bishop. When a surviving spouse and close family members made radical changes in their lives following the death of a loved one, further grief and unhappiness always seemed to follow.

Had he striven so hard to keep the outward forms of normality in his and his children's lives that he had developed a kind of blindness? If everything looked the same, could he then pretend nothing had changed? Was he freezing time in a grief-stricken frenzy to preserve the life he loved? From the start, dealing with Cathy's death had been difficult enough without facing change and confusion as well. He'd been so sure that was the right approach both for his girls and for himself. Had he really only avoided reality? Or had he carried the concept too far? What was best for his family three years ago might not be best today.

The telephone shattered his deep contemplation. The judge reached for it and after listening for a moment handed the instrument to Brad. It was his answering service informing him he was needed at the hospital. Missie Madison was in labor. A pang of regret made him hesitate. If he could only continue this conversation with his father, perhaps he'd know which way to turn. He wasn't on call, but he'd promised Missie that when her time came, he'd be there for her. All of his patients were important to him, but he felt especially close to this young woman who had endured endless tests and procedures in her quest to become pregnant, then had miscarried so many times. Her cheerfulness and quiet determination had never failed to lift his own spirits.

"Go ahead, son," the judge said as Brad hung up the phone. "The girls can stay here tonight. You can pick them up tomorrow."

"Thanks, Dad. I'll just let them know, then go straight to the hospital."

When Brad reached the hospital he found Missie scared and crying. She huddled on the bed in the center of one of the comfortably decorated birthing rooms of the Women's Center, tears streaming from her eyes. Through three miscarriages and the traumatic months leading up to this night, she'd remained strong and determined to bear a child. He'd been impressed by her faith each time she tried and failed, and tried again. He'd checked her only yesterday and though she was three weeks short of her due date, he felt confident the baby was large enough to survive well on its own and had told her so. He had expected she would be elated to reach this final chapter in her long wait.

He smiled as he greeted her, then turned to her husband. "Hello, Ken. I need to examine your wife, but I suspect it's the real thing this time. You just might be a father before Christmas is over."

The young man grinned nervously and shook Brad's hand before turning back to his wife. "I got a hold of your mom." He tried to comfort her. "The roads are good, so they'll be here in a couple of hours."

"Dad's coming, too?" When Ken nodded his head she burst into fresh tears.

After examining his patient and assuring her everything was progressing normally, he attached a fetal monitor, then took the chair beside her bed. She continued to cry.

"Missie," he spoke gently. "I can give you a shot of Demerol if you like. You expressed a preference for as little medication as possible, but if the pain is too much there won't be any harm to you or your baby if we take the edge off the pain."

"No," the young woman gulped. "It's not so bad."

"I've seen you take this much pain in stride before, Missie," Brad tried to reach the source of his patient's fear. "If it's not pain, then something else must be bothering you."

Ken moved closer to take his wife's hand as she struggled to speak. "I want a baby. You-you know how much I want a baby. I've dreamed for years about a tiny baby, with sweet little hands and fat cheeks, all dressed in white satin. But it— it has never been real. This," she placed one hand on the mound of her abdomen. "This isn't just a *baby*; this is a person. I've never let myself think about a real child, just that picture-book infant in white satin. I . . . I took a nap this afternoon and when I woke up the contractions had started and I knew nothing would ever be the same again. In a few hours I will be responsible for a person. This baby is real and he needs someone who knows how hot bath water should be and if he's sick or just crying and what to do when he won't eat. He needs someone who can teach him how to walk and to pray and to help him with his homework. I don't know a lot about the gospel; I never got really active in the Church until I met Ken. And I never went to college. I don't know how to be a mom. I don't know enough, and I'm not good enough."

Her slight body tightened with another contraction and Brad watched the monitor until the peak ebbed. Then, placing his hand over Missie's and Ken's joined hands, he spoke to them both.

"This baby is coming whether you're prepared or not. Babies do that," he chuckled. "But I think you're far more prepared than you think you are. You've gone through several intense disappointments and it's only natural your mind has tried to protect you from pain. It's done that by focusing on your pregnancy, on the here and now, so you couldn't see beyond this point. It's a rather common tendency for women who have suffered multiple miscarriages, as you have, to believe that if you don't dream or hope too much, you won't get hurt again."

A part of Brad heard his own words as if from a distance. Later he'd take them out and examine them more closely. Some prompting told him it wasn't only women like Missie who developed this strategy of self-preservation.

"Babies are really highly adaptable," he attempted to assure his patient. "They make a lot of allowances for inexperienced parents. There will be classes here at the hospital that will teach you how hot bath water should be and I'll only be a phone call away, as will both your mothers. Ken will help you, and you'll learn together. You don't have to know everything at once."

Missie attempted to smile through her tears, but he could still see a hint of doubt.

"Ken," Brad went on. "I think I saw your parents out in the hall. They're welcome to come in, if you both want them here. If you don't, I'll send them to a waiting room. But I think it might ease Missie's mind and yours, too, if you invited your father in here for a few minutes to assist you in giving your wife a priesthood blessing." He'd met Ken's father a couple of times and knew from Missie that the man served on the high council in the Winder Stake.

After assuring Missie he'd be back shortly, he left the room and found himself alone in the doctors' lounge. Sinking onto a deep sofa, he leaned his head against its back, his arms spread wide on either side. As he stared at the ceiling his eyes drifted shut and he found himself talking to God. For the first time in longer than he cared to remember, he sensed that a real presence was listening to him and hearing the turmoil of his heart.

At last voices penetrated his solitude and he lifted his head as two other doctors entered the lounge.

"False alarm," one laughed. "Every Christmas one of my ladies indulges in too much turkey and fruitcake, and mistakes heartburn for labor pains."

"Know what you mean," the other doctor laughed. "Only mine turned out to be the real thing. Her husband panicked and drove her to the emergency entrance instead of here and I had a heck of time getting her over here before Junior made his entrance."

"A quick one, huh?" the first doctor asked absently as he peeled off his scrubs.

"The baby came fast, but that wasn't the problem. The ER is a nightmare tonight. Doc Attitude's got her hands full with not only the usual Christmas mishaps, but some drunk plowed into a van full of kids. She's pulled in half a dozen orthopedic surgeons, and she's got every doctor and nurse on call running full tilt. The mother didn't make it and it looks pretty touch and go for a couple of the kids."

Some drunk . . . the mother didn't make it. Brad screwed his eyes as tightly shut as he could make them. But the words bounced around inside his head. Another drunk had cost a man his wife, the children their mother. It was Cathy's senseless death all over again. Rage built until he felt he might explode. He fought the urge to run to the ER, to confront the drunk, to literally tear him apart.

A voice spoke softly in his ear. *You haven't forgiven him, but in the end it's really God you're angry with.* His father's words sobered him. Was he angry with God? Was his life stymied because of his inability to forgive? Surely it was asking too much to expect a man to forgive a drunk whose self-indulgence had cost him his wife and his children their mother.

He needed to get back to Missie. He nodded briefly to the other doctors and left the lounge, anger still seething beneath the surface of his mind.

He sensed a difference in the birthing room the moment he walked through the door. Ken's and Missie's heads were close together, and they were talking softly with no sign of tears. An aura of peace and gentleness surrounded them.

Missie looked up and met his eyes. "Thank you," she whispered. "Your words helped and I needed a blessing to remind me to have faith. I'll be okay now." She patted her swollen abdomen and added, "We both will." Her eyes clouded again and she seemed to struggle for words. "My dad is coming. I didn't know until . . . I should have told . . . Oh . . ." She gasped as a contraction gripped her body.

This one was long and hard. When it finished, Brad checked Missie's progress and was satisfied to find she'd dilated to a six. She had a ways to go, but as another contraction began to build he knew her labor would go faster now. Between contractions Missie and Ken talked and planned. Sometimes she laughed softly and after each contraction she gently teased Ken about how serious he'd become.

As the contractions became harder and more frequent it was Ken's turn to look scared. Brad could hear the fear in the young father's voice as he struggled to remember all he'd been instructed in prenatal classes about coaching his wife. Brad had watched as many first-time fathers standing awkwardly in unfamiliar surgical gowns had faced this same struggle. Some opted out, some passed out, a few enjoyed every minute, but most, like Ken, faced a million terrors that blossomed into a keener awareness of life and the love they bore for their wives.

Missie's labor continued with greater intensity and for longer than Brad had expected, though he could see no reason for alarm. And at last Missie consented to an epidural, more, Brad suspected, to relieve her husband's pain than her own.

At last the baby's head crowned and Brad turned to the nurse at his side, instructing her to adjust the mirror so that Missie wouldn't miss any part of her baby's arrival. After taking his time, the baby suddenly appeared in a great rush. The tiny head shoved its way clear, and the small, slick body followed before Brad could suction the mouth and nose. A high, thin wail filled the air without any encouragement on Brad's part.

As he placed the baby on Missie's abdomen, a nurse's voice quietly noted the time. Eleven forty-two p.m. Missie had her Christmas baby. In moments the cord was severed and a nurse reached for the baby. She gently suctioned the remaining mucous and dried him thoroughly before wrapping him in a receiving blanket and handing him to Ken.

Long years of practice made Brad's movements smooth and efficient as he attended to the afterbirth and stitched the few small tears left behind. He laughed with his patient and her husband and took delight in the tears of joy that coursed down their faces as they examined their long-awaited son. Then Brad lifted the baby into his own arms for a cursory inspection. He'd check the baby more thoroughly in the nursery.

The baby was small, a little more than five pounds, he guessed, but his heart and lungs seemed to be functioning normally. Impulsively he cradled the infant in his arms. In a moment he would place him in the heated crib prepared for his journey to the nursery. A feeling of awe and wonder filled his heart, a sensation much like that he'd experienced as he'd held each of his own children in his arms for the first time. Each new life seemed to be a message from God telling the world of his love. A burden seemed to slip away from Brad's shoulders as the tiny, scrunched face stared owl-like into his own, and

Brad thought of that long-ago Christmas baby. Peace filled his heart and he knew that all that had happened in his life had not happened because his Savior didn't love him. A gentle calm filled his soul as faith and hope replaced the darkness he'd harbored for so long.

A sound caught his attention and he turned toward the door. Two women stood there. One had eyes only for her daughter, the other stepped to Ken's side to give him a hug. Ken's father threw Brad an apologetic glance. "A nurse told us it was all right for us to come in," he said before he stepped to his daughter-in-law's side and bent to kiss her cheek.

The other man remained in the doorway, his stance wary, his face drained of color. For a moment Brad couldn't breathe; his mind refused to assimilate the obvious. The drunk who took Cathy's life stood before him. He was Missie's father. Silence screamed in his ears and for one insane moment he wondered if the nightmare Susan faced this night in the trauma center was this man's fault, too.

The baby in his arms stirred and a whimper reached Brad's dazed senses. This precious infant was the monster's grandchild. No, the man wasn't a monster. Brad looked into his eyes, and without a word being spoken he knew the depths of despair that tormented the other man's soul. For the past three and a half years, Brad had not been the only one suffering.

Brad had been glad when Cathy's killer had been sent to prison and angry when he'd been released after only thirty months, but prison wasn't this man's ultimate punishment. He had to live night and day with the knowledge he'd taken a young woman's life. Not a day passed that he didn't face the knowledge that a family was without a mother because of him. Every day he'd had to face the loss and hurt in his own wife and children's eyes. He was a man who knew the gospel, had held the priesthood, and who knew the eternal value of families, a man whose faith hadn't matched his convictions and he'd yielded to weakness and temptation. That was his hell.

Brad felt the hatred and anger drain away His father was right; he'd been only half alive, simply marking time, as he waited for the world to stop and let him off. This man wasn't responsible for all that was wrong in Brad's life. Neither was God. The fault was in his own failure to grasp life and live it fully with faith in God's love.

Lightness filled Brad's heart, telling him it was time to let the past go. At last he could forgive. A sudden need to be with Susan filled all the empty spaces of his being.

With careful, measured steps he walked toward the figure clinging to the door jamb. Brad saw the man's fingers whiten as he braced himself, but Missie's father offered no defense. Vaguely, Brad heard the collective indrawn breaths of the family behind him.

"I think it's time you met your grandson." Brad placed the infant in a pair of shaking arms. Missie's father made no attempt to disguise either his gratitude nor remorse as his eyes met Brad's one last time before Brad turned to walk away.

Twelve

SUSAN FELT A PRICKLE DOWN HER BACK, AND without turning she knew Brad stood in the doorway watching her remove splinters of what had once been a lovely, glass tree ornament from a four-year-old's knee. His presence didn't disturb her concentration; instead she felt a renewal of the energy which had begun to lag.

Damage to the knee didn't appear to be as extensive as she'd feared earlier. The child had cried himself to sleep, and she was grateful he continued to sleep without sedation. Some of her patients weren't so fortunate.

She thought of the brother and sister she'd transferred to the Primary Children's Medical Center, the mother whose body had been picked up only minutes ago by the mortuary, and of the husband who still wasn't out of surgery. If he survived, he, like Brad, would face raising a large family of children alone. Three other children lay in various rooms of this hospital while only the baby, a four-month-old infant tightly strapped in an infant carrier, had survived unscathed. The inebriated driver's body had already been claimed by his heart-broken wife. Along with the two deaths, the day had been filled with holiday-related accidents and family disputes, making a mockery of Christmas cheer in the trauma center and draining the stamina of her staff.

She finished her delicate task and twisted her shoulders to ease their ache as she stood at last and turned toward the door. Brad was no longer there, but she'd known he'd gone. She'd felt him leave just as she'd sensed his arrival. For a moment she regretted he hadn't waited. It would have felt good to feel his arm around her and to lean her tired head against his shoulder for just a moment. But it was probably for the best. This had been a strange day, and she was feeling vulnerable. It would be better not to see Brad until she'd had a chance to armor herself once again.

It had started with Ashley. They'd talked for almost half an hour this morning when the child had called to wish Susan "Merry Christmas" and coax her to go with them to her grandpa's house for Christmas dinner. She'd wanted so much to say yes. A part of the lonely child who had never spent Christmas with cousins or grandparents ached to experience a large and noisy family celebration. But she feared she wouldn't be welcomed by Ashley's sisters and she wasn't certain Brad would want to hear from her on a day that must be full of memories of his dead wife.

She'd laughed when Ashley told her about the ruffled dress and matching anklets Brad had given Bobbi and chuckled when Ashley described Michelle's attempt to hide from her father the purple nail polish one of her friends had given her. Yet she felt sad for them. Brad was a loving father caught up in a welter of confusion made worse by his overloaded sense of responsibility, and Bobbi was a fourteen-year-old girl who wasn't certain whether she wanted to go forward or backward. Michelle complicated the equation in her headlong rush to grow up too fast. Susan wished there was a way she could help Brad's daughters through their transition from girls to women, but she recognized she was the last person they would want to help them—except Ashley, who truly wished to be Susan's friend.

Ashley's call had left her touched by the girl's candor, yet oddly unsettled. Long after she'd hung up the phone and checked in at the hospital she found her thoughts returning to the child at odd moments. She wondered that she felt such empathy for Ashley and questioned why she identified with her as she'd never done with another child. As Susan reflected on the question, little bits and pieces of her own childhood interspersed with what she knew of Ashley. She remembered her own hurt as she'd realized she couldn't talk to her mother. She'd camouflaged her loneliness behind an air of indifference to the real world around her and found her solace in books and dreams. Ashley, too, suffered from loneliness, left without a mother and left behind by her older sister Michelle. Fantasy and the world of print had become her refuge.

Repeatedly Susan found herself imagining how it would be if Ashley were her daughter and they were spending Christmas together. Brad kept intruding in the picture, and she found herself reluctant to push him away. Over and over she had to remind herself she couldn't afford to dream about Brad or Ashley or family Christmases. She had a job to do.

A jarring clatter disturbed her thoughts. From the corner of her eye, she saw a nurse stumble, scattering the contents of the tray she held. The woman scrambled to collect the objects rolling across the floor. As she reached for the last roll of tape she looked up to see Susan watching her. Fear coupled with embarrassment flashed across the nurse's face and a pair of scissors slid off the tray as she grappled for the tape. Susan's first impulse was to reprimand the nurse and to remind her that every item on the tray needed to be re-sterilized. Something held back the sharp words; maybe it was the day. Though her family hadn't placed much importance on celebrating Christmas, the day had always brought her an awareness of her Savior.

Perhaps in empathizing with Ashley, she empathized with this nurse, too.

She reached out a hand to the other woman, who reluctantly accepted her help in regaining her feet.

"I'm sorry. I'll take—"

"Yes, take the tray back," Susan interrupted. "Then go lie down for a while. It's quieter now. I'll send someone for you if we heat up again."

The nurse stared back dumbly and Susan hid a smile. Doc Attitude didn't have a reputation for overlooking mistakes or for noticing that nurses were human.

"Look," she explained. "I'm not unaware you started at seven this morning. With the high volume of holiday disasters we've seen today, I know you got pressed into working a double shift. I also know you have children. Therefore you were up half the night playing Santa Claus and back up before five to watch them open their presents. You're tired. Go get some sleep while you can." She turned on her heel, leaving the open-mouthed nurse behind.

She knew the story would be all over the hospital in less than ten minutes. Plenty of people would say Doc Attitude had finally cracked. She didn't care. From deep inside came a voice she'd ignored for a long time. If that voice sounded suspiciously like Brad's, then so be it. She didn't have to be perfect. When Jesus said, "Be ye perfect," he wasn't talking about a way of life; he was talking about a journey. Mistakes could be forgiven.

She sank into her office chair and stared fixedly at a calendar on the wall. Could mistakes be forgiven? Even mistakes as serious as those she had made? The gospel she had grown to love taught that repentance was necessary. Long ago she'd determined that repentance and forgiveness went hand in hand, and when her parents rejected her plea for forgiveness, she'd resigned herself to remaining unforgiven. Why had she assumed that because her parents wouldn't forgive her that neither would her Heavenly Father? Was Brad right when he said that God had forgiven her, that now she only needed to forgive herself? His words weren't much different from the words of a bishop in the little college-town ward she'd attended while going to school. He'd cautioned her that forgiving herself would be the hardest part, but that failure to do so would show a lack of faith in God's promise to forgive all those who truly repented and forsook their sins.

A flash of insight told Susan that, in a strange way, finding her son had become part of her quest to finally forgive herself. Only the knowledge that she hadn't damaged the life she'd carelessly brought into this world would enable her to complete the process. She had sought forgiveness from her Father in Heaven and from her parents; now she had to know if there was a chance her son would some day forgive her. Only then could she at last forgive herself.

After a scant six hours of sleep, Susan returned to the hospital to an almost quiet ER. A little after nine she was summoned to the telephone.

"Susan, I have to see you." Brad's voice held a note of urgency. Her heart skipped a beat as she wondered if something had happened to him or to Ashley. She had to stop this, she berated herself. Ashley was assuming too much importance in her life. As was Brad.

"Is something wrong?" she questioned.

"No," he hastened to assure her. "But I do need to speak with you where we won't be disturbed. Can you get away from the hospital for a few hours?"

"I think so. Would you like me to meet you somewhere?" Was she being foolish to agree to meet Brad? His voice alone filled her with a longing that didn't go well with her determination to keep a distance between herself and him.

"No, I have a patient at the hospital I need to see this morning. When I finish, I'll stop by the ER. I'll see you in half an hour."

Susan hung up the phone, then went searching for Dr. Giles. When she found him she asked him to take over for her for a couple of hours. He seemed pleased she'd asked. He had recently indicated his readiness for more responsibility, and she thought she might be wise to encourage him to do just that.

Susan felt self-conscious leaving the hospital with Brad at her side. Tongues would wag, but suddenly she didn't care. Some feminine instinct took infinite pleasure in being seen with the tall, handsome object of so many women's fantasies.

Brad threaded his way through traffic, avoiding the interstate and its massive construction delays. When she realized he was headed toward his own home a sense of trepidation filled her heart. She wasn't sure she wanted to meet his children again—except Ashley. She'd love to see Ashley.

"The children are with my father this morning." He seemed to read her mind. "Mrs. Mack is visiting with her daughter for a few weeks, so no one will interrupt us." As he reached his driveway, he pushed a button on a small remote and the garage door opened. He drove the car inside and parked beside the gleaming 1931 Ford that Holland was restoring. Briefly she wondered if Holland's obstetrician had given her the little gas mask she'd sent for and if it had worked for her.

Two months ago, she would have been suspicious of Brad's intentions at this point. Now she knew better. Trusting any man was a new experience in her life, a concept that only three months ago she would have dismissed as ridiculous. How or why this certainty of Brad's integrity had developed she couldn't pinpoint, but nevertheless it was there.

He led the way into the house through the kitchen door and headed for his study. The room surprised her by its air of familiarity. With its blend of old-world comfort and formality, it reminded her of the dream room she'd envisioned as a child caught up in fairy tales and English novels. A massive desk with the rich red patina of age dominated the room. Matching floor-to-ceiling book cases covered three walls. The fourth wall showcased a fireplace with a tall, narrow window on either side. Instinct told her that Brad, rather than Cathy, was responsible for the room's decor.

Brad led her to a pair of wingback chairs with a cozy view of the backyard. Authenticity called for a rose garden, but a patio complete with redwood table and gas grill met her eye.

She turned her attention to the man seated across from her and was surprised to see he appeared nervous.

"You're being very melodramatic." She attempted to lighten his somber mood and at the same time still her own erratic pulse.

"I've found your son," Brad stated baldly.

"My . . . You've found him? Where . . . ? How . . . ?" Joy and excitement exploded through her heart. Brad had found her son! Suddenly she sobered. Brad didn't share her joy. Something was wrong. Was he dead? Or ill?

"What is wrong?" She turned fierce eyes upon Brad. "Is there something wrong with my baby?"

"No, no. He's fine. I didn't mean to frighten you," he hastened to assure her. "I'm just not sure that I've done the right thing in tracing him for you. I've involved other people, traded on long-standing friendships, and used data intended for other purposes to access information that by law should be confidential. If any harm comes to that boy, if his family is hurt, or you suffer because of my actions, I'm not certain I'll ever be able to forgive myself."

"Brad, please. I won't hurt him. But I have to know. Is he well? Is he happy?"

"I'll tell you all I know." He sounded resigned. "I've gone this far and I've no intention of backing out now." He reached across the short gap separating them and took her hand in his. For a moment he played with her long capable fingers, then giving her hand a gentle squeeze, he began.

"Your son went to a young couple who lived in Kaysville at the time of his adoption. He was sealed to them in the Ogden Temple six months later. The father was employed at Hill Air Force Base, the mother was an elementary school teacher. The boy broke his collarbone jumping his bicycle over a platform he and some friends built when he was six. He cut himself quite severely in the fall, as well. His blood was typed, but no transfusion given.

"A year later his adopted mother's father passed away, leaving her a small ranch in Wyoming. The father quit his job and they moved back to the area where they'd both grown up and enrolled the boy in school in a nearby small town. Two years later the family adopted another child, a little girl with a cleft pallet. The little girl began a series of treatments at Primary Children's Medical Center when she was two months old. The boy has earned excellent grades all through school and currently plays varsity basketball at the local high school."

Brad's voice fell silent and several minutes passed before Susan could speak. A long-held pressure began to let go. Her baby was alive. "Thank you," she whispered.

Tears began to trickle down her cheeks. With one hand Brad reached to brush them away and from somewhere inside her a dam burst. Brad's arms came around her and he pulled her to her feet and into his arms. He held her while she cried for the little girl who had been alone, for the baby she'd carried and sheltered and loved for too short a time. She cried for the mother who had walked away from that baby, promising him a better life, and perhaps she cried for the woman who'd sacrificed everything to be a doctor and who now wondered if her career was enough. She cried, too, for Robbie, the young boy who never had a chance to become a man but who had set her on this journey to find her son.

Brad held her until her tears subsided. Tenderly he stroked her hair and massaged the tense muscles in her shoulders. This woman had endured too much. Only an indomitable inner power, the strength of her soul, could have carried her so far. A weaker woman would have yielded her dreams to her father's demands; a weaker woman wouldn't have accepted the blame for her youthful folly and walked alone with only her Heavenly Father beside her in her search for atonement for her sin. She certainly wouldn't have found the strength to walk away from the one person, her baby, whom she might have expected to give her the love she craved.

Brad took her hand and led her to a small sofa where he could sit beside her. At last she lifted her face and asked, "Do you know what they named him? At first I wanted to give him a name, something I could secretly call him, other than 'Baby,' but I knew a name would be too personal. It would bind him to me in a way that would make it harder to let him go. So I never did."

"Are you sure you want to know his name now? Nothing has changed, you know. You have no claim on him and knowing his name may only remind you of your loss."

"Brad, I can't explain it. For more than fifteen years I've done everything in my power to block out thinking about him or speculating about how he looked at various ages. I convinced myself my career was everything and that my baby belonged to a closed chapter of my life. Robbie opened that chapter."

She blinked back fresh tears and continued on a determined note, "I've felt especially close to my Heavenly Father these past few months and felt his support and approval of my quest to find my son. I appreciate the help you've given me. You've not only found my baby, but you've helped me see so much more than I ever did before about faith and about myself. I know you don't approve, but something tells me I need to see this through to the final page."

"And knowing your son's name is necessary?" Brad questioned, and for a fleeting moment she thought he held something back, something she didn't know to ask. Solemnly she nodded her head.

"All right." He sounded resigned. "His names is James. James Blake Christopherson."

"James," she repeated softly. "Jimmy. Or probably just Jim by now." She spoke with a touch of wonder in her voice.

He smiled, then sobered as he braced for what he knew was coming next.

"I want to see him."

"Susan, you can't," Brad argued. "For a boy his age to meet his natural mother could be traumatic. He may feel he has to choose between you and the mother who has raised him. Teenage boys are often protective and defensive of their mothers. You can't put him through that kind of dilemma." *Teenagers are often highly judgmental and critical, too,* he added silently, remembering Bobbi's assessment of Susan. If her child condemned her for her youthful rebellion as his daughter had, Susan would be hurt unbearably. He couldn't allow that to happen.

But he knew arguing would be futile. Susan had enough information now that she could find the address and make the trip to Wyoming to meet her son without Brad's help. The best he could do is make certain he was present when they met. If Susan needed him, he would be there.

"All right, I'll make the arrangements, but I want your word you won't try to contact him on your own. I won't be free to leave until after the holidays when Mrs. Mack returns."

"I can—"

Brad cut her off. "I know you can find him now on your own. But I've been in on this search from the beginning, and perhaps, like you, I need to see it to the end. Do I have your promise?" He held his breath until she slowly nodded her head and whispered her acceptance of his terms.

Brad returned Susan to the hospital, then drove to his father's house to collect his children. As he drove, his thoughts returned to his conversation with Susan. His feelings were mixed. It was good to know he'd brought her news that made her happy. Holding her in his arms had been a bonus he hadn't planned on, but it had strengthened his desire to make her part of his and his children's lives. Now her determination to see her son concerned him greatly.

He hadn't told her all he knew about the boy. He hadn't told her he was no ordinary teenager and that there was a good possibility the boy's relationship to Susan might someday be highly publicized. What he had discovered, some enterprising reporter would likely discover some day as well. He couldn't help wondering how the boy would deal with that or how Susan would handle the publicity. Achieving stature in a male-dominated field such as medicine was hard enough for a woman, and he wondered if knowledge of Susan's past indiscretion might add fuel to the bigoted minds of board members like Charles Gunther. He shuddered at the damage premature publicity could cause both Susan and her son.

He had to think of his daughters, too. He wanted to marry Susan, but how would they react to learning their stepmother had given birth to an illegitimate child and the whole world knew of it? He didn't want them to be ashamed or embarrassed because of Susan. His hope was that they would come to love and respect her and want her to be a part of their family. If they accepted her, then learned of her son and were confronted with all their friends' and acquaintances' scorn, what would happen to his family? Would people grasp the surface details of Susan's past and presume that by association his daughters lacked a commitment to chastity? Would his daughters question whether chastity really mattered?

A rocky road might lie ahead, but his newly strengthened faith told him to trust that Susan should be a part of his and his children's lives. He would have need of all the faith he possessed to convince her and his children they should be a family.

Thirteen

LIKE A HUGE BOILING POT, THE CLOUDS ROILED
and twisted, blackening the sky. Gusts of wind sent tumbleweeds skit-
tering across the highway and threatened to send Susan's car tumbling
after them. The heater sent a steady stream of warm air into the small
vehicle in contrast to the freezing January temperature on the outside.

Susan glanced sideways at Brad, who appeared to be sleeping
beside her. Tender regret touched her heart at the sight of his dear
face relaxed in sleep. If only . . . No, she mustn't dwell on what might
have been. He must never know she loved him. Once more she
wondered if she'd been wise to accept his offer to accompany her
today. In truth, he hadn't given her a choice in the matter.

When she'd insisted she only wanted to slip into the gym where the
boy would be playing, just to see him once, then quietly leave, he'd
cautioned that a strange woman alone at a small-town basketball game
would draw too much attention. He theorized that a couple traveling
through the town and stopping for a night would be more likely to
choose a local basketball game for a night's diversion than a woman alone
would. Perhaps he suspected she might fall apart at the sight of her son,
and he felt it his duty to be there to help her through a crisis situation.

Perhaps he came along to protect her son. She knew he was
uncertain he'd done the right thing by helping her locate her child. At
first it was a game, an interesting mystery, but once the child's identity had been confirmed, Brad had seemed to withdraw. She sensed he
knew something she didn't about the boy who was her son. He questioned whether they had a right to proceed any further, and his reluctance aroused her suspicions.

If she could assure him she wouldn't actually contact the boy or reveal her identity to him or his adoptive family, Brad would accept her determination to see her son more easily. But she couldn't promise that because she didn't know what she would do when she saw him. If his home conditions were like Robbie's had been, she couldn't possibly stay out of his life. At the time she signed the papers giving up her child, she'd been promised he would go to a two-parent, LDS home, and that he wouldn't be an only child. Now she needed proof that that promise had been kept.

Whatever Brad's reason, she was glad he was with her. A stab of pain caught at her heart as she wondered if they would continue to see each other after tonight. He never referred to the disastrous trip they'd made to his cabin and he'd made no attempt to kiss her again. She sighed, remembering that kiss. She might be naive where men's emotions were involved, but she knew he had been as deeply affected by that kiss as she had been. Could there be a chance for them if his daughters didn't despise her; if he wasn't still in love with Cathy? It was useless to speculate. Even without Cathy or his daughters, no man with the spiritual commitment and standards Brad possessed could love a woman who had given herself to a man in a drunken bout of self-pity, then given away her child so she could further her own education.

She squinted at the road ahead, searching for the turnoff.

"Turn your wipers on."

Startled, Susan glanced at Brad then quickly back to the windshield. Chagrined, she reached for the lever to set her windshield wipers in motion. She'd been so deep in thought she hadn't noticed the spatters of rain gradually obscuring the glass. She clicked on her headlights, too.

"There it is." Brad pointed to a glimmer of lights off to the right.

When they reached the small motel where Brad had made reservations, he carried Susan's bag to her room first before returning to the car for his own. When he asked her if she'd like to go somewhere for dinner before the game, she declined. Now that she was in the same town as her son and would actually be seeing him in less than an hour's time, she was too nervous to think about food. Brad left and returned a few minutes later with a couple of cans of fruit punch.

"You might not want to eat, but an empty stomach isn't a good idea either." He thrust a can in her hand. She knew he was right and forced a swallow down her throat. It tasted too sweet, like thick syrup. She felt herself shudder, then fought to stifle a giggle. Years ago she'd gone through a phase where she'd read every English novel she could get her hands on, and always, whenever any crisis arose in those books, the remedy was sweet tea. The more severe the crisis, the more sugar was added to the tea. Might fruit punch be Brad's answer to English tea? Did he think she was bordering on shock? The thought sobered her, giving her that slight edge she needed to prepare herself to see the boy she'd given away all those years ago.

Brad refused to arrive early at the gym. He insisted it was better to arrive after the bleachers were nearly full and the game was ready to start. With a hand at the small of her back, he guided her to a spot midway up on the home team side. Her heart beat rapidly and her skin felt flushed. Anxiously she scanned the home bench looking for a sturdy, dark-haired boy. More than half the team qualified. She panicked, wondering how she would recognize her son.

"Relax." Brad seemed to read her mind. "The players will run out onto the court one at a time as their names are announced over the loudspeaker. The visiting team is always introduced first."

Suddenly the school band broke into a drum roll and a voice came over the speaker. One by one the lanky youths dashed toward the center of the floor as each was announced. A second flurry of drums announced the home team, and Susan wiped her damp hands down the sides of her pants.

"John Perry!" Applause swept through the crowd as a young man ran forward. Susan's hands curled into fists, and her nails bit into her hands as she strained to hear the next name.

"Clay Cantrell!" Again the applause.

"Gary Woodward! Blaine Glendowski! Justin Anderson! Ben Renteria!"

Brad's arm settled around her shoulders and his hand tightened against her upper arm. She heard him mutter something she didn't quite hear, but she knew he shared her concern. He'd explained earlier that the bench or substitutes were introduced first, then the announcer would work his way up to the starters or best players on the team. Her son was fifteen, a sophomore; he should have been among the first players introduced. In a larger town a fifteen-year-old wouldn't even qualify for the varsity team. Could he be ill? Perhaps he wouldn't even be here tonight!

"J.B. Christopherson!" The crowd erupted in a frenzy, the drummer gave the bass drum a few good smacks, and shrill whistles split the air; several cheerleaders somersaulted onto the boards, then hastily withdrew. Brad's fingers bit into her arm. Puzzled, she let her eyes follow Brad's to the tall youth striding onto the floor. The boy was well over six feet tall and towered over his teammates as he grinned and waved to the crowd. A shock of light brown hair fell across his forehead and he swiped it away with the splayed fingers of one hand.

A sudden chill swept up her spine as the boy's name registered in her mind. J.B. Christopherson. The last name was right, but she'd been listening for James or Jimmy. Her first thought was that this boy must be her baby's adopted brother. But, no, J.B. had to be short for James Blake. Could this tall, young athlete be her child? There must be some mistake. Her baby was chunky with dark hair and ruddy skin. She turned shocked, questioning eyes to Brad. She must have voiced her doubts aloud.

"There's no mistake," he whispered. "I know you were expecting a boy more like Robbie, but this young giant truly is your child. Most babies start out with dark hair, even many blonds, and you can't judge much from a newborn's complexion. Stop seeing him in terms of his father, and I think you'll likely notice similarities to other family members."

Susan turned her face back toward the basketball court. For several seconds her eyes failed to focus, then slowly they returned to the young man crouching in the center of the court opposite a smaller boy. Both were intent on the basketball held in the referee's hand. When the official tossed the ball, J.B. easily spiked it to a teammate who handed it off for the first two points of the game.

In the ensuing minutes she watched intently as ten boys moved the ball from one end of the court to the other and back again. J.B.'s size lent his team an obvious advantage. He was a head taller than any other boy on the court, and he was remarkably well filled out for a boy so young. She didn't know much about basketball, but even she could tell J.B. caught more balls than anyone else. He also threw more through the net on his team's end of the court than anyone else did.

A whistle sounded and she watched the other boys line up on either side of the basket while J.B. stepped to a line bisecting a circle in front of the net. He glanced toward the basket as though measuring the distance, then raked his fingers through his hair and she saw her own nervous habit. As she watched the young man more closely, she acknowledged that both her parents were tall and that at 5'11" she was tall for a woman. J.B. was taller than her father, who was 6'4", though he lacked the finely defined bones both she and her father carried. She remembered her mother's solid Scandinavian build and recognized her carefully controlled movements in the way J.B. launched the ball toward the basket.

She bowed her head in silent acknowledgment. J.B. was the young man her baby had become, but that knowledge didn't bring her the satisfaction she had expected. There was no rush of maternal feeling. Was there nothing of Tony in the boy? Tony had abandoned her before he'd even known about the baby, but for fifteen years it had been his image she saw each time her mind had turned to her baby. Memories of Tony as they'd grown up had kept a fresh picture in her mind of her child in spite of her efforts to squelch thoughts of him. Now she knew the child she'd sheltered in a secret place in her heart didn't exist. J.B. was a stranger.

When halftime came Brad bought her a hamburger from a booth manned by members of the pep club, which she ate without tasting, her mind drifting between memories of her parents and sharply focusing on J.B. It wasn't until someone two rows ahead mentioned J.B.'s name that she became aware of her surroundings once more. Unabashedly eavesdropping, she strained to hear the conversation. In moments, what she'd already begun to suspect was confirmed. J.B. was some kind of local hero. His hometown was expecting him to carry them to a state championship. College recruiters showed up regularly to watch him play.

When play resumed Brad started explaining the game to her in soft whispers. If he'd done the same during the first half she'd been unaware. Perhaps the shock was wearing off. She could watch the young man now with almost a sense of detachment. The score for his team was double that of their opponents, and she felt a stirring of pride in his accomplishment. Tony would have been proud of him, too. Tony had loved sports, and his desire to play football or baseball had been a constant source of conflict with his parents.

With the beginning of the fourth quarter, she realized the game was nearly over. When the final buzzer sounded, could she walk out of here without looking back? Should she? She was satisfied her son was being cared for and receiving opportunities he would have never known in her father's house.

Residual bitterness from her own childhood reminded her that J.B. certainly wouldn't have been a basketball star in her hometown. Her father would have been delighted to see him become such a big, healthy, young man. But he would have used the boy's strength as a free farmhand and punished him severely had he attempted to spend his time playing "some foolish game."

She wished she could see J.B.'s parents and know once and for all that they were the kind of people she'd envisioned raising her child. She'd like to see his little sister.

A commotion on the floor drew her attention. A player from the other team shouted something at J.B., and the referee blew his whistle and made a quick hand gesture. Instantly the opposing coach stormed onto the floor, shouting at the referee, who pointed at the bench, indicating that was where the coach should be. Once the coach and the angry ball player were off the floor, J.B. was allowed two free shots.

"That's called a technical foul," Brad explained as the first ball sank through the net. "The ref called one on the other player and one on the coach." A groan rose from the opposite side of the gym.

When the second shot passed cleanly through the net, too, a cheer arose from one side of the room and disappointed moans from the other.

In seconds the game resumed and Susan watched as one of J.B.'s teammates dribbled the ball down the court, then tossed it to him. J.B. turned and arced the ball high to slide it once more through the net.

"Three pointer!" An enthusiastic crowd screamed their approval. Suddenly an object flew through the air and slammed into the side of J.B.'s head. He staggered against a teammate and they both went down in a tangle of arms and legs.

Susan and Brad jumped to their feet, but their vision was blocked as the home crowd strained for a better view. Shouts and snarls competed with the referee's whistle for several minutes, then a hush gradually fell over the crowd. Frantically Susan stretched, trying to see better.

"He's still on the floor," Brad let her know. "His coach and a tall thin man are arguing with a woman in a fire department uniform. She keeps shaking her head."

"I'm going down." Susan headed for the aisle.

"Don't." Brad caught her arm.

"I have to," she whispered back in a bleak voice. "I'm a trauma surgeon." Brad followed her as she plunged into the crowd.

As they worked their way forward, a strained voice announced over the speaker system that the game was over and the victory had been awarded to the home team. The crowd was encouraged to disperse quickly and warned that due to blizzard conditions the freeway had been closed. The visiting team would spend the night at a motel, and two local churches would help with emergency accommodations for those stranded in town.

A police officer blocked her way as Susan reached the gymnasium floor. He motioned for her to turn toward the door, but she shook her head. Brad could see Susan wouldn't take no for an answer. He almost felt sorry for the officer. If the officer knew Susan, he'd know only a crazy person would dare come between her and her patient.

"Lady, they're doing all they can." The gray-haired officer spoke gently, but left no doubt that he didn't intend to allow anyone past him. Brad could see a small crowd gathered around J.B.'s prone form. The other injured boy sat with his head resting on his drawn-up knees.

"Is there a doctor with him?" Brad asked as he clasped Susan's arm.

"No," the officer responded sadly. "We don't have a doctor in this town. Paramedics are the best we can do, but they had to transport a woman in labor to the hospital earlier this evening, and they haven't made it back yet. The coach is trying to reach an off-duty paramedic from the fire department who's home with the flu."

"How far to the nearest hospital?" Susan snapped.

"Only about fifty miles, but it might as well be a hundred with this storm. The highway patrol said it's too risky to move a patient right now, but they'll let us know and provide an escort as soon as there's a chance a vehicle can get through."

"Get my bag." Susan tossed Brad her car keys and neatly sidestepped the officer. Her long strides carried her purposefully toward J.B.

"Wait a minute," the officer roared and lunged after her. Brad reacted instantly, stepping between him and Susan.

"Let her go. She's a trauma surgeon." Seeing the other man's skeptical look, he added, "We're both doctors."

The officer glanced toward Susan's hurrying figure, then back to Brad. A mixture of emotions spread across his face. "You can verify that?" he asked. Brad reached for his wallet.

The older man studied his ID carefully then lifted his eyes to Brad. Brad answered the question there. "I'm an obstetrician. She manages the trauma center at a Salt Lake City hospital. Believe me, she's one of the best."

"Then don't just stand there," the older man spoke in a choked voice. "Do what she said. Go get her bag. That's my grandson over there." He indicated J.B. with a nod of his head.

Brad rushed toward the parking lot and stopped in dismay. Snow mounded every vehicle, making identification nearly impossible. Wind and snow narrowed visibility to a few feet. Tucking his chin inside the collar of his coat, Brad stumbled through knee-high drifts to the approximate area where he remembered leaving Susan's car. Leaning down, he brushed aside the snow obliterating several license plates until he found a Utah plate.

When he returned with the needed medical bag, he found Susan supervising the coach and a volunteer firefighter as they shifted the young basketball star to a long banquet-style table like those used for ward dinners back home. A woman clutched the young athlete's hand, and hovering near her was the tall man he'd noticed earlier with the coach. The police officer stood nearby, holding a girl of six or seven tightly in his arms. She was weeping uncontrollably. J.B.'s teammates formed a silent background.

Several thick athletic towels lay in an alarmingly large pool of blood. Scalp wounds tend to bleed profusely, but the amount of blood appeared excessive to Brad's eyes. No wonder, he thought, as he noted a thick compress extending across the boy's temple to his eye. This wasn't just a scalp wound as he had assumed. If the boy lost an eye, his future would change drastically. There would be no state championship, no basketball scholarship, and no NBA draft.

A large black case stood open at Susan's feet. She had obviously availed herself of the fire department's well-stocked emergency supplies. Susan's eyes met his across the table, revealing no personal stress, but only a cool professionalism. His already high estimation of her professional abilities increased another notch.

"He struck his head hard when he fell. I'm sure he has a concussion. I don't believe it's serious, but it could be, due to the loss of blood from the wound. The projectile was a jagged beer bottle, and it hit with a considerable amount of force, leaving splinters of glass in the wound. The cut is deep and will require extensive repair." Her tone was matter-of-fact. "You'll assist?"

Brad nodded his head as he reached for a pair of latex gloves lying on top of the emergency case. Susan reeled off a list of supplies she would need, and the firefighter scrambled to pull them from the box.

Brad stepped to the officer's side and spoke quietly. "Get the child and the boy's parents out of here." Raising his voice he asked the coach to take his team to the locker room. He then knelt to extract several items from Susan's bag.

The woman protested leaving her son's side, but taking her arm, her husband coaxed, "Come on, Ruth. We're in the doctor's way."

Taking a deep, shuddering breath, Ruth leaned over the still form on the table to kiss his forehead. "I love you, Jamie," she whispered. Raising her head, she looked squarely at Susan. "God bless and guide you," she spoke in a choked voice. Then she turned to walk slowly away beside her husband, pausing every few steps to glance back longingly at her son. When they reached the officer who was still holding the little girl, J.B.'s father reached for the sobbing child.

"I'll take her, Dad," he said gruffly. "I know you're still on duty."

"I'll be right here," the older man assured them.

"I'm Philip Chambers, principal here," a voice came from behind Brad. "Our custodian remembered we have some portable theater spot lights. We'll set them up if you'll tell us where you'd like them. Electricity is none too dependable around here during a blizzard."

"We have a generator in the truck. We can operate lights, too," the firefighter spoke up. "I'll send someone to set them up."

"Thanks," Brad responded, then turned his full attention to Susan. They took turns scrubbing in the nearby locker room before donning fresh gloves from Susan's kit. No flicker of emotion betrayed her secret as she turned to her task. Her actions were smooth and controlled, and only Brad suspected what that supreme calm cost her.

Brad restrained J.B.'s left arm to the side of the gurney, then found a suitable vein in the back of the boy's hand in which to insert the hollow needle. As he did so, the firefighter set up an IV stand. In seconds life-giving fluid dripped into the unconscious boy. With a nod from Susan, Brad carefully injected anesthesia into the IV. J.B. was unconscious, but he couldn't be allowed to awaken or move while Susan tended to his injury.

Working together with a precision that seemed strangely familiar, Brad anticipated Susan's needs. Over and over he mopped the wound to allow Susan an unobstructed view of her work. Slowly, meticulously, she picked out specks of glass, then drew together the ragged tear. As she applied delicate sutures, Brad reached for a towel to wipe her damp forehead. It was with a sense of relief he saw the tear closed and the bleeding restrained to a fine line of tiny, bright beads along the stitch line. Only then did he notice that the power had indeed gone out and the only light in the gymnasium was that of the powerful emergency lights and spotlights trained on the spot where J.B. lay.

"He's lost a lot of blood," Susan spoke for the first time as she at last closed the external wound. As her eyes above the mask she wore met Brad's, he saw the worry there. He didn't want to even think about what losing this patient would do to Susan. The boy had his coach to thank that he was even alive. The man had lost no time applying pressure to the wound. The coach and firefighter had slowed the bleeding considerably, but hadn't been able to stop it completely.

. "Will he lose his eye?" came a trembling voice from behind them. Brad turned and felt instant compassion as he viewed the police officer's pale face. Before he could answer, Susan spoke abruptly.

"The projectile severed the patient's eyelid; I've repaired that. There's only a faint scratch on the cornea. It will be irritating for a few days, but should heal quickly. He should see an ophthalmologist as soon as possible, but I don't expect any negative repercussions to the eye." She stepped away from the folding table that had served as an operating table. "Now I'd like to examine the other boy if you don't mind." She turned swiftly to a spot at the edge of the light where the coach sat on the bottom row of the bleachers with his arm around a youth of about seventeen with dark curly hair. She motioned for someone to focus one of the lights on the pair. Brad noted the irony that this boy appeared more like the son Susan had expected to find.

Brad continued to monitor J.B.'s blood pressure and pulse as Susan used the ophthalmoscope from her bag to check the other boy's eyes as she had earlier checked J.B.'s. She scrutinized several bruises then taped both an ankle and a wrist.

"Are his parents here?" she asked the coach.

He shook his head.

"Dad had to stay with a mare that was foaling," the boy volunteered. "And Mom has a cold, so I came in by myself tonight. Is J.B. going to be okay?" The worry was evident in his voice.

Susan ignored the boy's question as she turned to the coach to hand him a packet of Tylenol and tell him to find the boy a bed for the night. "Nothing is broken and he doesn't have a concussion. He should rest for a couple of days, then he'll be fine."

"And J.B.?" The coach pursued the boy's question.

"His recovery won't be so quick. He should be in a hospital."

"Susan," Brad spoke softly. "He's exhibiting symptoms of shock." Susan stepped quickly back to the patient as Brad gave J.B.'s vital signs.

"More Ringer's lactate," Susan ordered and he increased the flow. "Is there any way to locate a blanket and heat it?" she asked, turning to the firefighter. "We need to keep him warm to fight off shock."

"I have blankets in the truck," the uniformed woman responded before running from the gym to collect them.

"There's a clothes drier in the Home Ec room across the hall," the coach volunteered. "We sometimes wash and dry uniforms and towels there. If we've got enough extension cords to reach from the generator powering these lights, it won't take long to heat blankets." Several figures who had hung back in the dark rushed forward to follow the coach's instructions.

In moments the firefighter was back with three blankets. Susan draped one over her son while someone followed a flashlight across the hall with the other two blankets.

Susan and Brad stayed by their patient's side as the night dragged on. At regular intervals they traded the blanket covering the boy for a newly warmed one. The wound continued to bleed more than Susan felt it should, and he knew she was mentally weighing the possibility of more surgery under the crude circumstances surrounding them.

At some point the Christophersons returned to the room. They hung back, staying out of Susan's way, and Brad wondered if she even knew they were there until suddenly she turned and spoke with fierce intensity to the woman behind her.

"Mrs. Christopherson, take his hand. Talk to him; say what's in your heart. I can mend his body, but only you can make him want to stay alive."

Ruth didn't hesitate. She was instantly beside her son. Her husband stood behind her with one hand on her shoulder. Sometimes his voice joined hers as she entreated her son to wake up. Her voice was gentle and sure as she told her son of her love for him. For more than an hour she recounted experiences they'd shared, reminded him how much his little sister needed him, and talked of his hopes to someday be drafted by the NBA. She spoke of his patriarchal blessing and his commitment to serve a mission. She only paused when J.B.'s father and grandfather placed their hands on his head to administer to him. Their quiet faith touched Brad's heart, reminding him of a time when he credited faith more than medical know-how with bringing Cathy through her struggle with cancer.

"The plows are here! They've brought the ambulance!" a voice shouted as several running figures emerged from the darkness. Susan immediately began preparing her patient to be transported. She glanced once at Brad with a question in her eyes.

"Go with him," Brad said. "I'll follow with your car."

"He needs blood desperately," she murmured. "It's a small hospital and blood supplies are low following the holidays. What if—"

"Don't worry," he whispered as he wrapped his arms around her. "He'll have his donor. When he was a little boy and broke his collarbone, his doctor wanted to give him a transfusion but couldn't because no blood of his type was available. It's available now; his blood type is the same as yours."

"But mine is AB negative. Hardly anyone . . . and even a parent and child don't necessarily—"

"I know." He kissed her gently. "Perhaps this is the reason you had to find him."

The paramedics completed the transfer in record time, and Brad glimpsed Susan on one side of J.B. and Ruth on the other as a paramedic slammed the door and raced for the driver's seat. Brad turned and sprinted for the parking lot.

J.B.'s teammates materialized out of the night to push and shovel a way for the car to reach the road where the snowplows had cleared a path for the ambulance. Several boys volunteered to accompany Brad, just in case he needed some help on the way. Brad declined their offer, but couldn't help comparing the anxious boys and their willingness to aid their comrade with the sullen faces of the gang members who showed up for Robbie's funeral, then left as quickly as possible afterward.

Fourteen

SOME DISTANCE AHEAD BRAD SAW THE AMBULANCE skid, then right itself. He wished he didn't need to stop at the motel to collect his and Susan's bags. He'd much prefer to stay right behind the ambulance where, if Susan needed him, he'd be close. But they both needed to change their blood-spattered, sweat-soaked clothes. Besides, it might be too much for Susan to return for their bags once she left J.B. at the hospital.

At the motel he hastily grabbed their overnight cases and as he returned to the car he found a large four-wheel-drive Explorer waiting behind Susan's car. J.B.'s father leaned his head out the passenger window to shout, "We'll follow you."

Brad could see the coach hunched behind the steering wheel. He nodded to the two men as he seated himself behind the wheel of Susan's Intrepid. He was glad the car had front-wheel drive and all-terrain tires, but wished he were driving his own four-wheel-drive utility.

Wind lent a fine glaze to the snow, which made the long slopes treacherous and slowed driving speed to a crawl. Long skid marks in several places increased Brad's concern for the ambulance's occupants ahead. Forcing himself to concentrate on driving, he cautiously followed the steep terrain. Several times he felt the car skid and he automatically corrected it. But once, unable to correct the skid quickly enough, he plunged into one of the high mounds of snow left by the snowplow.

Switching to reverse, he tried to rock the car free. When that failed, he reached for the door handle. Before he could step outside, the two men who had been following him reached his door.

"Stay inside," the coach yelled. "We'll push." In minutes the car was free and they were on their way again.

Brad gazed anxiously down the road as the car began to move. The ambulance had chains, but a layer of fresh snow had obliterated all signs that it had passed this way. No glimmer of red lights could be seen in the distance.

Some distance ahead, a sudden jolt slammed Susan to the floor. Gasping for breath she pulled herself upright and reached for her patient. He emitted a low moan, then lapsed into silence once more. To her horror she saw the bandage extending from his crown to his eye turn bright red with blood. The force with which the ambulance had crashed against some snow-shrouded object alongside the road had started the wound bleeding again. She wondered how much more even a young, healthy heart could take.

Frantically she applied pressure, then when the bleeding seemed to slow, she rebandaged the wound. Once more she checked his vital signs and chewed her bottom lip. Losing more blood had cost him too much. Suddenly she felt angry. She'd lost Robbie, in spite of all she'd done to prevent his life from bleeding away. She wouldn't lose this boy the same way.

"Hold this!" She suddenly snapped at Ruth as she grabbed the woman's hand and showed her how to keep the pressure steady. "And pray like you've never prayed before," she added more gently.

Susan made her way to the front of the ambulance and slid into the seat next to the paramedic. He turned worried eyes toward her.

"Keep your eyes on the road," she ordered. "You have a radio in this thing. Tell me how to contact a doctor at the hospital we're headed toward."

"Click the button next to the microphone," the paramedic responded. "Dr. Baird, the Christopherson kid's doctor, is already at the hospital and he's monitoring this frequency."

She pressed the button and spoke tentatively, "Dr. Baird?"

A baritone voice immediately growled back, "What's going on? Are you the doctor they said was coming in with J.B.?"

"Yes." She didn't take time to introduce herself further. "The patient is bleeding again. I can slow it, but not stop it. Is he anemic, or does he have some blood disorder?"

"J.B. has tended to bleed heavily as long as I've known him. He's been tested, but there's been no disorder found."

"Set up a transfusion for as soon as we reach you."

"Doctor, I've called Salt Lake and Denver. Neither has his blood type on hand. He's AB negative. It may not be possible to transfuse until we can get blood flown in from Washington. I set up a reserve for him there when I first discovered his blood type, and there's a potential donor in Salt Lake—"

"My blood will match."

"Your blood will match?" Susan could feel the hope and the suspicion in the other doctor's voice.

"Just be ready!" She punched the button on the speaker, then scrambled back to her patient.

When the nightmare ride ended, Susan followed the gurney bearing J.B. into the hospital. The white-jacketed doctor who strode quickly toward them took over as they rushed down a hall. At the entrance to the room where he would examine J.B., he pointed Susan to an adjoining room. As soon as she stepped through the door a lab technician led her to a gurney and instructed her to lie down. He lost no time having her blood drawn and typed. After the technician left the room, Dr. Baird entered and stood beside the cot where she lay, a grim expression on his face.

"The blood matched?" She waited for his confirmation.

He nodded his head. "I'm not a believer in coincidence," he told her.

"I'm not either." She met his gaze squarely. "But I do believe God places people where they're needed, when they're needed."

"The Christophersons need that boy."

"I won't argue with that. He needs them, too." It took all of the control she could muster to not look away from Dr. Baird's searching eyes.

"There's no question you saved the boy's life, but what are you going to do now?" There was a look of compassion in his eyes. She squared her shoulders before answering.

"Go back to Salt Lake." She paused before going on. "Doctor, I'd appreciate it if no one knew I was the donor."

Dr. Baird reached for her hand and held it for several minutes. When he spoke, he struggled to hide deep emotion.

"The Christophersons are good people. I went to school with

Blake's sister and have known the family all my life. They had a hard time when they found out Ruth could never bear a child. It got so Ruth couldn't face teaching other people's kids. Our whole community, even the non-Mormons, held a fast for them when we heard their ward in Utah was having a special fast day for them, praying they'd be able to adopt a child.

"When the Christophersons moved back here, that kid went right to our hearts. He's a pretty special kid, all right. You might think it's just because he's a basketball star and the whole town loves a winner. But it's more than that. To Ruth and Blake, and little Julie, he's a miracle."

Dawn arrived, turning black to gray, and a chill wind continued to blow as Brad arrived in Evanston. Leaving their vehicles in the parking lot, he and the two men who followed him hurried up the steps and entered the small regional hospital. The coach and Christopherson seemed to know where they were going, so Brad followed.

Ruth Christopherson saw them coming and ran to meet her husband. As his arms closed around her, he asked, "J.B.? Is he all right?"

She nodded her head and began to cry. Between sobs she explained that J.B. needed a blood transfusion and the woman doctor had taken care of everything. She'd spoken with their doctor en route over the paramedics' radio, and Dr. Baird had everything ready as soon as they'd arrived. Their son was being cared for just across the hall.

"Where is Susan?" Brad asked.

"You mean the woman doctor? I think she's still with J.B. and Dr. Baird," Ruth responded. "I'm so glad you and your wife were there tonight," she went on. "She saved his life. Dr. Baird told me that without her prompt action he wouldn't have made it. I want to thank you both properly, but I'm embarrassed to admit that in all the confusion and worry I never learned your names."

Caught off guard, Brad was unsure how to answer. She assumed he and Susan were married and it might be best not to tell her the truth. But he wasn't in the habit of lying, either.

"Brad is my name," he responded. "Brad Williams."

"Brad and Susan Williams." She reached to shake his hand. "I'm Ruth Christopherson and my husband is Blake. Thank you. There's no way we can repay you for all you did for us tonight. You-you gave us our son."

Brad swallowed and shifted uncomfortably, knowing that where Susan was concerned, she'd given them their son twice. He was saved the need to respond by a nurse who interrupted to speak to the Christophersons.

"Excuse me," she said. "Your son is starting to wake up. Dr. Baird said it would be all right for you to be with him now." Ruth immediately fled across the hall with her husband right behind her. The coach looked around uncertainly, then decided to follow his star player's parents.

Brad found himself alone in the small waiting room wondering where Susan was and how she was handling all this. Would she be able to walk away from her child now? And had the boy's doctor put two and two together and guessed the odds of an AB negative donor being available by chance?

"Brad?" His head shot up and he swiveled toward the doorway where Susan stood, leaning against the door jamb. He rose to his feet, and as he walked toward her he noticed how pale and exhausted she looked. She shouldn't have been allowed to leave the blood donor area alone. He suspected someone had tried to stop her, but then, he couldn't fault a mere nurse or lab technician who lost an argument when Susan turned into Doc Attitude.

"Are you all right?" he questioned as he placed his arm around her. She leaned her head against his shoulder and closed her eyes. Twenty-four hours of being awake along with all the stress of seeing her son, then helping him through a major crisis, followed by donating blood, had left her drained. A lesser woman would have collapsed long ago.

"Come on," he urged. "I think it's time to leave."

"I can't leave until I know he's out of danger," Susan battled fatigue to argue.

"Dr. Baird is with him. You're too tired to be of use to anyone right now," Brad countered. "Let's check into a motel for a few hours' sleep, and I'll leave word for Dr. Baird to call the motel if there's any change in J.B.'s condition."

Reluctantly she nodded her head in agreement and he helped her to her car. She barely managed to stay awake while Brad drove, searching for a motel.

With the roads closed for most of the night, the motels were full. Stranded motorists occupied every available room. Brad drove around until he spotted a motel where a trucker was pulling out, then rushed inside and was told if they were willing to wait for the room to be cleaned, they could have the room just vacated. Wearily, Brad agreed.

When they gained access to the room, Brad was glad to see it contained two beds. He was tired enough to fall asleep on the floor or in the bathtub, but he'd definitely prefer a bed. He encouraged Susan to crawl into one bed while he brought in their bags. On returning to the room he found she'd fallen asleep, fully dressed, lying across the nearest bed.

Gently he loosened her clothing, removed her shoes, and pulled a quilt over her before collapsing on the other twin bed.

A tap on the door awoke Susan a few minutes past two in the afternoon. Through sleep-dulled eyes she noted that the other bed was rumpled, but empty. She peeked at her watch and was surprised to see she'd slept for six hours. She stumbled to the door, and after confirming Brad's presence on the other side, pulled it open.

"Hi." He stepped into the room and handed her a Styrofoam mug of hot chocolate. "I just checked with Dr. Baird. He says our patient is sitting up and taking small amounts of nourishment. A local ophthalmologist has looked at his eye and found no problem, but he has made arrangements for him to be seen at the University Medical Center in Salt Lake in a couple of days. Ruth is staying with him until he's released, which should be in a couple of days. His father is on his way back to the ranch to see about his stock and to be with the little girl." He paused for just a moment then continued, "I called the highway patrol. The road is open between here and Salt Lake, but another storm is expected in a few hours. We should be on our way as soon as possible." He appeared sympathetic, though determined, as he spoke and she noticed his eyes didn't quite meet hers.

"All right. It will take me about a half hour to shower and get dressed." She knew her response surprised him and she wasn't sure she could explain why she wouldn't insist on seeing J.B. again before they left. She wasn't certain she knew the answer herself. It was just something she'd awakened knowing. It was time to leave; she'd learned all she'd set out to know about her son. He was safe in Ruth's hands.

"I'll get us some hamburgers to eat on the way, or would you rather have pizza?" Brad reached for the door.

"Hamburgers are fine," Susan smiled as Brad flashed her a relieved grin. When the door closed behind him she carried her small case into the bathroom. In seconds she was luxuriating under the hot spray.

As the water washed away the sweat and fear of the night, she thought about the boy, J.B. He was a fine young man and she'd picked up enough from conversations around her to know he was likely headed for fame in collegiate basketball and probably professional play as well. That he was adopted was common knowledge, and given the modern media's penchant for digging up details of famous people's pasts, it was possible that if he became famous enough some day his relationship to Susan might be exposed. She could handle that, she decided; she hoped he could, too.

Other things she'd learned about her son interested her more than the possibility of embarrassing publicity. He liked animals and had a dog and a horse of his own. He'd participated in a project to restore eagles to a little-known wild canyon and planned to major in veterinary science in college. His interest in medicine pleased her. Though he bore no physical resemblance to Tony, she was glad he had inherited his father's interest in animals and sports.

He and his little sister were close and he'd spent hours teaching her to ride. When she was recovering from the various surgeries to repair her birth defect, he found time to read and play games with her. He'd soon be an Eagle Scout and his future plans included serving a mission. He was a son any mother could be proud of. But he wasn't her son; another woman claimed that honor. That thought didn't depress her as much as she had expected.

Leaning forward, she let the fine, sharp spray beat against her shoulders and the back of her neck, easing the tension that bunched her muscles there. Her emotions were a jumble; she needed time and peace to assimilate all she'd learned and all she felt. It would take months, perhaps years, to reconcile the past with the new reality she had found.

Straightening at last, she finished her shower, dressed, and was ready when Brad tapped on the door once more.

"Would you mind driving?" she asked as they carried their bags to the rear of the car. "I haven't had as much experience driving on snow as you have."

"No, I don't mind." Brad stowed their cases in the trunk before walking around to the driver's side of the car. Susan was already inside with the seat tilted back and dark glasses in place when he slid into the driver's seat.

As Brad drove he occasionally glanced at his passenger and wondered what she was thinking or if she was sleeping. She had spent such a long time looking for her child; to have to leave him again must be nearly unbearable, he thought. It surprised him that she hadn't insisted on returning to the hospital to see him once more before leaving Wyoming.

Removing one hand from the steering wheel he briefly touched one of her hands. "I'm sorry, Susan," he said gently. "If one of my children had suffered what J.B. went through last night, it would be nearly impossible for me to leave her side. The thought of being in a different state at such a time is unthinkable. If it weren't for the approaching storm . . ." He let his voice trail off.

"It's strange, Brad," Susan's voice barely carried to his ears. "J.B. is everything I've ever wanted him to be, but I discovered last night he's not really my son. The baby I knew so briefly and the child I imagined through the years are far more real to me than that great, strong young man. J.B. is Ruth Christopherson's son."

"Are you really okay with that?" Brad questioned.

"There was a time during that endless ride to the hospital that the driver lost control coming down one of those long, steep grades. The ambulance sideswiped a snow bank with enough force to jerk Ruth and me off our seats and pitch J.B. against the restraints holding him to the gurney. The jolt started his wound bleeding again and though I did everything I knew how to do, I wasn't sure I could save him. But Ruth never doubted. Her love and prayers pulled him through, and I knew then that though I will always love my child, there is someone who loves him more. I also realized that because of the great love she has given him, I will love her forever. She did for him what I couldn't all these years, just as her love pulled him through where my skill wasn't enough last night."

"It still must be hard to leave him," Brad commented quietly.

"Yes, it's hard, but . . . I'm not sure I should even say this. You may think I'm out of line to feel the way I do."

"Why would you hesitate to tell me something? I want you to share your feelings with me." He felt a moment's hurt that Susan felt reluctant to confide in him something that was obviously important to her.

"You know Ashley came to see me a few days after our snowmobile misadventure," Susan began hesitantly.

Brad nodded his head.

"Since then she has called me three or four times a week."

"She's what! I'll put a stop—"

"No, please don't," Susan cut in. "I told her she could call me and I enjoy her calls. We've gotten to be good friends. In fact," she admitted shyly. "I've come to care a great deal for your daughter." Susan paused, then went on, "Once when I looked down at the back of your head as you mopped blood so I could suture, I knew you were thanking God it wasn't your child we were working on under such crude conditions and I found myself echoing your prayer. For just a moment I saw Ashley's face before me and I felt my hand begin to shake. Then it suddenly popped into my head that a doctor isn't supposed to treat his or her own child, but I'd be all right because that boy wasn't really my child. Ashley is more my child than he is."

He couldn't believe he was hearing Susan right. And why hadn't he known? Ashley hadn't mentioned her growing relationship with Susan. He'd assumed because she helped Bobbi sabotage the snowmobile that she shared her sister's resentment toward Susan. Oddly, he didn't feel any resentment on Cathy's behalf that Susan had developed strong feelings for one of her daughters. Instead it pleased him. Ashley needed a strong female role model with a mind as quick as her own. And perhaps Susan needed a child such as Ashley.

A warm feeling filled his heart and he recalled Susan's words as she'd described her feelings toward Ruth and suspected they might equally sum up Cathy's regard for Susan. Someday he would tell Susan that.

A small piece of his heart lifted as the possibilities flooded his mind. If Ashley had formed a friendship with Susan, was it possible his other daughters might do so eventually as well? Michelle apparently saw nothing wrong with his interest in Susan and the two smaller girls only needed to get to know her better. Bobbi was another matter, but he could hope, and in the meantime he'd do everything possible to bring them together.

Susan drifted to sleep as he drove, and Brad found his mind filled with plans to ease Susan into his children's lives. If he had to enlist Ashley's aid, he had no qualms about doing so. He just hoped Susan didn't have plans to ease him out of hers.

Fifteen

A SENSE OF UNREALITY PERVADED SUSAN'S LIFE as she returned to the hospital the next day. Over and over she tried to reconcile the two images of her son. It seemed impossible to picture that the chubby, dark-haired infant she'd sheltered in her heart had turned into the tall athlete he had become. Numerous times she reached for the telephone to call the Wyoming hospital, then stopped. Dr. Baird was an efficient, competent doctor, and the Christophersons were the parents she'd prayed would raise her son. If a tiny part of her heart continued to dream of the day the boy would be an adult and might come looking for her, she'd grant herself that much. But for now he had his own life to live, and she had hers.

Unfortunately she no longer felt satisfied with her life. She wondered if she'd be happier in a larger city such as Los Angeles or Chicago. She'd interned in Chicago and knew how busy trauma centers there could be. Being busier and dealing on a daily basis with more dramatic emergencies no longer appealed to her. Perhaps she should turn to the peace and quiet of a more rural area. But her stubborn heart resisted going anywhere. It was while contemplating what she would do with the rest of her life that Brad called.

Hearing his voice brought whispers to her heart of what she'd really like to do with her life. Before she could still the tiny voices clamoring to be with Brad, she found herself agreeing to have breakfast with him on Saturday.

After she hung up the phone she chided herself for being a fool. Surely she'd learned long ago not to hope for the unobtainable.

The following Saturday they met at a pancake house near the

hospital. He'd asked if he could pick her up at her apartment, but she'd insisted on driving her own car. His children would be with him, and she wanted to be able to leave if the outing turned uncomfortable. In fact, she probably should have turned his invitation down, she told herself ruefully, but she couldn't. Since their trip to Wyoming, it had become increasingly difficult not to be around Brad. She admitted that the opportunity to see Ashley again was an added incentive.

When she arrived at the restaurant she found only four of Brad's daughters with him. She didn't question why Bobbi hadn't come, nor did Brad attempt to explain. Kelly acted shyly toward her, but Heidi chattered as freely as Ashley. Michelle was more reserved than her sisters, but not unfriendly.

After breakfast they went sledding at Sugarhouse Park. Riding a sled seemed an unlikely activity for a woman of Susan's age and position, but Ashley wouldn't allow her to hold back when she would have demurred.

"You have to ride with me," Ashley insisted. "Heidi can ride with us, too, then we'll be even.

Susan watched Brad seat himself behind Michelle and Kelly on a sled. His long legs extended around the girls and he braced his feet against the front of the sled. Tentatively she seated herself behind her young friend and Heidi. Following Brad's example, she tucked her feet securely against the front slope of the sled.

Kelly and Heidi whooped and laughed as they rushed down the hill and Susan soon found herself joining in their shouts of laughter. As Brad's team swept past them, Ashley shouted, "No fair!" The next time down the hill, Ashley traded places with Michelle, insisting her dad's team was faster only because he and Michelle were heavier than Susan and herself.

The sun shone brightly and the snow turned mushy before noon, but Susan felt reluctant to end the fun when Brad said it was time to leave. His eyes met hers and she knew he shared her reluctance to end what had turned out to be a most pleasurable morning.

"I have a birthday party to go to," Heidi informed her importantly. "That's why we have to go."

"I promised to get her back in time," Brad spoke apologetically to Susan, while something in his eyes offered her a promise as well.

Feeling suddenly breathless, she whispered, "You should keep your promise."

"Doctor Susan," Ashley spoke up. "What time do you have to be at the hospital?"

"Not until three," she answered.

"Then will you take Michelle and me shopping? Michelle's birthday was yesterday and Grandpa gave her money for her birthday."

"I'd love to go shopping with you," Susan answered without thinking. "If it's all right with your dad," she tacked on hastily.

"Sure, it's all right with me," Brad responded. "If you're certain you want to go, but I warn you, shopping with Michelle isn't good for your health."

"Daddy!" Michelle protested. "You're the one who is impossible to take shopping. You should have seen the clothes he bought me for Christmas." She turned to Susan. "He bought them in the *children's* department, so I had to take them back and he wouldn't let me buy anything I liked. Anyway, I have all these credit slips and I really do need new clothes."

Susan felt a moment's panic. If Brad hated everything she helped his daughter choose, would he decide not to see her again? The fierce pounding of her heart told her she would care a great deal if Brad chose to end their relationship.

Anyway, what did she know about teenage clothes? *You know a great deal about how a young girl feels when her clothes are all wrong. When you were thirteen you knew very well what you would have worn if you'd been allowed to choose.* A voice from her heart brought back a flood of memories reminding her of the way she had felt when her parents sent her to high school dressed like a six-year-old from another generation.

"If you'd rather not . . ." Brad's voice was full of understanding. Her gaze wandered over his face, noting the rosy color the cold added to his cheeks. She felt an urge to place her hands on either side of his face and feel the cold turn to warmth. When her eyes met his, he seemed to be asking for something more than a shopping trip with his daughter. Something stirred deep inside her, telling her that whatever Brad needed from her, she wanted with all her heart to give it to him.

"I'd like to go." She continued to hold his gaze. "That is, if you trust me?"

"Yes, Susan, I trust you." His words were like a caress, gently opening a door held shut against morning light for far too long.

Shopping with Michelle and Ashley turned out to be more fun than Susan had expected. Michelle was easily diverted from her more outrageous selections, and she expressed enthusiasm when Susan pointed out styles that enhanced her hair and eyes. Michelle's taste ran to more flamboyant styles and colors than Susan would choose for herself, but Susan could see they suited the young girl. She just hoped Brad would approve.

"I'm thirsty," Ashley wailed as they passed the food court.

"Okay, I'll buy us all drinks, then I'm afraid I'll have to take you home, or I'll be late for work," Susan agreed.

Soon all three were gathered around a round metal table sipping Sprite through straws.

"Do you think I'm too young to wear makeup?" Michelle suddenly asked Susan. Susan felt a moment's panic. She had a pretty good idea what Brad's opinion of makeup on a thirteen-year-old might be, but she also knew how tantalizing young girls found the stuff, especially if it were forbidden.

"Makeup doesn't really have much to do with age," Susan began carefully. "Little girls Kelly's age get into their mother's makeup and play grownup, but they don't fool anyone. And sometimes girls as old as you are do the same thing. They put on lots of eye liner and bright lipstick thinking they can fool others into thinking they're more grownup than they really are. They don't realize that all that makeup makes them look more than ever like children playing grownup. Then too, sometimes the makeup they use damages their skin, aggravates acne, or stains their clothing."

"You wear makeup," Michelle pointed out.

"Yes, I do, but not all of the time. My skin is very fair, like yours, but I spend most of my time indoors, so when I go outside I need a moisturizer. I use lipstick or lip gloss for the same reason. As a doctor I scrub so much, I don't have time to worry about makeup while I'm at work. Besides it sometimes spreads germs or if it's perfumed it might irritate someone, so I never wear makeup at the hospital."

"I was hoping you'd talk Daddy into letting me wear makeup, but you won't, will you?" Michelle asked glumly.

"Makeup is dumb," Ashley added her point of view.

"No, makeup isn't dumb," Susan smiled and reached out to place a hand on Ashley's shoulder. "Most women want to look their best and often makeup can cover flaws or enhance a woman's features, helping her to feel more confident of her appearance. The trick is to learn what and how much each person needs. Girls your age need very little. Most teenage girls experiment and that's okay if they study what works best for them and they're careful where they wear it."

"Will you talk to Daddy?" Michelle pursued.

"All right," Susan consented. "But you will have to promise that whatever rules he sets, you'll follow. If he agrees, I'll take you to visit a cosmetologist who can explain how to apply makeup, what colors suit you, and the appropriate times and places to wear it."

"Thank you!" Michelle squealed as she jumped from her chair to give Susan a hug. Susan's heart pounded. She could easily care for Michelle as much as she cared for Ashley. Though the girl had given her father a bad time recently, she was really very sweet. Her mad rush into life needn't be a bad thing if someone who cared guided her steps and steered her clear of the pitfalls. She wished . . . No, she told herself sternly, taking two girls shopping for a few hours wasn't much on which to base a mother-daughter relationship.

By the time they left the mall, Susan had to hurry in order to be to work on time. She caught herself humming as she walked through the hospital door and hid a smile at the sight of the startled look on Corbett's face.

As winter drifted toward spring, Susan and Brad spent an increasing amount of time together. Sometimes they went to dinner or a concert, just the two of them. Occasionally they got together with Brad's friends, but most frequently they took Brad's children with them wherever they went or watched a video at the Williams' home.

Susan's friendship with Ashley and Michelle became steadily more important to her. Frequently she found herself daydreaming about sharing Brad's life and becoming a mother to the two girls. From time to time thoughts of J.B. came to her mind, and she wondered how he was doing and if his team had gone on to win the state championship. Steadfastly she kept thoughts of her son from intruding into the idyll she imagined with Brad. She also took care to keep her feelings for Brad from becoming apparent to her co-workers at the hospital, though Gines and Corbett both hinted they were curious about the changes they'd seen in her.

One bright spring afternoon she found herself walking hand-in-hand with Brad through Temple Square. The tourist season hadn't yet begun, and only the hardiest flowers were in bloom, keeping the number of visitors low.

"Brad, I think I'd like to take out my endowments," Susan confided as they paused to look at the Christus, highlighted through the windows of the North Visitors' Center. "I've talked to my bishop and he approves."

"I think that's a wonderful idea," Brad responded.

"I've thought a lot about what you once said about forgiving myself and decided you were right," Susan continued. "My bishop encouraged me to go to the temple a long time ago, but until recently I never believed I had a right to that blessing. I can't pinpoint any exact moment when my feelings changed, but they have. It's as though the past belongs to a different me. The new me thinks more about the future than the past, and I no longer feel unworthy to enter the temple."

"I hope that when you think of the future, that future includes me," Brad whispered softly. "I want you to be my wife. I love you. I'd like to be by your side when you go to the temple and for all eternity."

Her first instinct was to say yes; nothing would make her happier, but there was still much that hadn't been resolved.

She was quiet so long that Brad prodded her gently, "Surely my proposal hasn't taken you by surprise. You've known for some time that I love you, and though you've never said it, I believe you love me, too."

"I do love you," she whispered. "But I'm not certain that is enough. If you and I were the only ones who would be affected by our marrying each other, I wouldn't hesitate to say yes."

"I can understand any woman being leery of becoming an instant mother to five children," Brad teased with a wry smile.

"Brad, you know I love Ashley and Michelle. Few things would make me happier than being their mother, and I get along well with

Heidi and Kelly, but you know Bobbi isn't ready to accept me."

"No, she's not, but I feel our relationship is right and that in time she will accept our marriage."

Susan took a couple of steps away from Brad, then turned with her arms wrapped around herself as if warding off the cold. "Brad, I think I have to reach some kind of positive understanding with Bobbi before I can marry you. But it isn't only Bobbi who concerns me. I can't provide your children with the kind of stable home environment Cathy did. Even though I honestly believe children do best when they have a mother who stays in the home with them, I don't think I can give up my career. Medicine has been my life and my dream for too long for me to suddenly abandon it."

"I'm not asking you to give up your career, though I'm hoping you'll consider cutting back on the number of double shifts you work. And with two incomes," he smiled beseechingly, "I see no reason to dispense with Mrs. Mack."

"What about Cathy?" Susan lifted her chin to look him squarely in the eye. "We haven't talked about her much, and I'm not sure whether she and I can share you."

Brad smiled a lopsided smile and reached to recapture her hands. "That's certainly a very flattering picture from my point of view; after all I suppose most men dream of having two gorgeous women, a redhead and a blond, fighting over them. But I don't think you need to worry about Cathy accepting you. I think she knew before I did that I would love you, and I believe that she wants us to be happy together. The question is, can you accept her?"

"I don't know." She withdrew one of her hands from Brad's and ran her fingers through her hair. "I met Cathy a few times and I know what others have said about her. It seems she was pretty near perfect. I can't measure up to that. It may sound petty, but I can't imagine spending eternity following the two of you around, always being the odd third."

Brad saw the bleakness in her eyes and longed to comfort her. But what could he say, when in truth he knew very little about how second marriages worked themselves out on the other side? He'd heard enough about the long-ago polygamous marriages of some of his ancestors to know that sometimes those marriages worked out fine, but sometimes they'd created a lot of jealousy and disharmony. He lifted his eyes to the spires of the temple as though asking for help.

An unexpected peace descended on Brad. A feeling of love and acceptance filled his heart. No, bickering and jealousy wouldn't exist in heaven. His faith in a just God assured him that if he loved both women, and they all three lived righteous lives and trusted in the Lord, they would be happy.

"Susan, I've never denied my feelings for Cathy. I expect to love her forever. My feelings for you are equally strong. And in my eyes you're pretty perfect, too. I don't want to even consider eternity without either of you by my side. I can't help believing that if we do our part, and trust in God, that when the day comes that the three of us are together, our love and respect for one another will be so vastly enhanced there will be no room for either you or Cathy to feel left out. Your experience with Ruth Christopherson tells me you are capable of that kind of love. There's much I don't know or understand, but I trust in God's concern for the personal happiness of each of us."

"Oh, Brad." Suddenly she turned into his arms and her slender form shook with barely suppressed sobs. "I want to marry you, but I'm afraid."

"Afraid?" He stroked the back of her hair.

"I've been pretty much alone for most of my thirty-five years, certainly all of my adult life. I'm afraid I'll let you down, and that I won't know how to be a mother to your children."

"You won't let me down," Brad whispered. "Trust me on that one. And as far as being a mother goes, I don't expect you to become an instant mother to five half-grown girls. I'm only asking you to be my wife and give them a chance. For now, all I ask is for you to be a friend to them."

"Will you give me time to win Bobbi's approval before I say yes?" Susan whispered against his shoulder.

Reluctantly Brad agreed. He'd been trying for months to get Bobbi to go on outings with him and Susan and the other girls, but she steadfastly refused to cooperate.

Two days later Susan parked her car in front of Brad's house and climbed out. Nervously she tugged at her jacket zipper and took a deep breath. She opened the car door and just as she expected, the sound of a bouncing ball reached her ears. She hadn't been unaware of Brad's efforts to bring her and his children together, but this was the first time she had initiated the effort.

When she reached the makeshift basketball court in front of the garage she stopped. For several minutes she watched Bobbi dribble and shoot. When the girl became aware of Susan's presence, her blur of movement halted.

"Dad isn't here." She spoke tonelessly.

"I know," Susan attempted to keep her voice neutral and not give away her nervousness. "I came to see you."

"Me?" Bobbi revealed her surprise, which quickly turned to suspicion. "Why do you want to see me?"

"I hoped you might help me." She advanced a couple of steps toward the wary girl.

"Help you do what?" Susan suspected Bobbi's curiosity was at war with her instinct to refuse.

"I'd like to learn how to play basketball."

"Why?" Bobbi questioned in a belligerent tone.

"Lots of reasons," Susan answered as nonchalantly as she could manage. "Your dad likes basketball and he'd like to see the Utah Jazz play now and then, but since I don't know anything about the game he thinks it wouldn't be much fun for me. Then there's you. I'd like to attend some of your games, but I don't want to embarrass you by cheering at the wrong times."

"Why didn't you learn to play basketball in school? You're pretty tall." Bobbi sounded skeptical.

"My parents wouldn't let me play sports," Susan admitted.

"Why not?" Startled, Bobbi dropped her indifferent tone. She evidently couldn't imagine parents who wouldn't allow their daughter to play ball.

"My father was very strict. He believed play was the work of the devil," Susan answered as neutrally as possible.

"That's crazy!" Bobbi protested. "Didn't he think you should exercise?"

"He thought I got enough exercise cleaning house and milking cows."

Bobbi moved closer to Susan. "Is that why you ran away and had . . . ?" She stopped, embarrassed.

"It's all right," Susan looked around, then suggested, "Could we sit down a minute?"

"Yeah, sure." Bobbi led Susan to the kitchen step.

"Your father told me you knew about my baby," Susan spoke bluntly. "And yes, he was part of the reason I left my parents' home. I didn't want him to grow up the way I had. But I also wanted to go to college and become a doctor. My father would never have allowed me to do that if I'd stayed."

"But how could you give away your own baby?" Bobbi asked fiercely. "Didn't you love him even a little bit?"

"I loved him. No one will ever understand how much I loved that baby," Susan answered equally fiercely. "It was because I loved him that I knew I had to give him a better chance in life than I could give him by myself. Giving him up was the right thing to do. I know that now, though there have been many times in the past that I doubted it."

Bobbi did not let go of her disapproval easily. "Megan had Jason when she was just a year older than me and she was all alone. She didn't give him away."

"I know what Megan did," Susan responded. "She was very brave and strong, but she had something I didn't. She had a husband she could return to if she chose, and she had money to support herself and her baby while she went to school. I had nothing but a scholarship."

Bobbi's curiosity got the better of her. "Don't you ever wish you'd kept him anyway?"

"I don't think I had much choice. I've missed him and wondered about him over the years, but no, I don't regret the choice I made. He's living a much better life than I could have given him."

"How do you know he's happier living with strangers than with his own mother?"

"He isn't living with strangers. The people who raised him are his parents and they love him very much."

"Do you know where he is?" Bobbi's face showed her shock. "I thought adoptions were kept secret."

"They are, but something unusual happened not long ago and I learned where he is. I went to see him and your father went with me—" Bobbi started to interrupt, but Susan cut her off. "I didn't tell him who I am, but I watched him play basketball. Even I could tell he plays the game really well. He's another reason I want to know about basketball. Though he'll never live with me and probably never know I'm his mother, it will help me to feel closer to him if I learn about the activity he loves."

Bobbi chewed on one end of her long braid and stared thought-fully at the closed garage door. Finally she jumped to her feet and dusted off the seat of her jeans. "Okay, the first thing you have to learn is how to dribble the ball. See, like this." She bounced the ball with one hand several times, then tossed it to Susan. "You try it!"

Startled, Susan rose to her feet and gave the ball a tentative pat.

"No, like this." Bobbi demonstrated again.

Susan's second attempt was better, but when she discovered she had to learn to bounce the ball and keep Bobbi from taking it from her at the same time, she wondered if this had been such a great idea after all.

Her attempts to throw the ball through the hoop brought peals of laughter from both of them, but she did improve slightly before time brought a halt to their practice.

They sprawled side by side on the step once more and Susan felt a sense of elation. Bobbi's stiffness had lessened and her own awkward-ness had dissolved.

"You like my dad a lot, don't you?" Bobbi asked and Susan didn't miss the challenge behind the words.

"I do," she acknowledged.

"Are you going to marry him?" Bobbi continued her interrogation.

"I want to marry him," Susan admitted. "But I know you'd rather I didn't."

"I don't want another mother. I wish I could have my own mother back."

"Life doesn't work that way."

"I know. Sometimes I think life stinks." Bobbi rested her chin in one palm and continued to stare at the garage door.

"Your mom was pretty special," Susan went on, unconsciously adopting Bobbi's pose. "I could never be like her. I wouldn't even try. I don't like cleaning house, and I'm not a very good cook. I'm cranky when I work a double shift, and I'd collapse if the bishop asked me to be Primary president like your mom was. At the hospital some of the nurses and interns call me Doc Attitude because I'm bossy. I know I'm not very good mom material, but I love your father. If I marry him, I guess the best we can hope for is to be friends."

"You won't try any of that mom-stuff if you marry my dad?" Bobbi asked worriedly.

"What mom stuff?"

"Oh, like telling me to clean my room and what to wear."

"I might. I warned you I'm pretty bossy."

"What about hugs and things like that?"

"I'd say I know as much about hugs and that kind of thing as I do about basketball. I wouldn't know where to start. If you want any of that, you'll have to teach me," Susan responded candidly.

"I loved my mom an awful lot," Bobbi confided. "It seems sort of disloyal to let someone else be my mom. Jason and I talked about it. He and Megan used to live in Montana—that's where they met Allen. Jason used to pretend Allen was his father, even though Allen was just his mother's friend at work. Then, when Megan came back to Utah to be with Doug, Jason was happy to have his real father, but that didn't make him stop loving Allen. Allen was away in Alaska for a long time, but he came back and married Holland, and now Jason sees Allen whenever he wants to. But he says he'll never forget how he felt when Allen was all he had."

Susan looked at the disheveled teenager beside her, seeing more than the tangled hair and gangly adolescent body. The girl was fiercely loyal to her mother and troubled by the fear that she might forget her.

Susan leaned forward and clasped her arms around her knees. They sat without speaking, oblivious to the waning sunlight and the growing chill in the air. Susan wanted to say something to assure the girl that her fears were normal. She knew most people who lose a loved one eventually have trouble recalling the details of the loved one's face. To compensate, their memories of the time and experiences they shared become more perfect and idealized.

At last Susan spoke. "When I found my son I was glad he'd grown up to be a great young man and that he has had wonderful experiences in his life. He's happy and planning to go to college and on a mission. Knowing that pleases me a great deal. I'd feel terrible if he missed me so much he stopped growing and learning. I think your mom feels that way about you. She doesn't want you to spend your life missing her. She knows you won't forget her in your heart where it really counts. Besides, every time you look in your mirror, you'll see a part of your mother."

"I wish I didn't look so much like her," Bobbi muttered.

Susan raised her eyebrows; she hadn't expected that admission from Bobbi.

"I hate my hair," Bobbi went on. "It's too long and it gets in the way when I play ball. And it reminds me that Mom's hair fell out when she had cancer. I could get cancer, too. I read that daughters of women with breast cancer are more likely to get it than anyone else."

Understanding dawned for Susan. Bobbi was torn by divided loyalties. She'd loved her mother, but she resented that because of her, she was more likely to become ill or even die of cancer. She had watched her mother lose a breast and struggle through chemotherapy and its resultant damage to her appearance just at the time her own body was beginning to develop, which had created havoc with her confidence in becoming a woman. It might take years to overcome her ambivalent feelings toward her mother, Susan realized.

"Look, Bobbi." Susan surprised herself by placing one hand on the girl's denim-clad leg. "No one can promise you that you won't get breast cancer some day, but with the amount of research being done, eventually there will be better, less traumatic ways of dealing with it. Remember, too, that breast cancer didn't kill your mother. She was recovering, becoming beautiful again, when a terrible accident took her life."

"I know," Bobbi whispered and her bottom lip quivered.

"You know even if you cut your hair, you're still going to look like your mother," Susan reminded her. "If you decide to cut your hair it should be because you really want short hair."

The speculative look in Bobbi's eyes made Susan uneasy for just a moment. When she looked again the expression was gone and Susan credited her imagination with seeing too much. Brad's daughter had opened up to her much more than she had expected. It wouldn't do to undermine this budding relationship with anything negative.

"Will you take me to get it cut? I've wanted short hair for a long time," Bobbi pleaded. "It's not just because of Mom. My hair is too heavy and I hate braids, but I can't play ball with long hair flying every which way or a big, fat pony tail smacking me in the face every time I turn around."

Susan's spirits lifted. She'd made more progress with Bobbi than she'd dared hope if the girl wanted her to take her somewhere. She remembered the fun she'd had with Michelle and Ashley shopping at the mall. Bobbi might still be leery of accepting her as a stepmother, but they could be friends. And Bobbi really would look better without the heavy mop of hair that seemed to weigh her down.

"Okay." She smiled at Bobbi. "I'll make an appointment for Saturday. That will give you time to talk to your Dad and change your mind if you have any doubts."

Sixteen

"DADDY, COME SEE." KELLY TUGGED AT BRAD'S
hand. Excitement danced in her eyes. He laughed as he set down his
rake and let her pull him along. He felt almost as young and lighthearted as his daughter. Spring had arrived with a burst of sunshine,
and Susan had shown up at his house every day this week to practice
basketball with Bobbi. Earlier this morning they'd disappeared
together on some secret errand.

Bobbi never mentioned the time she and Susan spent together, but
Mrs. Mack had informed him of their daily practice sessions. She also
let him know she'd kept the other girls from intruding on the pair. This
morning Bobbi had vacillated between an air of suppressed excitement
and giddy fear. He'd love to be a fly on the wall this morning watching
the two of them, but some instinct had warned him all week to stay out
of the fledgling relationship they were building, though he'd love to
know what activity had Bobbi so wound up.

"See, Daddy! Mama's red flowers growed." Kelly pointed with
pride to the mass of tulips beginning to bloom in the big circular bed.
Then she scampered forward to snap off a large red bloom. "Here,
Daddy." She thrust the flower toward him.

"Thank you." He accepted the flower before picking Kelly up and
hugging her.

"Do you think Mama is happy now?" Kelly asked.

"I think she is," he answered softly. As he gazed at the flowers a
sense of quiet calm filled his heart, telling him Cathy truly was happy
now that he was happy and looking forward to each day again.

As he gazed over the flower bed an odd sensation enveloped him.

It was more than an awareness that Cathy was close by. It was as though they were at last bidding each other farewell, not forever, but for the length of his mortal life. He'd miss those quiet moments when he'd sensed her closeness, but something prompted him that she had a mission to serve and that she had been waiting for him to get on with his life before beginning that mission. He felt a touch of sorrow, then a lightening of his spirits. Cathy was his past and his distant future; Susan was now and always.

"Uncle Allen says he's going to name Dutch's little sister Tulip," Kelly announced importantly.

"Uh-oh!" Brad laughed. "I'll bet Holland doesn't like that idea."

"Holland said the baby is going to be named Amanda, and Allen better get used to it. She said she's not taking any chances either. When it's time for the baby to be blessed, she's going to have you, Daddy, bless her so Uncle Allen can't pull any sneaky tricks."

Brad chuckled and kissed Kelly on the top of her head. Briefly his thoughts went to Holland. He was glad her pregnancy was progressing well this time and that she was past the morning sickness stage. He didn't know if the little gas mask she wore while working on cars had worked or if her second pregnancy was simply an easier pregnancy.

The sound of slamming car doors reached Brad's ears and he turned to walk toward the front of the house, a smile on his lips. Susan and Bobbi were back from their mysterious trip. He rounded the side of the house with Kelly in his arms. His eyes went first to Susan. She was laughing and looked happier than he'd ever seen her before. Joy filled his heart as he sensed she would soon consent to be his wife. Then his eyes went to Bobbi and a gasp left his throat. Her hair appeared to be no more than two inches long. It tapered in the back and was cut out around her ears.

Slowly he set Kelly on her feet, clenched his jaw, and started toward his oldest daughter. She glared back at him defiantly. How could she do such a thing when he'd expressly asked her not to? And why hadn't Susan asked his permission? Susan's laughter stilled and she looked hesitantly between father and daughter.

A haze of red caught his eyes and he was vaguely aware of the crushed red tulip he still held in his hand. Only moments ago he'd experienced a letting-go between himself and Cathy. With blinding clarity he saw that Bobbi too needed a symbolic letting-go. Perhaps cutting her hair was the catharsis she needed to put away the past and move on. His steps slowed.

A whisper in his heart told him how he handled this situation might well determine his future happiness. He glanced at the tulip and acknowledged that if Cathy had taken any of their daughters to get a haircut, he would have thought little of it. He wouldn't have expected her to ask his permission. A larger truth exploded in his mind. Bobbi had set this up for the express purpose of determining how much authority her potential stepmother would have in her life. If he undermined Susan now, her position of authority in his home would be irrevocably damaged. He suspected, too, that Bobbi had also subconsciously attempted to discover whether or not he was ready to allow her to grow up. *He* was being tested.

"Brad, I'm sorry. I understood the two of you had discussed cutting her hair." Susan looked stricken.

"We did discuss it," Brad admitted wryly. He spoke to Susan, but his attention remained focused on Bobbi.

"I like it!" Bobbi skimmed her fingers against the short curls above her ears and visibly braced herself for her father's expected disapproval.

"Actually, I do, too," Brad spoke evenly. "It suits you. What I don't like is the way you misrepresented our discussion to Susan, and that you set her up to share the blame for something for which I'd already refused you permission."

"You're not mad at Susan, are you, Daddy?" It was Bobbi's turn to look stricken. "You didn't make Michelle take back any of the clothes Susan helped her buy, so I thought if she took me to get my hair cut, you might not be too mad at me." She turned to Susan. "Honest, I didn't mean to get you in trouble. I should have told you Daddy didn't want me to cut my hair, but I was only thinking about how much I wanted it cut."

"I'm not angry with Susan." Brad stepped forward to place an arm around Susan's shoulders. "And I'm not really angry with you either." He placed his other arm around Bobbi. "You are mature enough to decide for yourself how short or long your hair should be. Whichever one of you selected this style did well. I'm sorry I tried to force my preferences on you."

"I'm sorry, too." Bobbi brushed the back of her hand across her eyes.

"You look funny." Kelly cocked her head to one side and contemplated her sister's changed appearance. "Are you crying 'cause your hair got chopped off?"

"No, silly." Bobbi dropped to Kelly's eye level. "I'm glad my hair is short. Short hair won't get in my eyes when I play basketball and smart alecks on the other teams won't be able to pull it."

"Then why are you crying? Are you mad at Dr. Susan again?" Brad took a deep breath, hoping neither Susan nor Bobbi were ready to call off their new relationship.

Before Bobbi could answer, Heidi stumbled from the house crying. Michelle and Ashley followed. Bobbi rose to her feet and started toward Heidi, but the little girl threw herself against her father. She gripped his leg and sobbed as though her heart were broken.

"What's the matter, honey?" Brad gathered her against his shoulder and patted her back. "Are you hurt?"

". . . J-Jason—" She couldn't get any more out.

"What happened?" He turned puzzled eyes toward Michelle and Ashley.

"Heidi called Jason to see if he could come play," Michelle started.

"The dummy told Heidi he couldn't come over because he's taking Jennifer Stowbridge to a movie this afternoon," Ashley finished.

"Don't call each other names," Brad remonstrated automatically.

"Oh, Heidi," Bobbi suddenly wrapped her arms around her little sister. "I told you Jason is sixteen now. He's going to start taking girls his own age on dates, but he'll still be your friend just like he'll always be my friend. He'll still come by to play basketball, and he promised now that he has his driver's license he'll take you to the zoo one day."

Susan's heart ached for Heidi and she suspected that today would just be the beginning of a great deal of heartache for the child as she watched Jason turn into a man while she was still a little girl. Heidi would need a great deal of love and support to find her way to new friends and interests. Could she be the one there for Heidi? Susan wondered. Her eyes filled with tears as she admitted she'd like to be the one. She held out her arms and to her surprise and joy Heidi accepted the invitation.

As she held Heidi and whispered consoling words in her ear, her own emotions broke free. For the first time she experienced a quiet certainty that she could give Cathy's daughters all the love she'd longed to give her own child and all the affection she herself had been denied. She'd make mistakes; all mothers do, but with love on her side she'd manage. A silent prayer filled her heart that she'd have the wisdom and grace to be everything to these children Ruth Christopherson was to her child.

Kelly sighed and looked in exasperation at her sisters and Susan. "Is everyone mad at somebody?" she demanded to know.

"No, I'm not mad at anyone," Brad denied and the others seconded his denial. His eyes met Susan's over Heidi's head and he smiled. "Actually I'm about as far from being mad at anybody as I can get," he added.

"I'm not mad at anyone either." Bobbi stroked Heidi's back, saying words that seemed almost more for Susan's benefit than Kelly's. Bobbi turned and knelt in the grass beside Kelly. "I'm sorry Heidi is sad, but I think she's found a new mama to help her be happier."

"Am I going to get a new mama, too?" Kelly asked.

"I think so," Bobbi half promised as she raised her eyes to meet Susan's, a question in their depths.

"Good! I want Holland to be my mama," Kelly announced.

Brad winced and Susan had to fight to keep a chuckle from emerging.

"Holland can't be your mama," Ashley pointed out scornfully. "She's Dutch's mama and she has her own house."

"Our new mom would have to be married to our daddy," Michelle pointed out with a smirking glance toward Brad and Susan. "Holland is married to Uncle Allen, so she can't be married to Daddy, too."

"But I love Holland mostest," Kelly protested.

Brad swept Kelly into his arms and walked over to stand in front of Susan and Heidi. "I'd like Susan to be your mama. I know she'd love you and take really good care of you. Do you think you could let her be your mama?"

Kelly glanced dubiously at Susan and Susan's heart wrenched. Holland had been there for Kelly as long as Kelly could remember. Kelly had been only three when her mother died and Holland had cared for her even before that, during Cathy's long fight against cancer. Of course the child's first loyalty would be to the woman who had been a mother in all but name to her for so long.

"It's all right, Kelly." She ran a finger down Kelly's chubby cheek. "You love Holland and she loves you. I don't want to change that. Many children have more than one mother. If you like, you could have three mamas."

"Three?" Kelly looked skeptical.

"Yes," Susan continued as she held up three fingers. "There's your mama who went away to live in heaven. And there's Holland, who loved your mama and you so much she's been almost a mother to you. And I'd like to be your mama. I could live in your house and eat dinner with you. I could go to parents' night at your school and send pizza for your class on your birthday."

Kelly wrapped one arm tightly around her dad's neck and seemed to be considering. "Will you make me a new Halloween costume? I don't want to be a bunny anymore 'cause Ashley said I look like a dorky pink blob."

"I don't know how to make costumes," Susan admitted seriously. "But I could take you to a store and help you buy one you like next Halloween."

"Well, okay." Kelly suddenly leaned forward to kiss Susan. "You can be my mama."

Brad loosened one arm so he could hug Susan and whisper, "Can I take that as a yes?" Susan nodded her head. Suddenly they were joined by the other girls with Ashley yelling, "Group hug! Group hug!"

"Dr. Williams?" A voice broke through their noisy laughter. Susan peered past Brad to where a young man approached across the grass. Her heart caught in her throat. What was J.B. doing here? The doctor in her immediately appraised the long jagged scar running from the crown of his head, across his temple, and over his right eye. It looked red and frightening now, but would almost completely disappear in time. He looked directly at her, but it was Brad's name he called. Brad slowly turned, while Susan stood frozen in place.

Ignoring Brad, J.B. spoke again. "Dr. Williams, could I speak to you privately for a few minutes?"

Ashley was the first to react. "She isn't Dr. Williams. Daddy is Dr.

Williams." Eyeing J.B. suspiciously, she moved protectively in front of Susan. Heidi tightened her grip around Susan's waist.

The young man faltered as he looked back and forth between Brad and Susan. "Grandpa said . . ." He stopped, suddenly unsure of himself.

Taking pity on the boy, Brad set Kelly down and extended his hand. As the boy gripped it, Brad introduced himself. He then turned to Susan. "And this is Dr. Susan MacKendrick. We're both greatly relieved to see you looking fully recovered."

"Except for the Frankenstein scar," came a whisper behind him from Ashley.

"Thank you, sir." J.B. looked around nervously. "I want to thank you, both of you. Grandpa said I might have died if you hadn't been there. He thought you were both named Williams."

"In all the confusion I'm not sure my name was ever mentioned." Susan finally recovered her ability to speak.

"Did you sew him?" Kelly whispered loudly to Susan.

"Yes." Her whisper was softer and her eyes never left J.B.

"I think we better go to K-Mart for my costume," Kelly whispered back. "You really don't sew pretty."

"Please, ma'am—Doctor, could I talk to you alone?" J.B. insisted.

"Susan, take J.B. around to the patio," Brad put in smoothly. "The girls and I will go inside for a while."

Bobbi suddenly gasped and Susan knew she'd made the connection. "He's Susan's baby!" she whispered hoarsely to Michelle, but the words carried further in the clear spring air.

"No, he isn't!" Kelly rounded on her sister with a glare. "I'm Susan's baby, 'cause I'm the youngest. 'Sides, he's not a baby. He's great big."

J.B. blushed fiery red. "I'm sorry—ma'am. I didn't mean to cause any trouble. It's just that I figured out who gave me the blood transfusion, and well, I'm going to be a vet someday, so I study a lot about biology and genetics and . . . My blood type . . . Well, you know . . . I thought the donor might be a close relative. I talked to my mom—"

"Your mother knows you're here?" Susan asked.

"Yes. She said I could ask you." He glanced toward the street. "She and Dad are waiting in the car with my little sister."

"I'll go get them and take them inside," Brad offered. "You and J.B. go have your talk. Come on, girls. In the house," he raised his voice slightly. All but Kelly moved obediently toward the front door.

Kelly planted herself firmly in front of J.B. She looked up and for a moment appeared awestruck by his tremendous height, but not for long. Squaring her shoulders, she drew in a deep breath then let it out in one angry shout. "Go away! You can't have Susan be your mama! She's my mama. She promised!"

The inertia that had held her since J.B.'s arrival suddenly let go and Susan reached to soothe Kelly. "It's all right," she crooned to the distraught child. "J.B. has a mama; he doesn't need me. I won't go away, I promise. I'll stay right here and be your mama. But I would like to talk to J.B. for a few minutes."

"Kelly!" Michelle reached for Kelly's hand. Susan had been unaware the girl had returned for her sister. "Come on, Kelly," Michelle whispered. "Let's go look at my magazines. There are pages and pages of dresses for little girls who are going to a wedding. We have to find the prettiest one of all for you to wear when Susan becomes our new mama."

Obediently Kelly trotted away hand in hand with Michelle, chattering about the dress she would wear and wondering what Dutch should wear.

At last Susan stood alone, face to face with her son. Face-to-face wasn't exactly accurate Susan thought and stifled an hysterical giggle. Not many people could stand face-to-face with J.B.

"There are chairs on the patio," she spoke softly. He nodded his head and followed her around the corner of the house. When they were both seated, an awkward silence fell between them. At last J.B. blurted out, "Are you really my birth mother?"

"Yes," Susan admitted both joyfully and painfully.

"Is it all right if I ask some questions?" Her heart lurched when she saw the determined angle of his jaw, so reminiscent of her father.

"Yes, certainly," she agreed.

"Mom told me you gave me up for adoption because you were really young and poor. But you're a doctor and this house—"

"I was young, just a year older than you are now," Susan answered sharply, then continued more gently. "If you're really asking if I gave you up because I didn't want you, I promise nothing could be further from the truth. I wasn't a doctor then, just a very scared kid with no one to turn to. This wasn't my home either. The closest I came to having a home then was a room I shared with a series of roommates in the girls' dorm."

"What about my father? Is Dr. Williams . . . ?"

"No, Dr. Williams isn't your father. I didn't meet him until years later." Briefly she told him as much as she could about Tony. She was careful to describe his death as a hunting accident.

At last the boy fell silent, but Susan suspected he had one more question. He started several times then blurted out, "I don't know why you came to my game. Maybe you were just curious, but if you came to take me back, I won't go. You seem like a nice lady and you saved my life and all that, but my mom and dad really need me and I've got this little sister who gets scared if I'm not there when she has to go to the hospital."

"Sh-h . . ." Susan placed her hand on his arm. "Taking you away from a good home was never my intention," she assured him. "Even before you were born I wanted the best for you. I believed you would be happier in a stable two-parent home than with me. Then a few months ago a boy died at the hospital where I work. His date of birth was the same as yours. I learned that he had been adopted and that he had been badly neglected during his short life. He was the reason I went searching for you. I had to know whether you were loved and being cared for. I met your mother and have been grateful ever since that I had the privilege of giving her the son she'd fasted and prayed for."

"Thank you, I didn't mean to hurt your feelings, Mrs.—uh— Doctor . . ."

"Call me Susan," she smiled at the stammering young man. "Don't ever think you're being disloyal to me because you love Ruth. The Spirit testified to me that night we rushed you to the hospital that you were never meant to be mine. Right from the start God meant you to be part of the Christopherson family. You are Ruth's son."

"I'm glad you have other children," J.B. mumbled, "so you're not all alone."

"I am, too," she answered from the bottom of her heart and felt no need to explain that the girls belonged to Brad, not her. Soon they would be her daughters, too. "Would you like to go inside now and meet them?"

"Do they know about me? I mean . . ." Again he blushed from the tips of his ears to his shirt collar.

"Of course we know about you." A cool voice came from the sunroom door a few feet away. Bobbi strolled onto the patio and casually linked her arm through Susan's. "Mom doesn't keep secrets from us or treat us like babies. And you'd better not think anything bad about her just because she made one mistake when she was a mixed-up kid."

"I don't think anything bad about her," J.B. defended himself.

"You turned red like you were embarrassed." Bobbi leveled her eyes like daggers at the boy.

"Yeah, but . . . I can't help . . . Look, I think your mom is a really cool lady. You're lucky she's your mom."

"I think your mom is pretty cool, too." Bobbi's tone of voice changed drastically. "I heard you were a big basketball star."

J.B. ducked his head and grinned self-consciously.

"Want to try a little one-on-one?" she challenged.

"You're kidding!" J.B. sat up straighter. "You're a girl!"

"So glad you noticed," Bobbi retorted sarcastically. "Is that a yes or a no?"

The lanky youth unfolded himself from his chair and rose to his full height, obviously expecting Bobbi to be impressed. She looked him up and down, then turned casually to Susan. "Is he well enough to play, or should I go easy on him?"

Laughter sprang to Susan's lips. "He's just fine, Bobbi," she sputtered. "And it's a good thing, because you don't know the meaning of going easy."

She felt two arms wrap around her from behind, and she leaned back against Brad, savoring his warmth as the two lanky teenagers raced around the corner of the house with Bobbi's basketball bouncing back and forth between them.

"Are you okay?" Brad whispered.

"Yes," she murmured. "It wasn't nearly as difficult as I expected. What about the Christophersons? Are they upset?"

"No, they really aren't. I think Ruth has suspected the truth since January."

For several minutes they stood quietly, listening to the thump of

Bobbi's basketball and smiling at the good-natured verbal war being waged between their offspring. From somewhere inside the house came several giggles and an off-key rendition of "Teach Me To Walk in the Light," accompanied by a piano badly in need of tuning.

"What now?" Susan turned anxiously to Brad.

"I don't know," he admitted. "There's bound to be some bumps in the road, but with love and faith, we'll work them out."

"I love you," Susan sighed as she slipped her arms around Brad's neck.

"I did have something more romantic in mind for that moment when you finally agreed to be my wife," Brad spoke ruefully. "I intended to whisk you off to a jeweler, then out to a candlelight dinner to celebrate our official engagement."

Susan's laughter rang out. "Instead," she sighed, "since it's Mrs. Mack's day off, we'd better grab Ashley and head for the kitchen. Something tells me we're going to need a really big pot of spaghetti tonight. And you might as well know spaghetti is as far as my culinary skills extend."

"I like spaghetti," Brad murmured as he tightened his arms around her and his mouth found hers. She suspected he wasn't really thinking about spaghetti, and in seconds neither was she.

ABOUT THE AUTHOR

Jennie Hansen attended Ricks College and graduated from Westminster College in Salt Lake City, Utah. She has been a newspaper reporter, editor, and librarian, and is presently a circulation specialist for the Salt Lake City library system.

Her church service has included teaching in all auxiliaries and serving in stake and ward Primary presidencies. She has also served as a stake public affairs coordinator and ward chorister. Currently she is the education counselor in her ward Relief Society.

Jennie and her husband, Boyd, live in Salt Lake City. They are the parents of four daughters and a son.

Coming Home is Jennie's sixth novel for the LDS market. In addition to the two previous books in this series, *Run Away Home* and *Journey Home,* she has written *When Tomorrow Comes, Macady,* and *Some Sweet Day.*